NOT DEAD ENOUGH

Acclaim for J.M. Redmann's Micky Knight Series

Girl on the Edge of Summer

"Excellent storytelling and a brilliant character. This is one of only a few series where I reread all the books when a new one comes out… FIVE STARS and recommended if you like crime fiction with a heart— you may fall for Micky too."—*Planet Nation*

"The two mysteries themselves are interesting and have twists and turns to keep the reader entertained, and there are the usual fast-paced dangerous scenes…Overall, an entertaining read charged with action."—*Lez Review Books*

"We get to enjoy some well-plotted mysteries, some life-and-death rescues, and some despicably seedy characters. Redmann works through her action scenes with precision and balance, never letting them drag or sputter. The YA characters here are also well-drawn. They sound like teenagers, not forty-year-olds, and they act age appropriately as well. But at the heart of it all is Mickey–mostly smart (but sometimes stupid), looking forward without forgetting her past, and trying to reassemble her life with some bent and abraded puzzle pieces."—*Out in Print*

Ill Will

Lambda Literary Award Winner

***Foreword* Magazine Honorable Mention**

"*Ill Will* is fast-paced, well-plotted, and peopled with great characters. Redmann's dialogue is, as usual, marvelous. To top it off, you get an unexpected twist at the end. Please join me in hoping that book number eight is well underway."—*Lambda Literary Review*

"*Ill Will* is a solidly plotted, strongly character-driven mystery that is well paced."—*Mysterious Reviews*

Water Mark

***Foreword* Magazine Gold Medal Winner**

Golden Crown Literary Award Winner

"*Water Mark* is a rich, deep novel filled with humor and pathos. Its exciting plot keeps the pages flying, while it shows that long after a front page story has ceased to exist, even in the back sections of the newspaper, it remains very real to those whose lives it touched. This is another great read from a fine author."—*Just About Write*

Death of a Dying Man

Lambda Literary Award Winner

"Like other books in the series, Redmann's pacing is sharp, her sense of place acute and her characters well crafted. The story has a definite edge, raising some discomfiting questions about the selfishly unsavory way some gay men and lesbians live their lives and what the consequences of that behavior can be. Redmann isn't all edge, however—she's got plenty of sass. Knight is funny, her relationship with Cordelia is believably long-term-lover sexy and little details of both the characters' lives and New Orleans give the atmosphere heft."—*Lambda Book Report*

"As the investigation continues and Micky's personal dramas rage, a big storm is brewing. Redmann, whose day job is with NO/AIDS, gets the Hurricane Katrina evacuation just right—at times she brought tears to my eyes. An unsettled Micky searches for friends and does her work as she constantly grieves for her beloved city."—*New Orleans Times-Picayune*

The Intersection of Law and Desire

Lambda Literary Award Winner

San Francisco Chronicle **Editor's Choice for the year**

Profiled on *Fresh Air*, hosted by Terry Gross, and selected for book reviewer Maureen Corrigan's recommended holiday book list.

"Superbly crafted, multi-layered…One of the most hard-boiled and complex female detectives in print today."—*San Francisco Chronicle* (An Editor's Choice selection for 1995)

"Fine, hard-boiled tale-telling."—*Washington Post Book World*

"An edge-of-the-seat, action-packed New Orleans adventure… Micky Knight is a fast-moving, fearless, fascinating character…*The Intersection of Law and Desire* will win Redmann lots more fans." —*New Orleans Times-Picayune*

"Crackling with tension…an uncommonly rich book…Redmann has the making of a landmark series."—*Kirkus Review*

"Perceptive, sensitive prose; in-depth characterization; and pensive, wry wit add up to a memorable and compelling read."—*Library Journal*

"Powerful and page turning…A rip-roaring read, as randy as it is reflective…Micky Knight is a to-die-for creation…a Cajun firebrand with the proverbial quick wit, fast tongue, and heavy heart."—*Lambda Book Report*

Lost Daughters

"A sophisticated, funny, plot-driven, character-laden murder mystery set in New Orleans…as tightly plotted a page-turner as they come… One of the pleasures of *Lost Daughters* is its highly accurate portrayal of the real work of private detection—a standout accomplishment in the usually sloppily conjectured world of thriller-killer fiction. Redmann has a firm grasp of both the techniques and the emotions of real-life cases—in this instance, why people decide to search for their relatives, why people don't, what they fear finding and losing…and Knight is a competent, tightly wound, sardonic, passionate detective with a keen eye for detail and a spine made of steel."—*San Francisco Chronicle*

"Redmann's Micky Knight series just gets better…For finely delineated characters, unerring timing, and page-turning action, Redmann deserves the widest possible audience."—*Booklist, starred review*

"Like fine wine, J.M. Redmann's private eye has developed interesting depths and nuances with age…Redmann continues to write some of the fastest –moving action scenes in the business…In Lost Daughters, Redmann has found a winning combination of action and emotion that should attract new fans—both gay and straight—in droves."—*New Orleans Times Picayune*

"…tastefully sexy…"—*USA Today*

"An admirable, tough PI with an eye for detail and the courage, finally, to confront her own fear. Recommended."—*Library Journal*

"The best mysteries are character-driven and still have great moments of atmosphere and a tightly wound plot. J.M. Redmann succeeds on all three counts in this story of a smart lesbian private eye who unravels the fascinating evidence in a string of bizarre cases, involving missing children, grisly mutilations, and a runaway teen driven from her own home because she is gay."—*Outsmart*

By the Author

The Micky Knight Mystery Series:

Death by the Riverside

Deaths of Jocasta

The Intersection of Law and Desire

Lost Daughters

Death of a Dying Man

Water Mark

Ill Will

The Shoal of Time

The Girl on the Edge of Summer

Not Dead Enough

Women of the Mean Streets: Lesbian Noir
edited with Greg Herren

Men of the Mean Streets: Gay Noir
edited with Greg Herren

Night Shadows: Queer Horror
edited with Greg Herren

As R. Jean Reid, the Nell McGraw mystery series

Roots of Murder

Perdition

Visit us at www.boldstrokesbooks.com

NOT DEAD ENOUGH

by

J.M. Redmann

2019

NOT DEAD ENOUGH

ISBN 13: 978-1-63555-543-1

THIS TRADE PAPERBACK ORIGINAL IS PUBLISHED BY
BOLD STROKES BOOKS, INC.
P.O. BOX 249
VALLEY FALLS, NY 12185

FIRST EDITION: NOVEMBER 2019

CREDITS
EDITORS: GREG HERREN AND STACIA SEAMAN
PRODUCTION DESIGN: STACIA SEAMAN
COVER DESIGN BY SHERI (HINDSIGHTGRAPHICS@GMAIL.COM)

Acknowledgments

Writing a book isn't as easy as reading one. There are times I'd really prefer to be doing the latter. Especially when I come home from the day job of staring at a computer screen for most of the day and I'm tired and want nothing more than to turn my brain off, pour a glass of wine (okay, Scotch in the winter, vodka in the summer) and read a book instead of writing one. Sometimes that does happen. But really only Monday through Friday. Then I remember the world of friends and readers this life has given me and get back to writing.

My writer friends, all of us who struggle to get the words on the page amidst everything else life throws at us. Greg, Carsen, Ali, Anne, VK, 'Nathan, Jeffrey, Rob, Fay, Isabella, Dorothy, Jewelle, Ellen, and I know I'm forgetting some of y'all. You keep me sane, or as close to it as I'm likely to get. Also thanks to the authors who started so many of us on this journey and have been kind and generous to me, Ellen Hart, Katherine V. Forrest, Barbara Wilson, Dorothy Allison, Jewelle Gomez, and so many others.

I also need to thank the generous folks who have willingly supported my day job at CrescentCare, NO/AIDS Task Force by donating because I used a name of their choosing in the book. The support is greatly appreciated, and it really helps me come up with names. I hope you don't mind being all the murder victims. Kidding. No spoilers here.

A major thanks to Greg Herren for his editorial work and his calm demeanor, especially about those pesky deadlines.

Mr. Squeaky and Arnold because I'm a lesbian and we have to thank our cats. My partner, Gillian, who is better about the litter boxes than I am (also she's home more, just sayin') and that we can spend days at our respective computers working on our respective books. She makes me appreciate not having to do footnotes and an index.

There are many people at my day job who are greatly understanding about the writing career. Noel, our CEO, Reg, our COO and my boss for letting me run off to do book things. My staff is great and makes my job easy enough that I have time to write—Narquis, Joey, Lauren, Allison, and all the members of the Prevention Department. I would love to be able to write full time, but since I have to have a real job, I'm very lucky to have this one.

Also huge thanks to Rad for making Bold Strokes what it is. Ruth, Connie, Shelley, Sandy, Stacia, and Cindy for all their hard work behind the scenes and everyone at BSB for being such a great and supportive publishing house.

To all the women who dared to ignore society's conventions
and be themselves, to love who they wished to love.
Who left words behind as proof and gave us a place in history.
Sappho, Anne Lister, Annie Hindle, and so many others.

CHAPTER ONE

Snakes.

Have I told you I hate snakes? Make that motherfucking snakes. Or anything fucking snakes. Yeah, I don't generally use that kind of language in public, but that was the kind of mood I was in.

It had already been an annoying day. The only messages when I got to work were three all asking/not really asking if they could pay their bill a little later. Sure, pal, if you can arrange for the bank to take its time about my mortgage. Just around lunch, a potential client dropped in. I try to discourage drop-ins. There are people I can't (or won't) help, and it's so much easier to tell them over the phone. Even if they get pissy, they can't complain about the drive down here. Or be close enough to throw something in my direction.

But Mrs. Aimee Smyth had dropped in just as my stomach was starting to truly growl.

She was too well dressed for the weather, especially this time of day and this mission, a raw silk suit in a tropical turquoise, crisp white shirt, linen, I guessed. Jewelry that hung off every possible appendage, mostly gold with stones that tried but didn't quite succeed in matching her suit. All expensive, not very tasteful. She might have been dressed for a long lunch at Commander's Palace, but not a last day of July jaunt down to my neighborhood. The humidity made steam baths seem chilly. The last three days had been downpours of afternoon thundershowers. Today's sun added all that wet back to the air.

I was wearing a light blue V-neck T-shirt and off-white lightweight cotton pants, and I felt overdressed for the weather.

Seeing her in a long-sleeved shirt with a jacket over it made me itch.

She wasn't pulling it off either. There are some women who seem impervious to heat. They might glow a little on the worst days of August but are always perfectly put out, hair and makeup in place. Aimee Smyth wasn't one of those. Her makeup was starting to slide down her face, her hair too much unruly frizz to be the latest hairstyle.

She was trying too hard, and that always worries me in a client.

She wanted me to find her missing sister. A vague family feud, they'd lost touch. Now she wanted to find her.

"Why now?" I asked.

"It's time. We've been apart for too long," was her answer.

Lies are vague. Truth has sharp points that are jagged, that don't always make sense. A friend passed away, a cousin reconnected with a long-lost friend, my dog died—something usually triggers the search. Not just a vague notice of time.

She'd written a personal check from an out-of-state bank.

She also hadn't given me much. Her putative sister was named Sally Brand. Her maiden name, so presumably Smyth was Aimee's married name, although the one missing piece of jewelry was a band on her left hand. Aimee didn't know if she'd married or not, thought she'd probably stayed in the South, maybe the New Orleans area—again with only the vaguest of reasons.

Aimee was from Atlanta and was only going to be in town for a few days. She'd appreciate it if I could do this as quickly as possible.

"Why me?" I asked.

She was too ready for the question. "You were recommended," she answered.

She couldn't remember by whom.

I said yes. Summer is slow. The "can't pay the bill now" people were piling up. But I wasn't going to do a lot of work on the case until the check cleared.

After lunch—some leftover shrimp thrown on a salad—I started the case by looking her up.

Or trying to. Aimee Smyth should be just uncommon enough for me to find something. And just common enough to be confusing. I found more than enough A. Smyths and Smiths in the Atlanta area to be unhelpful. But no specific Aimee Smyth.

I even called the bank on the check, but they seemed to do Eastern time zone early closing, as no one answered the phone.

If I couldn't find the Aimee who had been sitting in my office, it was unlikely I'd find the long-missing sister.

That had eaten up most of the rest of the day. I'd stayed later than I'd planned, doing "just one more" internet search, until I noticed the sun tucking behind clouds. A variation in our weather—thunderstorms in the evening instead of the afternoon.

So now, standing in front of my home, it was just dark, long shadows from the rain-smeared streetlights.

And I was staring at a snake.

Okay, a poster of one, its flickering tongue pointed in my direction. "Lost python" with a big picture of the missing snake.

I looked at the bushes next to my entrance steps. Dense, perfect for hiding a snake. I live in a city, thank you very much, a mere two blocks from the French Quarter, and I can see the tall towers of the CBD from the small deck off the upstairs. Urban means no snakes should be lurking in bushes I had to walk past.

As I paused to glare at the shadows, looking for anything long and sinuous, I could feel the sweat drip down my nose. The dusk was still too new to get rid of the heat the sun had left, adding only humidity. Perfect snake weather.

Fucking snakes, I grumbled, then charged up my stairs, jammed my key in—missing twice, enough times to make me mutter "fuck" out loud again, before finally getting it in and the door open and slamming it louder than I'd intended as I closed it.

I tossed my briefcase, and gym bag, left over from good intentions of the morning that weren't carried out, on the chair I cleared off only when company came over.

It hadn't been cleaned in a month.

Then to the kitchen where I filled a go-cup with ice (Muses, I'm classy like that) then water and chugged half of it down.

Bedroom. Strip off the clothes, into ratty shorts and a T-shirt. No bra, needless to say.

Only then did I check the phone for messages. Nada. Do I still exist if no one calls me?

Ah, email. One from Torbin seeing if I'm free next weekend. And a group email from Danny and Joanne, asking about lunch tomorrow,

Tuesday. A not pleasant reminder that today was still only Monday, the week barely newborn and already way past its welcome.

I managed a quick yes to both before I contemplated dinner.

A few months ago, Danny, Joanne, and a few other women in the legal/law enforcement profession started meeting for monthly lunches. I got invited along as the "illegal" one, since I'm a private detective. It was mostly a fun time, occasional professional news and info. And work-related enough to be a tax deduction for my small business.

I hadn't seen Torbin, save for passing in the street—we lived on the same block—for close to a month. My ex, Cordelia James, was back in town. We had been together long enough for Torbin and her to be friends—and she had been close to Alex and Joanne before we got together. It was an unspoken rule that we traded off, to avoid any awkward meetings. She—and her new girlfriend—had been here for six months and I hadn't run into her yet. At least not officially.

Oh, I knew where she lived—uptown in the Touro area, worked—a new community health clinic, the girlfriend's name—Nancy Something Forgettable. I am a private detective, after all. What kind of car she drove—a blue Subaru Forester. Forgettable Nancy didn't have a job yet. Or was she going to be a lesbian housewife of New Orleans?

I didn't ask, my friends didn't tell.

Had I driven by her house? Yes, but late enough at night and I was in the area anyway. I was curious, that was all. The lights were all off, save for the obligatory porch light. A quick glance; I'd kept on driving.

I'd seen a car like hers, with a driver that could have been her, but it was the usual crazy New Orleans traffic, so I kept driving and didn't look back.

Sometimes I thought I should just show up or find some public event they would be at and go. Get it over with. New Orleans can be a small town, and when half my friends were her friends, too, it made for an awkward social dance.

At other times, I thought I should make this a game; could I avoid her for the rest of my life? Dash around corners just in time, jump out bedroom windows, or peel off in my car.

And then I'd have a couple fingers of Scotch and decide to let it go. It would happen or it wouldn't. We would be perfect fake Southern polite. My life would go on exactly as it was now.

It was an okay life. Business was doing reasonably well. *Summer is always slower*, I reminded myself. I was carrying the mortgages both on the house and on my office, the latter covered in good part by the hipster coffee shop that rented the downstairs. Bills got paid on time, a little put away here and there. I could afford the decent Scotch if not the really good stuff. But why pay a hundred dollars a bottle for stuff you're only going to convert to piss anyway?

I was still single and beginning to decide I liked it that way. I'd been dating a nurse for a couple of months; we'd hit it off, but our schedules kept getting in the way. She mostly worked nights. My hours were scattered depending on the job. She'd emailed me last week saying she's met someone at work; they had similar schedules and could do things together. If I wasn't hunky-dory fine, I would be soon enough. It had only been a few months; we had gone out maybe six or seven times. Spent the night together twice, still awkward and unsure. She'd been fun, but I wasn't sure she was the person I wanted to spend the rest of my life with. If that was the case, maybe it was better she found someone else and dumped me before I dumped her.

Right.

I took a slug of the Scotch.

In a nod to adulthood, I sliced up an apple and grabbed a wedge of cheddar. Supper.

And it was only Monday and every time I had to pee in the middle of the night, I'd have to check the toilet to make sure no snake had slithered into my sewer system. I took another big gulp of Scotch. Maybe grain whisky pee could keep the snakes away.

Chapter Two

I slept late-ish. For a weekday, that is. Didn't get to the office until around ten a.m. The first order of business was to make a pot of coffee.

Once I had a cup in front of me, I looked at the case for Aimee Smyth. She had hired me, paid after all. I checked my bank to see if the money had cleared. Of course not; it goes out very quickly, in very slowly.

Maybe Aimee Smyth wasn't her real name. That could explain why she was so hard to find. Or maybe she hadn't led the kind of life that leaves much of a track.

Summer is too slow, you're spending too much time on this case, Micky, I told myself. *Do what you're paid to do until you have a good reason to not do it.*

I did call the bank again. They weren't very helpful. Could not give out client information. Even to verify the check the client had written me was good. Annoying, but I had to give them points for security. Anyone could call up and make the same claim that I had to get info about someone's bank account.

I started the usual internet search for Aimee's sister Sally. I also slowly sipped my coffee. Aimee had claimed she was pressed for time, but until the check cleared, I wasn't going to bust my ass on this case. Most people are honest, but a few aren't, and there have been checks that have not cleared.

As elusive as Aimee had been, her sister was even more elusive. Why is it that no one searching for a lost person can ever be helpful enough to have their Social Security number? No, it's always "I think she might be in the New Orleans, maybe Slidell, area and her last name might have changed." (C'mon, really, you're still taking his name like you're his property? Feminism can't be over; it's barely started.)

In the hour and a half I had before my lunch meeting, I found nada on Sally, not even that she existed.

I glanced at the phone number for Aimee. After lunch, I told myself, I'd call her and see if she could scrape up any more info on her sister.

Then it was time to head uptown. They vary their locations, and this one was up on Freret Street, a strip with lots of new restaurants on it. And most of the major road construction in the city between me and there.

I was about ten minutes late. Respectable given I had to come all the way from downtown. They were ordering as I slid into the last remaining chair. A bottle of sparkling water was already in front of me. Either Joanne or Danny had ordered it. Both of them were capable of the betrayal. I had been contemplating a Bloody Mary, but my choice had been usurped.

"We can't stay long," Danny was saying, even as she ordered the fried catfish plate. The large one. Maybe she was taking the leftovers home to her partner Elly. Danny and I had been friends since college. She was now an assistant district attorney, well on the legal side of the group. She was sunny and stoic, attributes that got her through working in a criminal justice system she knew was far from perfect, especially for people of her skin color. And she could be more patient than I could ever hope to be explaining why she worked in the system to change it rather than fighting it from the outside.

Joanne was even more legal, a cop, actually a detective, now overseeing a homicide unit. Like Danny, she had her conflicts with the system, one that didn't welcome women, let alone lesbians. She could be as stoic as Danny and not let others see what it cost her, but not as sunny. Oh, no, Joanne was not a sunny person. Fair, honest, blunt. If you were sick, Danny would make chicken soup and bring balloons. Joanne would tell you you're probably not going to die and if you do, your troubles will be over. I preferred Danny's chicken soup (she could cook), but Joanne had pushed me to get over my whiny self on multiple occasions.

I did a quick glance at the menu, saw an oyster po-boy, and ordered that as the waitress was looking expectantly at me.

Joanne got a salad. But wavered enough to add fried oysters as a topping. Two more catfish lunches—what this place is known for—and one burger for the Midwestern transplant who did not do seafood. She was a new lawyer who worked with Danny. She also ordered a beer. I took a sip of my sparkling water.

"Why can't you stay long?" I asked.

A sigh from Burger Girl—so passive-aggressively nice—told me they had already covered this topic before I came.

"A nice juicy murder," Danny said. "No name, no ID, but well dressed enough that someone is going to miss her."

"It wasn't a robbery," Joanne added. "She had jewelry on just about every place you can have it, and nothing was disturbed."

"No sign of sexual assault, either," Danny added.

That explained why this was an interesting murder. The common motives seemed to be missing. I also enjoyed that both Danny and Joanne seemed interested in discussing it with me.

"But she was older," Burger Girl said. She had a name, but I couldn't remember it. That was more effort than she was worth.

"Maybe in her forties," Joanne said. She and Danny, both well into their forties, glared at her. "Not bad looking, but as you know, sexual assault has nothing to do with what a woman looks like. It's about power."

I took another sip of water. What were the odds? Forty-year-old woman with a lot of jewelry. I took another sip. "You don't happen to have a picture of her, do you?" I asked.

Danny was passing the bread, but Joanne looked at me, catching the suspicion in my tone. "Why?" she asked.

"Not here with us," Danny added, catching the current in the air.

What were the odds, I thought again.

Let's close this door. "I had a client who claimed she's here from Atlanta, wanted me to look for her sister. Forties, lots of jewelry, well dressed, raw silk turquoise suit when I saw her."

"Hair color?" Joanne asked.

"Black, probably dyed, but a decent enough job."

She and Danny exchanged a look. The door didn't seem to be closing.

Our food arrived.

Joanne said quietly to me, "Can you come with us after lunch?"

I nodded yes.

Then we got to hear all about Burger Girl's upcoming wedding, including how much every flower arrangement cost.

I was not unhappy to follow Joanne and Danny out, even carrying Danny's doggy bag of leftover catfish on the way to her car while she struggled with her briefcase and large handbag. We waved good-bye to Burger Girl, still rambling on about flower arrangements to the others who were caught behind her.

Danny did remember to take the doggy bag from me before we went to our separate cars. I'd have to figure out something else for dinner.

I followed them, thinking we'd be going to either Joanne's station or Danny's office.

But no, we were going to the morgue.

The Orleans Parish Coroner's office, aka the morgue, is not in my favorite area of the city, not even close. It's in Central City, a location that hasn't had a whiff of gentrification for blocks. Guess they figured people this poor wouldn't object to the dead bodies. Or else that it would save on travel time. It's an area with a high murder rate. Murder and desperation often go together.

Coming here in the steam bath part of the summer? Call this another "not enough aspirin and vodka in the world" day.

I scrabbled in my briefcase—no, I will not carry a purse—for what I hoped was a scented lip balm. Oh, great, rum cola, a giveaway from the last Pride festival, not a flavor I would have picked myself. But that was all I had. It was that or the windshield cleaning fluid.

I even contemplated just driving on, not following Danny as she turned into the parking lot. But like a good citizen, always willing to help the forces of law, I parked beside her, pausing only to rub some rum cola lip balm under my nose.

One whiff told me that was probably not a good idea.

I tried breathing through my mouth. Less of a good idea. The heat and humidity and trash can we were walking past smelled like rotting, rancid bananas. Or what I imagined they would smell like.

Joanne, who drives like a cop, was already waiting for us at the door.

Trotting behind Danny, I asked, "You're not going to make me look at a dead body, are you?"

"No, we're here for the fish tank in the lobby," she said.

It was too hot for sarcasm.

"If I barf, it's on you," I said as we mounted the steps to join Joanne.

She was already opening the door into air-conditioning.

But even the cold air couldn't hide the odors of…cleaning fluids? Bleach? Yeah, that was it, I told myself. It was just bleach I was smelling.

Both Joanne and Danny seemed blissfully unaware. Or were used to it.

Do not let your imagination get away with you, I admonished myself. *Bleach. That musty, chemical smell is just bleach.*

They led me through the security with practiced ease, and I got little more scrutiny than a bare nod. I had been hoping for blaring alarms and being denied admittance.

But no, we were striding down a too brightly lit hallway, scrubbed to gleaming white perfection. Just a hint of…bleach—I had to convince myself all I was smelling was something antiseptic and cleansing— nothing else.

The power of the mind is so annoying. Just because I'm in a place where all the dead bodies in Orleans Parish end up doesn't mean it smells like them. But that thought was lodged in my brain, and it wasn't leaving until I did.

I swallowed and surreptitiously rubbed some more rum cola under my nose. Now I was smelling rum cola bleach.

We turned a corner and Joanne opened a door, Danny following, with me having little choice but to tag along behind.

Smell was the first thing I noticed. More than bleach. Another hard swallow. Rapid, shallow breathing. So not what I wanted to be doing right after lunch.

Another thing I shouldn't be thinking about: What was roiling in my stomach. Oyster po-boys are only good going down.

Be clinical, be detached, view this as just another New Orleans experience.

Joanne and Danny greeted the people in the room—the live ones—like old friends.

There were several gurneys. Joanne led us over to one and, without asking if I was ready, pulled back the sheet.

It was her…but not her. Same age, hair, like a bad drawing of the woman who had been in my office.

"Is it her?" Joanne asked.

"I…think so," I answered. "But something seems different."

"She is dead," Danny pointed out.

Maybe that was it. I had seen a woman—briefly—in the animation of life, eyes roving the room, mouth and lips moving in speech and expression. This woman was still and silent, not even the whisper of breath left.

I tried to impose the two faces together, the one I'd seen and the one in front of me. One was a person and one a clay statue. But if it wasn't the woman from my office, it was someone who bore a striking resemblance to her.

"I think so. That's the best I can do," I said, turning away. "It might help if I could see her clothing and jewelry."

Joanne nodded and, mercifully, led me out of the room with the gurneys.

It was just bleach, that was all you smelled, I told myself as I followed them through another too bright hallway. But I knew that wasn't true. There had also been the distinct taint of mortality—we go this way but once.

Another door. This time I could smell the odor of stale clothing, last garments of homeless men found on the street, no one to claim their final belongings, the bloodstained shirts and pants, all the odors of life oozing away.

I looked down at the floor, another application of rum cola, on my lips this time but a wide smear. Maybe it helped; maybe it just gave me something to do. It felt like an hour but was probably only a few minutes when Joanne called me over to a table. She opened the box that was on it.

The clothes were the same, but even they seemed to have less color, or the bright fluorescent lights dulled the vibrant hues. I looked at the jewelry, the profusion of turquoise. One ring, a big rock, with small bands of lapis blue around it. I remembered looking it as she had talked.

"That looks like what she was wearing," I said, adding, "The ring is distinctive."

Joanne nodded and put the clothing back in its container.

Danny added, "That's helpful. It gives us something to go on."

Joanne threw her latex gloves in the trash, then led us out.

"What can you tell us about her?" she asked as we headed back down the hallway that seemed even brighter than before.

What could I tell them about her? She was a client—had been. What did I owe her in death?

I was silent long enough for Danny to prompt, "Your client's confidentiality ends at her death. Anything you know might help us."

"Yes, I know," I answered. "Can we go outside? I could use some fresh air."

"Sure," Danny answered. She seemed to finally notice that I wasn't as seasoned as she and Joanne were about dead bodies. She led the way as Joanne checked us out.

I crossed quickly to my car, gulping rum cola–infused air. And dust and the heat of asphalt and car engines. Just not…bleach.

"Are you okay?" Danny asked.

"Yes, I'm fine," I lied. I took another deep breath. I looked up at the clouds in the sky.

Joanne joined us.

I kept looking at the clouds as I talked. "She gave her name as Aimee Smyth." I spelled it out. Joanne took notes. "Said she wanted to find her sister. They had lost touch and she wanted to reconnect. She was in my office for maybe half an hour. She didn't have a lot of information, and what she did have was…vague. Sister was probably somewhere around here, maybe the Northshore. She claimed to be only in town for a few days. Said someone had recommended me, but couldn't remember who."

"And you took her at her word?" Joanne asked.

"I'm not the police," I said. "She wanted me to find someone. As long as it seemed reasonably legit and I have the resources, it's a case." Another breath, finally looking at them. "But yeah, something didn't feel right. I usually do a quick check of any new clients. Mostly everything checks out enough for me—they are who they say they are. And their credit report is good enough to make it likely they'll pay the bill."

"So you checked her out?"

"Yes. And I found nothing."

"Nothing to make you suspicious?" Danny asked.

"No, just nothing. No record of her. Or nothing that I could trace back to her. Plenty of A. Smyths—and Smiths in the Atlanta area, but no Aimee with her spelling. Check written from a small out-of-state bank. Nothing bad, but most people leave paper trails. I couldn't find hers."

"You think she faked it?"

"I don't know. If she did, she was good. Usually something comes up, the death certificate for the person whose identity they took, an address that doesn't exist. But nothing like that. It could be she was one of those paranoid people, no credit cards, locked everything down as tightly as she could."

"Have you found the sister?"

"I wasn't going to start looking until the check cleared," I admitted.

Joanne gave a dry chuckle. "No one said you weren't smart."

"I might be able to give you more if I look over my case file." I might be able to quiet my still-roiling stomach if I got out of the morgue parking lot.

"Okay, thanks, give me a call," Joanne said.

"Yes, thank you, Micky, this has been helpful. First break we've had on this," Danny added.

I nodded and got in my car, not waiting for them to get in theirs before pulling out of the parking lot. About a block down the street, I rolled down my window, letting the hot air in, but I needed real air, the distraction of the normal smells of summer.

Two blocks later, I rolled the window back up. Greasy fried chicken was not a helpful odor.

It might have been quicker, but I avoided the spaghetti around the Superdome and went up to Broad to head back downtown. There was a less than remote chance I might have to pull over to the side of the road, and it would be easier to do it on this route.

I grew up out in the bayous. Stumbling over a dead critter—or even killing one—was common. Why was my stomach acting like a roller-coaster ride? Time, maybe. And knowing. It's one thing to catch a whiff of decay, then see the dead gator, skimming by in a boat. Another to park in the lot of the morgue and know I was going to view a body of someone I'd known—albeit slightly. The minutes of walking down the hallway, knowing what was coming, not the random turn in a bayou.

And death out there was part of life, expected, the inevitable changing of the seasons. But this was too soon, too sudden. Too deliberate. The woman I had seen in my office was only hot and sweaty, not the gray, hollow face of someone in such poor health she was likely to turn up dead in a day.

And she had given me a quest—okay, a case. But it mattered to her. Someone lost; wanting them to be found.

It's not your case anymore, Micky, I told myself as I turned onto Esplanade. Instead of going back to my office, I headed home. Two bathrooms there instead of one. My stomach still wasn't sure which way it would go.

But it nagged at me.

Maybe I should try to find Sally to at least say her sister tried to find her before she died.

And maybe I'd do it if the check cleared.

CHAPTER THREE

Coffee made. My piled up desk stared at me. I could do invoices. I could do filing. I so didn't want to do either.

I looked at my bank account. The check still hadn't cleared.

I should just bundle up the case file for Aimee Smyth and drop it on Joanne's desk.

And come back to my invoices and filing.

I looked up the phone number she had given me.

Dialed it.

Maybe someone was looking for her. As heartbreaking as it was, leaving them in uncertainty was crueler than the truth. Aimee wasn't coming home.

Three rings. Maybe it was ringing in her pile of clothes in the morgue.

"Hello?"

It sounded like her voice.

I almost dropped my coffee before pulling it together enough to answer.

"Hi, this is Micky Knight. The private detective you hired?"

"I'm sorry, who?"

"Michele Knight," I answered.

"Oh, okay. Look, this isn't a good time."

"When would be a good time? There are some things I'd like to discuss."

"Can you find my sister?"

"No, not yet."

"Call me when you do."

"No, we need to talk. There is someone who looks a lot like you—it might be your sister—in the morgue. I need to—"

The phone dropped.

Well, that was smooth.

The phone was picked up again.

"I'm sorry, you have the wrong number." She hung up.

No one answered when I tried again. I tried from my personal cell phone, but still no answer.

"Well, fuck," I muttered. Someone had answered her phone. Female voice, about in the range of hers. But was it her? Or was the woman who had been in my office on the slab in the morgue? There was no way I could know for sure.

But then who the hell answered her phone? And knew about looking for her sister? And why the clumsy pretense of claiming it was a wrong number?

Not your case. Hand it to the police.

I waited only long enough to finish my coffee before heading to Joanne's station and dumping the copy I'd made of her case.

She picked it up.

"Not much."

"No," I admitted. "She didn't give me much. Said the best contact was her cell phone—the one she's not answering. Didn't fill in the address part of the form. And I hadn't really started looking." I gave her a rundown of the methods I'd used to look for both Sally and Aimee. Joanne nodded and took a few notes. She'd have to do it all over again. But she also had law enforcement resources that I didn't have access to.

I debated telling her about the phone call. Cowardice won and I left it out. It didn't add much and I'd only get the—well-deserved—lecture on messing in police business.

She nodded, thanked me, and it was time to go. It was a workday for her, and lingering disreputable private detectives wouldn't make it any easier.

Out in the street again. It still smelled like greasy fried chicken here. Oh, wait, there was a fowl place down the block. I was somewhat relieved to know the smell of chicken fat hadn't taken over New Orleans. Or my brain.

Duty done, it was time to head back to my office and pretend I loved, just loved, filing.

The pretense lasted about ten minutes if I included making another pot of coffee and taking a bathroom break.

Who in hell had answered the phone?

Not your case anymore, Micky. It's murder now, and the police don't play with murder.

But who had answered the phone?

Clearly I didn't love—or loathe—filing enough to be distracted from thinking about the phone call.

Just enough to only notice the sound of footsteps when they were coming up the final flight of stairs to my office. I'm the only one up here, so they were either way lost (a few coffee shop folks have sought the bathroom up here) or on their way to see me.

Filing did not put me in the mood for unexpected visitors.

Without a knock, the door opened.

And nothing would have put me in the mood for this unexpected— and unwanted—visitor.

Impeccably dressed as always, white pants, probably linen, loose and flowing, white shirt, sleeveless, showing arms that spent time at the gym but not too heavy on the weightlifting, to only hint at muscles, without being unfeminine about them. A deep navy belt added color and contrast to the outfit. Her hair was perfectly blond, as if just coming from a sun-kissed beach, twisted up in a chignon. Understated jewelry, a pendant necklace with a deep blue stone echoing the navy of her belt, matching earrings. A ring on her left hand. Well, that was new.

"I need your help," she said.

"I'm the last person you should ever ask for help," I replied. I stood up, as if I was about to go to the door and usher her out.

"I know that. Believe me, I do know that. But you're the only one who can help."

I wanted her out of my office. But, damn my inquiring mind, was also curious about what could possibly bring her to my door.

Karen Holloway had hired me, long ago, and hadn't been exactly up front and honest about her reasons. Let's just say it was messy in more ways than I cared to think about. Karen was also a first cousin to my ex, Cordelia. When we had been together, I'd occasionally run into Karen and her various lady friends at some charity function that

Cordelia was expected to go to, meaning I got dragged along. Since we'd broken up, I hadn't seen Karen, didn't even know if she was still in New Orleans or not.

The last place I'd expected to see her was here in my office.

"Only one, huh? What kind of betrayal do you have in mind this time?"

"Don't be like that! I've changed. Really, I have."

"Karen, what do you want?"

She started to cross the room toward me, but I put up my hand like a traffic cop. I wanted her as close to the exit door as possible.

"Can't I at least sit down?"

"No. You have two minutes. One second past, I will escort you out and call security if you don't leave. Use your time wisely."

I crossed my arms.

She did the same, then realized she was mimicking me and dropped them to her sides. "Why do you have to make it so hard?"

"Because you've made it so hard in the past. One minute and thirty seconds."

She gave a sour glance, then said, "As you may know, I've gotten into real estate—"

"What? Your trust funds aren't enough?"

The look soured even more. "After taxes, no, not really. Barely 100k a year."

She ignored my snorted opinion.

"I just made a deal on a house. A really good one, in the Garden District, just over a million."

"That should help your trust fund," I interjected.

"Don't use up my time."

I waved her to go ahead.

"A woman from out of town. Atlanta. She wanted to make it a cash deal, she seemed to check out, deposit cleared the bank okay, submitted proof of the other funds. We're supposed to go to closing tomorrow."

I glanced at my watch. "I don't do real estate cases."

"This isn't real estate. The woman's name is Sally Brand, and she listed you as her local contact."

I stared at Karen, then quickly looked away, out the window.

Karen may have been venal, but she wasn't stupid. I didn't want to give away what a bombshell she had dropped in my lap.

I coughed, grabbed a sip of water from the always present sports bottle on my desk. Recovered. Somewhat. "Did she say why I was her contact?" I added, "I've never met anyone by that name." True enough. I'd never met Sally, only her sister Aimee.

"I don't know. She gave me a pile of paper, and it was only on the last sheet."

"Really?"

"Yes, really. Real estate takes a lot of paperwork. I can't read over every word in front of the client. Look, she gave me all the contact info I thought I'd need. Home address, cell phone, home phone, business phone, two emails, one business and one personal. How was I to know she'd disappear and leave only your name?"

With a sigh I didn't bother to hide, I motioned her to sit down. Karen was wise enough not to smirk at her victory.

Barely letting her get seated, I began a barrage of questions. "What do you mean by disappeared?"

"What people usually mean. I can't find her, can't contact her."

"What have you tried?"

"Everything! I wouldn't be here if anything else had worked."

It was, as usual, going to take effort to get useful information out of Karen. I considered throwing her over to Joanne—they weren't exactly bosom buddies—since it was possible this was related to the murder.

But my curious—and not perfectly ethical—mind wanted to see what I could get from Karen first.

"Tell me exactly what happened."

With a few prompts, she did. Called her cell just to finalize a few details. No answer. Left a message. Two days ago. No call back. Called her work phone. Disconnected. Went to the hotel she was staying in— where they'd initially met. No one by that name was staying there. They couldn't tell her if anyone by that name or her description had stayed there. Confidentiality. Email to both addresses. No answer to the personal. Work bounced back.

Fifteen minutes later I said, "Yep, looks like she did indeed disappear."

"Thanks," Karen huffed, "I knew that. What are you going to do about it?"

"What am I going to do? Are you hiring me to find her?"

"She listed you as the person to contact as the last resort!" Karen seemed appalled that she might have to spend money and not get her problem solved.

"Without my permission. Or even notification."

"But why would she do that? It makes no sense!"

"Does it matter? You said the deposit cleared. The seller gets to keep it, right? So you find another buyer."

She huffed again. "It's not that easy."

"There are tons of people moving from Brooklyn who think our prices here are cheap."

"That doesn't help me if this falls through."

"You cut corners," I guessed.

"No! But we had several offers. I pushed for this one because it was full list and in cash." She twisted in her seat, not looking me in the eye. Oh, Karen, do you have to be so predictable?

"Even though it wasn't as solid as some of the others."

"They all were solid. At least on paper. Cash and full price. It seemed a no-brainer."

"So why did you have to push for it?"

"One of the other bidders was local; he bought his last house with us. But it was complicated. He'd have to sell that house to buy this one. He wasn't happy when we turned him down. So if this falls through… we lose this sale and have pissed off a repeat customer."

"Life in the real estate business is harsh."

"But why would she do that? Throw away a chunk of money to hold the property, then disappear?"

"Maybe something happened to her."

"Why? What do you know?" Karen asked. Amoral, yes. Stupid, no. She knew there was something I wasn't telling her.

It was too big a coincidence to think Aimee hired me to find her sister, and her sister randomly picked my name out of the phone book (online directory?) as a contact for a house she was buying. It seemed Karen and I had something in common—being pawns in someone else's game.

And a deadly one. There was a body in the morgue. Aimee? Sally?

Could the sisters look enough alike to pass for each other? Especially from a brief moment, like the one in my office? Or with a new Realtor? Switch the clothes and jewelry, and a family resemblance could be enough. Maybe they were even twins, although that sounded so soap opera weird. But why? Any contact would have worked as well—a hotel clerk, a waitress. Why hire a private detective and go through the motions of buying a house to create witnesses to an identity switch? The house deposit. My fee. Why did money have to change hands?

Karen was staring at me.

I could send her out of my office and claim I knew nothing. She wouldn't believe me for the very valid reason that I would be obviously lying. I could tell her she needed to talk to Joanne, but that might be a bridge too far for Karen—at the mercy of a police officer who didn't approve of her ethics.

Or I could tell her what I knew. Maybe in the small piles of information we both had, something would stand out. Or maybe it was my excuse to pursue who had answered the phone. Who had dumped me into this mess?

"A woman claiming to be Sally's sister hired me to find her. And someone who looks a lot like her turned up in the morgue."

Karen covered her mouth with her hand, shock on her face. "What? But her sister isn't my buyer."

"Unless she is," I pointed out. "I couldn't find much of a paper trail for the woman, like she didn't exist. She could have used a fake name."

"That's crazy!"

"You got a better explanation?"

"No, that's no explanation at all."

She was right.

Karen continued, "Are you sure?" Not waiting for my answer, she said, "That might be the best outcome for me." At the look on my face, "Yes, horrible for her and her family—I'm sorry and all that—but if she was killed, then it means I didn't screw up and pick a flake for a buyer."

"I'm so sorry for your loss," I said as sarcastically as I could.

"Oh, fuck your snotty attitude! Yeah, I'm sorry she's dead. I didn't kill her and I'd be happier if she were alive and taking possession of the house right now. She's not any more dead by my benefiting from it."

"It's one problem solved," I conceded, still leaving the sarcasm in my tone. "But it doesn't solve the larger problem."

Karen stared at me. "What are you talking about?"

"Why? Why would she hire me? If her sister was buying a house from you, she'd be easy to find. Just check the property records. Why would the woman claiming to be the lost sister put down a deposit on a house and list me as the contact?"

"It makes no sense."

"Not to us. But someone had a plan."

"But if she's dead, it got messed up."

"Unless that was part of the plan."

Karen stared at me. I couldn't tell if she thought I was crazy or was worried at where this was going.

"Think about it," I continued. "She hires me. Engages you to sell her a house. Actions long enough that we can ID the body—"

"I'm not looking at a dead body."

"You're going to have to," I told her bluntly, making no effort to be kind about it. "If it's your client and my client—who both gave different names—the police need to know that."

"Maybe the police do, but I don't," Karen protested. Then she saw the look on my face. "You're going to tell them, aren't you?"

"I'm not withholding information in a murder investigation. That's accessory after the fact." Yeah, I was laying it on thick. But Karen wasn't weaseling out of this one.

"Look, I didn't want to get involved in this—"

"Then you shouldn't have walked into my office and dumped this on my lap."

"She put your name down!"

"Not by my choice, remember? Karen, there is a con going on. Likely involving a murder, and we've both been unwittingly involved. My hunch is it hasn't played itself out yet."

"But the woman's dead. You've identified her."

"If that was their goal, have us ID the body, why did she use one name with me and another with you?"

Karen didn't have an answer.

I didn't either. But if their hiring us was to create two disinterested professionals who could say they saw this woman, why change the name? And the story? Aimee Smyth could have hired me to do a title search—claimed she had been burned before and wanted to be sure or some such. It would have been the same story, Karen and I backing each other up. But now we had to contradict each other. The same woman, but with two different names and two different stories. The only reason to put my name on the document was to make sure we linked up.

It made no sense.

That worried me.

My head hurt.

I sent Karen from my office, telling her to bring every scrap of paper she could, even telephone doodles, concerning Sally Brand back as soon as she could.

I stared at my clock, wondering how long it would take her to come back. It wasn't even lunch yet, and I already knew this was not how I wanted to end my day.

Chapter Four

April isn't the cruelest month; August is. The heat of the summer has oozed into every crack of the sidewalk, the relief of fall—not until late September or October for us—seems impossibly far away. The glower from the Gulf, its sunburned waters threatening monsters of wind and waves, a waiting game to see which fragile stretch of coast will be hit this time. We constantly scan the reports, following tropical depressions from far out in the Atlantic as if they're stalkers in our backyard. When you've seen what can happen, the worst that can happen, a city underwater, even when it misses you this time, you feel little relief, heartbreak for those it strikes. We wait in the heat and oppressive humidity and hope we're lucky this year—and that someone else is not.

Karen had brought her stack of papers. I had taken them from her and told her to go away; I'd call when I had something. She obeyed, I'm guessing because she was relieved I wasn't dragging her straight away to the morgue.

Gawd, I hate real estate. Too much paper, too many words to read. I had read them and read them again, the long day turning to dark before I finally gave up and went home. Even then I took the stack with me as well as my case file, to cross-reference and see if I could tease anything out.

Nothing.

No, plenty of things, but nothing that made sense, nothing that hinted at why they had come up with two conflicting stories and linked us so we would know those conflicting stories.

I had wanted to find something, a hint, a clue, a direction. Something. But the night had closed in and I found nothing.

Now I was back at my desk, staring out the window, delaying what I knew was the inevitable next step. Take Karen (I'd have to take her; I didn't trust she'd go by herself) to reveal the whole mess, with no answers, just our names sticking out like glowing neon on a dark day, to Joanne. And hope I could explain rationally that this had landed in my lap with the splat that tainted crawfish make as they pass through the stomach.

To complicate matters even more, the check had cleared.

I had been betting that it wouldn't, a clear con, an obscure out-of-state bank, odds were 99 to 1 against it. Of course it wouldn't clear. And now the money sat in my bank account, another bad-seafood-in-the-bowels feeling. My client wasn't answering the phone or emails, so returning it would be difficult. I supposed I could just take the money—something to compensate me for the mess I was now in, but that was ethically dicey. I could also keep working the case—try to find the sister who probably didn't exist, fail and call it a day. Or I could donate it to a good cause and appease my conscience, if not my bank account. The hipster coffee shop on the first floor paid the rent in hipster time, not bank time, and I preferred not to have to count my pennies to make sure my mortgage checks—home and office—didn't bounce.

With a sigh, I picked up my phone and dialed Karen's number. Suppressing an even greater sigh, I told her to meet me here at my office at ten thirty. To her protests, I said it was important, and unless she was dead she needed to be here. She seemed to have matured enough not to argue further.

Then I called Joanne and asked to meet her around eleven a.m., that I had more information on the murder and it was complicated enough to have to do in person. She wasn't happy either, but agreed.

That made it unanimous—none of us were happy.

I made the strategic decision to meet Karen on the street. She was, as usual, late. Five minutes, but five minutes in the steam bath summer of New Orleans only added to my unhappy meter.

"Where are we going?" she said, when I ushered her to my car.

I was astute enough not to answer until we were seat-belted and in motion.

"You'll see when we get there," I answered, coward to the end.

But Karen wasn't dumb. "I am not talking to Joanne Ranson! She hates me!"

I kept driving.

"If I have to do this—and I don't think I do—there has to be some other cop besides her to talk to!" Karen gave a dramatic sigh, the cherry on top.

"It's her case. You have to talk to her about it," I said, as I avoided a bicyclist going the wrong way while drinking a beer and listening to music on headphones. He had a death wish; I didn't have a dent-my-car wish.

"Can't we do a conference call?"

"No. Police like to talk to witnesses in person."

"But I'm not a witness! I didn't see a crime. Just your name on a piece of paper."

"Your client and my client are missing. There is a dead woman in the morgue who fits the description for both of them."

"But you ID'ed her as your client."

"As someone who could have been my client. Or her sister," I pointed out, now at a red light long enough to look at Karen. "Besides, Joanne will be professional about this. She'll ask questions. You answer them honestly and then it's over."

We both knew I was lying.

But I kept driving.

Karen pouted. "But she'll tell my cousin."

I knew who she was referring to. I ignored the bait. "So? You'll get points for doing your civic duty."

"I will get a lecture about not getting involved in grubby murders. I mean, that's why she dumped you, isn't it? Tired of the dime-store-novel messes you got into."

Ten years ago, no, maybe even five, I would be screaming at Karen, telling her she was a fucking idiot and other boring, clichéd insults. Now I was mature enough to hold my tongue, understand she was attacking me because she felt attacked. And to know that I'd get her back, but at a time of my choosing, not hers. Cold anger is much more dangerous than hot anger—it has time to think.

"You're too young to have ever been to a dime store," I replied, aiming for an annoyingly placid tone in my voice, and again looking at the road, one hand on the steering wheel, the other changing gears. Another reason to drive a manual car besides discouraging thieves who can't drive a stick—it occupies both hands, making it harder to wrap them around annoying passengers' necks.

"You know what I mean," she retorted.

"I know you mean to piss me off and make this as fucking difficult as you can, typical spoiled child." Ah, yes, a moment of keeping calm allows you to pick where to stick the knife.

"You fucking bitch! You don't know anything at all about my life!"

"I know you've always had a lot more money than I've had. I know you've never been hungry. I know you're careless with people and what happens to them after you're done."

"Fuck you!" Then she started crying. Not gentle tears of manipulation, but heaving sobs. Genuine emotion. But I couldn't tell which one—hurt that I wasn't playing nice, or her life wasn't its usually glossy finish? Or had I wounded her, too close to a truth she tried to hide?

Or something else that had nothing to do with this, except today was the trigger.

I found a napkin in my door pocket and threw it in her lap.

Whatever Karen was crying about, I couldn't fix it. Even if it was something I said.

Parking was not kind around Joanne's station. I ignored Karen's dabbing at her face with my crumpled napkin as I cursed a jerk who took two spaces.

"Why do you have to be so mean?" she asked quietly as I finally found a place two blocks away.

"Maybe I'm not mean, just honest."

"Really? You think you're different, but you're not. Judging, always judging. Making sure your way of life is better than anyone else's. You, and Joanne. And Cordelia. You're so much better than I am. So sure you are."

"No, different. That's all," I mumbled, surprised by her naked honesty. It was the last thing I expected from Karen Holloway.

"Oh, please, you never look beyond your superiority, like it was something handed to anyone and I don't have it only because I chose not to."

"You have made your choices, Karen," I pointed out.

"That's what I mean! You made those choices, too, but you had someone—someone who mattered—tell you that you were strong enough and smart enough and brave enough. I never had that. I was told I could be pretty, but not smart and not strong and certainly not brave. My mother was a trophy wife and I was raised to be just like her. 'Shut up and be pretty, Karen.' 'Your brother has opinions; you have a smile.' You didn't grow up like that."

"No, I didn't," I retorted. "I was raised by a hellish religious aunt after my father died."

"What about those stories of you fighting alligators on the bayou? Off on your own in a boat."

"Not that big a deal. No alligator fighting, just gliding by them as they sunned."

"On a boat by yourself."

"A small skiff, no more than a mile from home."

"I wasn't allowed to be on those little paddleboats in City Park by myself. My legs weren't strong enough, they said. I believed them. For a long time. On my own? Even a small skiff, even less than a mile from home? Not possible. Not even in the dreams I was allowed. I never got to find out I could glide by an alligator and come home safe on my own. The best things money could buy didn't make it less a cage."

"I'm sorry," I said. "None of us get dealt a perfect hand."

"No, we don't. I thought I had everything I needed—a new car, expensive clothes. Anything money could buy. It took me a long time to see how crippled that comfort made me. You, Joanne, Cordelia, all your friends. The things you do in your everyday life terrify me. I can't find missing people, or heal a wound, or arrest someone—there are too many voices in my head telling me I can't do any of those things."

"Then stop listening to those voices."

"I tell myself that every day. On a few days, I take a step farther than I ever have before."

Karen was right. I had judged her as if she could and should live my life, never considering the unseen damage done by her lavish cage. But she was the only one who could repair it. The best I could do—and it wasn't much—was to be kinder and less judgmental.

And we still had to talk to Joanne.

"I'm sorry, Karen. There were many things I was told as a child, harmful, vicious things, but not that I couldn't be strong and smart. But none of us can change the past."

"I know. But I don't want to do this in a way I don't think you'll ever understand."

"No, probably not. But I'll do my best to keep Joanne focused on neither of us did anything wrong."

I opened my door, letting the heat blast in.

We walked the two blocks silently.

I hoped that Joanne would at least make us wait long enough for most of the sweat to dry; it was dripping down my nose after the first block. But no, she had to be prompt, ushering us into her office almost the minute we arrived.

She gave Karen an appraising look, then pushed her glasses up and looked down at the papers on her desk, doing her best to deny me a clue as to what she was thinking.

"A woman claiming to be Aimee Smyth hired me to find her missing sister, Sally Brand. Someone named Sally Brand just put money down on a house but failed to show at closing and, for reasons neither of us can figure out, put my name in her paperwork as the contact of last resort."

At Karen. "You're the Realtor?" Not really a question.

Karen just nodded.

Joanne looked at me. "And she contacted you first?"

"Yes. My name was in her paperwork. She had no reason to suspect anything criminal at that point. Only when we got together and compared stories—"

Joanne cut me off. "You identified the body as that of your client." A statement, but with a question lurking in it.

"I identified her as someone who looked like my client—a woman I met only once—and who had clothing and jewelry like my client wore."

Joanne threw questions at us, rapid fire, everything from the minute-by-minute time line to when we'd met with Sally/Aimee to the details of Karen's real estate license.

I could see why Joanne was doing this, why she had to go over every detail. This case had gotten a whole lot more complicated. It wasn't just a dead woman now—maybe a tourist who'd taken a wrong turn into tragedy. Find a hopped-up robber, probably a kid who panicked. Ugly, sordid, but not complicated. Instead of finally having some idea of who this woman was, now everything was up in the air. Did Aimee Smyth or Sally Brand even exist? If so, was one of them the dead woman? And why this elaborate setup? Put money down for a house, give me a check that cleared (yes, I admitted to that. Joanne merely grunted in reply).

Karen had started out nervous, and now every question Joanne threw her way hit her like a jolt. Her hands were everywhere, smoothing her skirt, fiddling with her phone, brushing her hair back. Now they were starting to shake. I'm sure Joanne was aware, but she didn't pull back. If anything, it made her push harder, aim more of her questions at Karen. Who drove to the house? Who else was there? What was she wearing? What did she say to Karen? What ID did she provide? Why hadn't she done a better background check? I tried to answer when I could. Or at least remind Joanne that we did all the normal things that people do, and most of the time it turns out okay. We didn't know we were dealing with criminals. By the third time I mentioned this, Joanne gave me a hard stare, told me she was aware, but a woman was dead and we were involved. Like it or not, she added, as if she knew I was about to point out we didn't ask for this.

Our eleven a.m. meeting slid past one p.m. I finally demanded a bathroom break. Reluctantly, Joanne gave it to us, but she walked with us both to the toilet and waited outside the door. I wasn't sure if this was standard, she just wanted to stretch her legs but had a bladder of steel, or if it was another tactic to rattle Karen. Or all of the above.

When we came back to her office, she sat staring at her notes for a long time. Finally, she said, "I need you to look at the body."

Karen blanched. "No, can't I just look at a picture?"

"No," Joanne answered. "We need to know if we're dealing with the same woman or if your buyer is different from Micky's client." With a barely perceptible softening, she added, "I'm sorry, I know this isn't pleasant, but we need to know."

I chimed in. "It's quick, only a minute or so."

"Mick, I need you to go with her. I want you both to look at her and see if you see the same woman."

"I don't know if I can add—"

"It's quick, only a minute or so," Joanne echoed, not even smiling as she captured me with my words. "We really need to verify if this is the same woman or two different women."

I saw her point but fervently did not want to return to the morgue.

Cutting off our last escape, she called in a patrol officer to drive us there.

Reluctantly, I followed the patrol officer, behind him to let Karen follow me. I didn't want to see the look on her face. I only knew she was still following from the sharp tap of her heels on the linoleum floor.

But he ushered us both into the back seat, not trusting either of us to be up front where the shotgun and radio were.

"This is the last time I do the right thing," Karen huffed as I slid in beside her.

"You and me both," I muttered, although I suspected we were better off with Joanne aware of the mess we were in. I couldn't see through to why they were doing this—what was the payoff? What did they gain? And why involve both me and Karen?

The car jolted over a pothole. New Orleans' Finest didn't include the back seat accommodations.

New Orleans, alas for trips like this, is not a large, spread-out city.

We were parking at the morgue before I even thought to look for the lip balm to rub under my nose. Now I couldn't do it without being obvious. I found a tube, this time tart cherry cola, and offered it to Karen.

She gave me an odd look.

"To rub under your nose."

She gave the tube an odder look. "I don't think tart cherry is going to help." And she waved it away.

I put it back in my pocket, not wanting to look like the wimp who needed it to get through only a few minutes at the morgue. Tart cherry isn't my favorite flavor anyway.

"What's that smell?" she said as she got out of the car.

"Your nose," I replied.

"No, it's not. It doesn't smell good."

"Oh, the fried chicken place down the block. They might need to change their grease."

"Oh." Then, "Are you sure?"

"Yes," I said. "Remember, I've been here before."

The officer was already walking to the door, and we had to hurry to catch up with him.

Karen didn't look like she believed me about the chicken. I wasn't sure I believed myself. Tart cherry cola lip balm didn't seem like it would help the mix.

We were led in, then down the long (it seemed to me) hallway. Ten feet in, Karen gripped my hand tight enough to cut off circulation. The woman did work out at the gym.

"It'll be quick," I whispered, a promise to both of us.

Needless to say, it wasn't. We had gotten here too quickly—in my opinion. They had to take time to retrieve her body and set up the viewing. We were left in the long hallway trying to convince ourselves the smells were only rancid fried chicken overlaid with bleach and disinfectant. Almost enough to make me wish I'd gone ahead with the tart cherry cola.

Just as I was hoping they'd tell us to go away, the patrol officer tapped me on the shoulder. I never did get his name—a mumbled Derrick or Dwayne, but I wasn't sure enough of which to call him by it.

We were led into the room. Karen gripped my forearm with her other hand, two places my circulation was now cut off. Her whole body shook as she took a deep breath.

The attendant folded back the sheet.

Was it the woman I had seen? The last time, the clothes and jewelry had influenced me; they were the same, so she had to be the same. But now? With whatever game this was, the clothes could have been switched. I stared at her, the slack muscles, flesh now a dull faded pink, sliding into gray. She ticked off the boxes, same approximate age, hair color, facial features.

But...something felt off. Me? Knowing what I know now? Or just the wide chasm between animated life and silent death?

A small mole under her right ear. I closed my eyes and pictured the woman in my office, attempting to freeze on her face. I didn't see the mole. But was it a trick of memory? Wanting to see a difference and finding this tiny discrepancy?

Karen made a sound from the back of her throat that would have signaled hairball in a cat. "I need to get out of here," she said, her words battling to get out over what else wanted to get out.

"Let's go, we've seen enough." I turned and, still attached by her double-handed grip, pulled Karen with me.

The hallway seemed even longer, Karen huffing air to quell her nausea.

The last few steps turned into a trot to get outside. I needed Karen to get enough fresh air to be able to let go of me; otherwise I was far too close.

She let go of my forearm as she gasped for breath but held on to my hand. I tried to subtly shift to be as far from the vomit range as possible. Laundry is one of my least favorite chores.

After about a minute of gasping, she wheezed out, "I never thought fried chicken would smell so good." She was still taking deeper than usual breaths.

I considered cracking that it was the crematorium but realized my stomach wasn't its usual happy camper, on the line between unsettled and roiled. If Karen threw up, I'd likely join her, and I couldn't move far enough away from myself to keep my clothes clean.

"Yes, it does. And some fresh air. It's over and done. You did pretty well."

She managed a weak, wavering smile. Then took another huffing breath.

"Did you recognize her?" I asked.

Karen took another breath. "Yes, I think so. It—she—looked like her. But..."

"Did she have a small mole under her right ear?"

Karen frowned, as if thinking, finally saying, "I don't know... maybe."

"Picture the woman in your office. Can you see it?"

She looked off, held still for a moment, then said, "I don't know. She had long hair she kept flipping out of her face."

"Picture her in that moment, the hair off her face. Can you see a mole?"

Karen was again silent, her eyes on the ground. "No...maybe...I don't know." Then vehemently, "I can't think about her anymore. I keep seeing...that body, that face. I need to think of something else. Quickly." She sucked in air.

"Okay, let's move on. Um...seen any good movies lately?"

She looked at me. So it wasn't the best change of subject.

I tried again. "There's a disturbance in the Atlantic."

"Coming this way?"

"Too soon to tell. A depression, medium chance of development into a tropical storm, but the track is still too far out to sea to know if it'll come into the Gulf."

One worry replaced with another. Discussing possible storm tracks got us through long enough for the patrol officer to rejoin us, seeming to finally remember he was our ride out of here.

Even so, Karen continued mouth breathing all the way back to Joanne's office. But the Fates were with us. She was out, had left a message for us to call her with our information.

We were again in the sunshine and fresh air—hot and saturated with humidity as it was. Still better than the chill of the morgue. Karen followed me.

As we got to my car, I said, "Where do you want me to drop you?"

"We need to go back to your place."

"Look, I'm pretty busy—"

"My car. That's where my car is."

Damn, I had done that to myself, hadn't I? I motioned her to get in, hoping her nausea had truly passed. Cars are even harder to clean than clothes.

I was searching for a safe topic—not too clearly idle chatter like movies, but not our current situation, as that might produce more nausea. I was saved by her phone ringing.

Karen looked at the screen, then quickly answered. "Hi, Holly! I'm so glad you called. I've had a rotten day. I had to go to—"

I only got her side of the conversation, with enough long pauses to indicate Holly was a talker more than a listener. Karen answered with a series of, "Yes, I understand," "Yeah, I get it," "You're right," and a few strings of, "Yeah," "Uh-huh," and "Yes."

Finally, Karen, "Yes, I understand. I know you do important work. Why don't we go out someplace nice? You can tell me about your day and I'll tell you about mine? Would that be okay? Or maybe tomorrow or the next few days if that doesn't work?" Her tone was tentative; a supplicant asking for what she feared would be refused. Not a tone I often heard from Karen.

A long pause, then Karen said, "Yes, that would be great! Around seven? I can pick you up?"

Again a pause, then Karen said, "I'm not sure. I'll see where I can get reservations. Yes, I'll let you know." She said good-bye, made a few kissy sounds, then put the phone away with a look of satisfaction. I could almost hear her thoughts—*I have a serious girlfriend and look at me.* I pretended not to hear what her expression was saying.

"Sorry about that," she said to me as she put her phone away.

"Girlfriend?" I guessed. I was curious—not about Karen's girlfriends; she was rich and good-looking; she always had a bevy of them—but mostly Karen had seemed the dominant partner, the one with the looks and the money and therefore the control. She would tell, not ask.

"Yes, and I know what you're thinking, but Holly is different. She's a social worker. Works for a food pantry down in Chalmette. She isn't impressed by my money."

"Just going out to a nice place to sort your day?" Oh, wait, I said I'd be nicer to Karen. Oh, well.

"We don't do it every night," Karen said defensively. "But she's such a good person; she deserves an occasional night out."

I didn't say what I was thinking—and it was none of my business—but from the admittedly one-sided phone call, it sounded like girlfriend Holly wasn't willing to listen to Karen's morgue trauma unless she got taken out to an upscale restaurant. And Karen was too love (lust?) blind to see through her do-gooder façade to the manipulation beneath. But that was merely my cynical viewpoint on it, and I was hardly in a position to judge other people's relationships. Not that it stopped me. But my vow to be kinder did keep me from saying it. "What's her name? I know a lot of social workers."

"Holly Farmer," Karen answered.

"That's her real name?"

"What's wrong with it?"

"It's sort of like Wendy Beach, April May, or Rose Gardener. Did she grow up on a holly farm?"

"I don't think holly is farmed," Karen answered. "And no, she grew up in a small town in Georgia. Her mother was a teacher and her father the local doctor."

"Wow, you've met her parents already?"

"No, she's told me about them. Tragically they died in a car accident when Holly was eighteen. She's been on her own ever since."

"How long have you known her?" Did I really care? No, but we were almost back to my place, and another question or two would fill the time.

"We've been together only three months. She moved here shortly before then and was new in town. We were jogging together on the levee, got to talking, and I offered to show her around. The rest is history," Karen finished with a smile. Then she had to add, "Cordelia even approves of her."

Cordelia, her cousin. My ex.

I pulled up beside her car. "Enjoy your dinner tonight." Then I looked at my watch.

Karen got out, still smiling.

I gave her a bare second to clear the door, then drove away, although only a few yards, parking on the other side of the street. This was my office, after all, and I had work to do. I stared down at my phone while Karen got in her car, as if I had important messages that needed to be answered immediately. I waited until she had turned the corner and was out of sight before getting out. The phone had only told me what I already knew, it was hot, would stay hot, and the humidity required swimming lessons.

In the twenty feet to my door, sweat was again dripping down my nose. As I entered, I was hit with a heavy chai tea smell. Must be the special of the day. Not a chai or tea person, I hastened up the stairs to get above the smell, arriving at my third-floor office door out of breath and sweating even more.

I made a pot of coffee, more wanting the aroma and the caffeine than the heat. I managed to scrape up enough ice cubes from the old office fridge to pretend it was iced coffee. And even remembered to refill the ice trays so next time (and in New Orleans summers, there would be many next times) I would have enough ice to not have to pretend.

Then I sat at my desk watching the ice cubes rapidly melt as I huffed the coffee aroma to get all the other smells of the day out of my nose and brain.

I needed to call Joanne, but I hesitated. Could I truly remember the mole or not? If she wasn't the woman who had been in my office, who was she? Was it possible there was an innocent explanation? Or not one as messy as it looked? Woman getting away from an abusive spouse? Hired me to see if she could be traced here, but had to use her real name for real estate? Gone far enough along with both before the spouse/ex tracked her here and killed her?

But why put my name on Karen's real estate papers?

It made no sense.

My phone rang. Caller ID said it was Joanne. Reluctantly I picked it up.

"How was your trip to the morgue?"

"Karen didn't throw up in my car. Best news of the day." I left enough silence to force Joanne to ask what she wanted to know. Not playing nice today.

"Was it the same woman?"

"Yes, no, maybe. Was it the woman in my office? Probably. Could be a sister? Maybe. Or one of those improbable coincidences of people who look amazingly alike."

"Don't go all soap opera on me. Was she the same woman Karen saw?"

"Again, yes, no, maybe. I got Karen to not upchuck, trying to get details through nausea was hard. Yes, she looked like her, but again it could be someone who resembled her a lot."

"Any clue if she was the same woman?"

"Yes—"

"No, maybe," Joanne finished for me.

"The corpse—the woman in the morgue had a small mole behind her right ear. I've been trying to picture the woman in my office, trying to call up that patch of skin in memory—to not add it. But…memory is stubborn. I can't be sure. I asked Karen as well and she wasn't sure. Couldn't press because of that nausea thing. You can question her further when it's your carpet at risk."

"Thanks, maybe I should go to her house for the follow-up."

"Let the maid clean it up?"

"You are in a pissy mood."

"Going to the morgue—again—with Karen Holloway crushing my arm in a death grip and threatening to throw up in my car for the entire trip back isn't a mood booster."

Joanne grunted, as close as I was likely to get to acknowledgment that I had a point. "Okay, thanks, I'll catch up with Karen later."

"She may not be in; she's going somewhere 'nice' with her girlfriend."

"That's a bit more buddy-buddy than just nausea in your car."

"Not really. Girlfriend called while we were driving, and I got to hear the whole conversation. Karen was happy to babble on until we got back to her car, luckily before we got to their favorite sexual positions."

"Don't be too snarky. Holly seems okay, maybe even good for Karen."

"You've met her?" Too late. Of course they had met. Joanne's partner Alex had been friends with Cordelia since high school, and the two lesbian cousins often found themselves at the same social gatherings. I hastily continued, "Well, good luck. I'll probe my memory and see if anything surfaces. I'll call you if it does."

"Okay, Mick. Catch you later."

I stared at my phone. What the hell had I got myself tangled in? I had been fine living my single life, not thinking about Cordelia and how I'd messed that up—the past is stone, it will not change. Now it all came roaring back—I was single and Karen Holloway had a nice social worker girlfriend—my one-sided eavesdropping wasn't a good standard to judge her by. It's so easy to see what we want to see. The call had been during work hours, maybe Holly thought she had a moment, then ended up handling a crisis while talking to Karen to explain what I'd heard as her talking a lot. Joanne was a good judge of character—and had actually met her, unlike my overhearing a phone conversation where I had to guess at everything she said. The imp of perversity was sitting on my shoulder—back to judging Karen with standards that made sure I was better.

Instead I got to be like the kid outside the closed—permanently closed to me—candy shop, being aware of all the things I was left out of, the awkward social dance my friends were doing. They were all still friends with her. And her new partner. Wife? Would I even know? I wasn't going to be a big enough asshole to make them choose sides, especially since they weren't likely to choose me. I realized I was the odd girl out, uncoupled, the single amongst all the settled pairs. Joanne and Alex, Danny and Elly, even Torbin and Andy, all had to decide which of us to invite, even for a casual meet-up after work for drinks.

Maybe I should just call her up, say, "We need to meet, figure out how to be friends enough so our friends don't need to dance around us. So Danny can send out a text to say meet at her place after work and not have to remember to leave out either my name or yours."

Yeah, right. Perhaps the best person I could be would be able to manage that. But I wasn't the best person I could be at present, and I wasn't even sure how to get there from here.

I wasn't going to call her. Maybe tomorrow. Next week.

Next year.

Besides, it was her choice to come back to New Orleans. If she'd stayed away, there wouldn't be a problem.

Instead I did something entirely frivolous and borderline unethical, and searched for info on Holly Farmer.

And found nothing. Okay, very little. Maybe I was slipping; this was what I was supposed to be good at, finding people. First Aimee Smyth and now Holly Farmer. Admittedly it wasn't an "I'm being paid for this" search, more a whim, bored search. Someone named Holly Farmer lived in a house in the Irish Channel. She bought it three months ago. Maybe her dead parents had left her well off. Most of the social workers I knew were moving into the Holy Cross area, the Lower Ninth because it was what they could afford. The Irish Channel, close to the river and nicely uptown, had gentrified quickly after the disaster speculators had moved in, buying damaged property after Katrina and flipping it.

Of course I have a house in Treme, now also a high-price area. But I moved here a long time ago, well before Katrina when it was considered an "are you sure you want to live there" neighborhood. I couldn't afford it now.

And this was all a waste of time. Maybe Holly Farmer (really, who names their kid that?) was the perfect girlfriend for Karen and they would live happily ever after.

It didn't affect me and I didn't care.

It was close enough to five o'clock to end this workday. Not that I had done much actual work.

I headed home but only parked in front of my house before heading to my favorite watering hole, Riley and Finnegan's, a down-at-heel bar, still holding to the scruffy Rampart Street feel even as the bright shiny streetcar, recently revived, rolled past. It was queer/punk/whatever. Even the name over the door had been lost to time. Now some called it Finnegan and Riley, which had changed to FAR, and that had morphed to Far Bar. Usually a younger crowd, but that was okay. I could chat with Mary Buchanan, the barkeep and wise counsel all around. Plus the best burgers in the Quarter, and we had all taken vows of silence to never tell a tourist that. It was a place you could talk if you wanted to talk or be quiet and nurse a drink. And, I had to admit, it was not the kind of place Joanne, Danny, or Cordelia would frequent—graffitied on the outside, a banged-up metal door as the grand (not) entrance, it looked like a dive bar's dive bar.

"Hey, Micky," Mary greeted me. "What's your poison?" I petted Miss M, the bar cat, sitting regally on the bar at the end nearest the door to guarantee anyone who entered would give her the attention she deserved.

I ordered an Abita draft and told her to add a burger when it came time for a refill. Then I found my preferred booth in the far front corner, where I could see who came and went but still be enough away that there was no to and fro traffic. My plan was to do some people watching to get me through the burger, enough beer to mellow the evening. And then probably go home and read. Exciting no, distracting, yes.

The burger, when it came, was hot and juicy, perfect with another cold beer and thick cut fries, in my air-conditioned bubble away from the sticky humidity outside. Back when Cordelia and I were together we'd occasionally do what we'd called fancy date night and go out, sometimes to the grand old places like Commander's Palace, Dooky Chase, or Antoine's. Sometimes the newer ones with the hot chefs. Sometimes we'd do not so fancy and come to, well, someplace like this, or one of the neighborhood po-boy places.

I missed the ease of it, coming home saying "I don't want to cook, do you?" and then heading out. Now plans had to be made, dates set. No spontaneous outings. The friends I went out with weren't in the same place, didn't eat in the same kitchen, didn't live in the same part of town. It became easier to go out on my own, find a place like R&F, where I fit in as much as I fit in anywhere.

I noticed an older man standing by the bar—well, closer to my age, but older for the usual crowd that came here, those just barely able to drink (legally) searching for the excitement of the night, not yet coupled, first job or maybe second, or still chasing degrees, adult life had just begun, the seeming freedom of it before being weighed down by the responsibility that came with freedom. They were seeking the connections of the night, new people, new possibilities, so many directions to travel because their journey had barely begun. I watched him as he poured a glass of Chardonnay from a bottle beside him. Sometimes older people came here to seek the young, maybe for an ego boost at best, but to prey on them with the differences in power between someone with three roommates and a bike for transportation and someone with a newer car, a home not shared other than by choice. Predators. I watched him, but he seemed content to top up his wineglass, pet Miss M, and chat with Mary.

Maybe he was here for the same reasons I was, to be someplace besides the same walls staring back at me.

Maybe Karen was right, my profession had jaded me, made me look for the suspicious, constantly calculating the dangers. Older guy in a bar had to be here for picking up the barely old enough to vote. Seeing that as the first reason, slowly finding others, mainly by looking at my face in the mirror, an older woman, could be here for the same reasons.

Except I knew I wasn't here specifically to pick up someone twenty years younger.

But what if one of those young women came over here, started talking, seemed interested, consenting? Would I really turn her down if she was appealing? Blind myself to the ways our ages changed who we were and could be? My house, job, car, money in the bank, not enough, but a reasonable enough pile to get me through a few slow months, earned through years of saving. She wouldn't have the years to save that kind of money, the years to pay off a car note, a mortgage, to pay for the meal or bar tab without having to worry it would come from next month's rent. Even a little power can be alluring. Buying someone a beer could be that little power. If I wanted someone to go home with, the fission and allure of attraction, would I turn it down?

I finished the last fry. The point of coming here was to distract myself, stop thinking about my problems and enjoy the fun of watching how many people were wearing purple or beer T-shirts. Have a good burger with enough beer to smooth the evening out and then go home to sleep. Not to sit here contemplating the ways I judged others for the same flaws I had, to wonder if my rationalizations were any better than theirs were.

I got up, leaving my half-finished beer to mark my place, taking the hamburger plate back to the bar.

Right next to where the older man was standing. It was still early, the bar wasn't crowded.

"Hi," I said as I handed the plate to Mary. "I don't think I've seen you here before," I said to him. To Mary, "Great burger as always. How do you do it?"

"Oh, we just let the cat lick the plate. Adds the extra flavor," she replied.

I smiled at her, then turned back to him, wanting to see if he'd reply. Maybe he was a nice guy, or maybe I was right the first time. I wanted him to realize he'd been noticed.

"Nope," he said easily, "haven't been here in far too long." Not a local accent, my guess was Northeast.

"Why this bar?" I asked.

"I own it."

"Ah." Then, "Are you going to renovate it?" Be part of the gentrification taking over Rampart Street. Give the young and not so well off one less place to be.

But he said, "Why? Is there something wrong with it the way it is?"

"No, I love it just the way it is, a place that scares the tourists away."

"Something wrong with tourists?"

"No, some of my best friends and all that—but I live around here and I like being able to stop by for a good burger and beer without being overrun by straight tourists looking for the 'authentic' New Orleans."

He held up his hand for a high five. After we completed the ritual, he said, "I live in New York but love New Orleans. Since I like my vino," he raised his glass, "why not own a bar? Last owner is a friend, but he's getting older and wanted out. I was crazy enough to say sure, why not? He gave me a good price. I just had to agree to keep it the way it is, pay decent wages, and always bow to the bar cat."

"Is he a suitable new owner?" I said, turning to Mary, although I pretty much knew the answer.

She gave him an appraising look, then said, "He's okay, but no one will ever be like Catfish."

"I could take that as a compliment or an insult," he said. "Either goes well with wine."

"So, new owner, what's your name?"

"Byrnes, Rob Byrnes."

"Hey, Rob," Mary said, "Micky is a private eye. She might be able to help you."

"Really?" Rob said. He picked up his bottle and glass and motioned us back to my corner table. He also signaled Mary to bring another beer for me.

Yeah, it was after hours, but I never turn down work, not in the summer when it's slow.

Once we were seated, he glanced around to make sure no one was within earshot. "Okay, Mary vouches for you, I'm good," he started. "We had two overdoses right around here last week. Yeah, we keep naloxone here at the bar just in case."

"Sad but true for a lot of places around here."

"Except I think someone is dealing out of the bar. Hot stuff, laced with fentanyl."

I shook my head. It was too easy to slip up. A bad job, bad breakup, bad luck in life, and you get caught in a trap. Then I got professional. "What kind of security do you have here?"

"That's the balancing act. I don't really want cameras all over the place. A lot of the people that come here aren't out to their families. This is the one safe space for them. A camera could take that away."

"What about outside?"

"I don't know. Some don't even want to be seen coming in the door. Maybe I could have two entrances, open the back door."

"Then you'd have to control two different entrances, your staff would have to watch both. Better to stick with just one. Why do you think it's out of your place?"

"One of the ODs was a regular here. She's okay—wouldn't have been if Ali, the night manager, hadn't been quick with the naloxone—and smart enough to use a second dose to overcome the fentanyl."

"Ali Cook?" I asked, noting her name down in the notes app on my phone. This was a case and I was working.

"Yep, that's her."

I'd met Ali a couple of times. A grad student in public health. The overdose victim had been lucky. Not everyone knew to do a second dose of naloxone if the first didn't work, a more common occurrence with fentanyl. "Would it be okay if I talked to your staff?"

"Yeah, sure. But how will that help? I don't want drugs here in the bar—it's illegal for me and the staff, could lose our license. Also don't want people using my space to prey on these kids—we can call them that, right? But at the same time, I don't want a big mess, police in here busting people. I'm making it difficult, aren't I?"

"No, you're being real. Too many of us aren't safe in the so-called safe world. Bullied at school, catcalled dyke in the suburbs, kicked out of bathrooms in shopping malls because we don't tick off all the right gender markers. It can be hard to find space where you feel okay to be yourself. Law and order too often means protecting the right people from the wrong people. You don't want this to be anything goes to the point of everyone for themselves. But you also recognize the usual security measures might mean making it not feel safe for the people that desperately need a safe space."

"So, what do we do?"

"Would you consider outside cameras that face down the block, so they can keep track of who's coming and going, but not directly cover the door? Also, the back area, where you have the garbage cans. No customers should be there. You get to decide if you want to turn the tapes over to the cops. Some straight guy hassles a transwoman and she kicks back—no tape, no one saw anything."

"You're telling me to not fully cooperate with the police?"

"I'm private. I'm not bound by the rules cops are. Plus I'm queer. I've been stopped for no other reason than I was leaving a dyke bar."

We talked over a few other things, adding some outside lights. "It doesn't have to be bright white, but enough to light the area so it doesn't invite shooting up." Training the bar staff in what to look out for. Having Ali make sure they were all trained on using naloxone. I agreed to hang around and watch, not much more than my usual, but I'd be more vigilant. I told him I'd look up prices on cameras and lights for him tomorrow and get back to him.

We chatted at the bar for another beer's worth of time. Mostly about the differences between New York and New Orleans. "Be careful.

Forty degrees may sound not so cold, but the high humidity here makes it feel like cold, dead fingers are everywhere."

I watched as we talked but didn't see anything that looked suspicious. The usual crowd was filtering in, waiters off the afternoon shift, a group of young lesbians in softball shirts, all matching, a team or they didn't like having to think about what to wear.

But no quick hand movements that might indicate a drug deal. No one who came in scanning the crowd with a hungry look. Friends who knew friends, transwomen, transmen, some with makeup and bulging biceps, or skinny wrists and beards. Pink hair, blue hair, shaved heads. Black, white, mixed race, mixed couples and groups.

After what was probably one beer too many—Rob insisted they were on the house—I headed home.

There wasn't much more I could do tonight on my new case. I'd get going on the camera and security lights tomorrow. I could hang out at the bar but might better spend my time skimming through the camera footage, see who I pegged as a likely dealer and the times they were around.

It was a hot, muggy night, the long hours of summer leaving the final faded pinks and purple of sunset in the sky. And therefore a hot, muggy walk home.

CHAPTER FIVE

I'd emailed Rob several possible packages of security cameras and lights—most basic bottom line to super deluxe and two options between them—before noon.

Last night had been a take another shower and go to bed night, so I was up bright and early. After I sent the information to him, I busied myself with drinking more coffee and dreaded filing and billing. Paperwork is so not my favorite task. I became a private eye, my own one-person business, to get away from people telling me what to do. The problem with a one-person business was there was no one to delegate to. And if the odious tasks didn't get done, it was my bottom line they came out of.

It had been a struggle in the early years. My current office had also been my living space and there were times it took eating rice and beans four days out of five to scrape up that one monthly rent. It always seemed to be a balancing act. I couldn't count on a steady paycheck, and clients were sometimes slow to pay their bills. I'd learned, not always the easy way, to plan for the worst case, to save when I could. I'd worked hard, not been too picky about cases. Of course it had been easier when I was with Cordelia, two incomes, her steady doctor paychecks. I turned down the real rat-ass cases—divorces, always messy; bosses paying minimum wage to catch employees stealing a bag of French fries— forgo the private eye and pay them enough not to go hungry.

But now it was just me again. A house mortgage and now the building mortgage. Two big bills that had to be paid every month. The coffee shop ("specialty coffees and teas shoppe") on the first floor covered most of the mortgage, the computer grannies on the second floor, the rest. But that didn't cover repairs or maintenance. Do you know how much it costs to replace the air-conditioning units in a three-story building? I do. Hello and good-bye home equity loan. Termite contract? Forget the new computer.

I was happy to have Rob's case but liked his cause enough not to charge full freight, something I really couldn't afford to do. But this was what I had saved for.

While waiting for him to get back to me, I continued my search for Sally Brand and Aimee Smyth, suspecting both were futile. I wanted to check out the hotel where she had putatively been staying, but Joanne had that information as well, and she would not thank me if I dropped by.

Not your case anymore, Micky, I told myself. Except the check had cleared. If it was what it seemed, some con game, why throw real money into it? Maybe they hadn't intended me to keep it, but something interfered.

Like a real murder in the midst of a con game? You don't make people happy when you cheat and steal from them.

I re-did every internet search I'd done before, this time looking for a liar and grifter, not just a client.

Lunch, a barely remembered to be eaten turkey sandwich, came and went and I kept searching. Different spellings of the names, different locations, broad and wide searches that yielded too much information and narrow targeted ones that gave too little.

Then something. The Brande family of Atlanta. Not the biggest, but not the smallest either, of crime families. Four brothers from a small town in Georgia moved there in the fifties. Started with illegal alcohol sales—get your hooch on the way to church. Most places aren't as liberal as New Orleans in where and when you can get booze—grocery stores, gas stations, lemonade stands, elves in potholes.

The Brandes didn't seem to be the brightest of lights. The four brothers, then their sons did time in jail. Then the sons of the sons. Big-time enough to go to jail, but small-time enough to not stay there too long. Drugs and gambling got added to the booze. More male children went to jail, then back out to the family business. But business was good enough to buy several houses in the Buckhead area—they called it the family compound, but pictures showed a few strung-together houses of the mini-mansion variety with a high wall around them. A wall the neighbors fought as an eyesore. They won their case, but in true scofflaw style, the Brandes didn't take it down.

Ah, domestic violence charges started popping up. Walls had multiple reasons to keep prying eyes away.

About ten years ago, there seemed to be a family split, a bitter one, from the escalating reports of bar fights and violence. A fire at the Buckhead place—cause listed as unknown, possibly arson, but the authorities got little cooperation from the Brandes. No charges were filed.

Eight years ago one of the older Brande men was shot, a drive-by. Ended up in a wheelchair. No arrests were made. But four months later, another shooting, this time in a parking lot of one of their favored watering holes. Two cars were destroyed, but only minor injuries. After that about every year there was at least one shooting, rarely causing more damage than minor injuries. The usual arrests for bootlegging, drugs, and bookmaking continued.

As did the domestic violence.

About three years ago it stopped. Truce? Or had one side won?

This was all fascinating, and had eaten most of my day. But in the scant mentions of the women, there was no Sally or Aimee of any spelling. Women, usually blond and big busted, showed up mostly in wedding photos. These were mostly the posed newspaper announcements, so they only told me what the male Brandes looked like. They didn't rule out Aimee as being related, but no clear family trait like the same nose or eyes. But I did stumble on a few photos— ah, the age of the ever-present camera phone—that showed what the Brande women looked like—some taking after their blond mothers, but some had the darker hair and wide brown eyes of the fathers. Could that have produced Aimee? Not a no, but not a yes.

Sally Brand might have been just a coincidence, a similar name. Even Sally and Atlanta didn't prove anything. Maybe they were connected. And maybe I had wasted an entire day, and the petty criminal Brande family had nothing to do with this.

I debated calling Joanne and letting her know of this possible connection.

But the day was late and I left the debate for the morning.

Rob had texted asking if I could bring a printout of my suggested security plans to his bar. Customer service is not my middle name, but

I'd make an exception in this case. Especially since it so neatly met my wishes—an excuse to leave the office before the proverbial office hours ended. (Yes, I'm my own boss, but I try to impose reasonable work standards on myself.) And an excuse to have another beer or two and still call it doing my job. Win-win. And it would ease me into the weekend. Yeah, sometimes I worked the days most people were off, but if I could I tried to take a break. Slow summer gave me breaks.

The hipster coffee shop smelled of pumpkin and cinnamon. Insulting smells for the bare beginning of August here. We are so far from cool fall temperatures that they feel like unicorns. It was a slow time, so maybe they were experimenting with their upcoming specials. None of it made me more likely to eat/drink there.

As usual, I parked by my house. I probably wouldn't find parking much closer anyway, and even if I did, by the time I left, all the parking near my home would be taken by people wanting to go to the French Quarter and spend a lot of money, but none of it on parking. They would take the nice, well-lit and maintained spot in front of my house and leave me the dark end of the street under the constantly shedding fir trees.

I headed to the bar, toting an envelope of specs for Rob.

He was there, as promised, the bottle of Chardonnay beside his glass.

"I hear you like good Scotch," he said, pointing to one of the bottles on the top shelf.

Ethically I should have said no, but I don't have the kind of ethics to refuse fifteen-year-old single malt, especially one with a nice hint of smoke and peat. I don't eat raw oysters in August, but I will drink Scotch, that was about it as far as my ethics were concerned.

Once my drink was poured—a generous pour, thank you, Mary!—we moved to my usual table in the corner.

I pulled the specs out of the envelope and spread them across the table, walking Rob through the various plans. After questions about the pros and cons, he decided to go with the higher middle plan, a choice that pleased me. It wasn't as bare bones as the bottom ones and had a fairly decent camera as well as a panic button for the bar, office, and back room. The garbage and loading area out back would be well lit, with two cameras to be able to see the entire area as well as onto the street outside.

We had gotten up to walk around, me suggesting possible places to put the cameras and lights.

Rob was reasonable, asked good questions, and we were soon back at the table signing a contract.

I used my phone to quickly type an email to Lisa/Valerie, the Electric Girls. I had worked with them for years to install security systems and they were my first choice, if they were available. It was after business hours, but this way they'd get it first thing in the morning.

And then it was time to sip the Scotch. Rob went back to his Chardonnay at the bar—he was more gregarious than my far corner table permitted. I watched the people come and go. I got another Scotch, paying this time, although opting for the same one Rob had bought me, more than I'd usually go for. But it was a nice whisky, smooth and smoky, and I didn't want to switch to something lesser.

The sun set and the evening passed. There was no snake curled up on my doorstep when I got home.

CHAPTER SIX

S aturday and Sunday passed and I was again staring at a Monday. The morning quickly lost its place in my best morning of the week competition. The cloying pumpkin spice smell had wafted up my stairs and was now hovering outside my office. The blinking light on my answering machine was a message from Karen wanting to know if I'd made any progress on "our" problem.

And it was too early in the morning to spike my coffee.

My second message made me want to break that rule.

"Come talk to me." Joanne. No hint about what, and that's never good from her.

First a pot of coffee. A big pot. Neither had said to call back immediately. And even so, immediate was in the eye of the beholder.

Just as I took the first sip, my phone rang.

I stared at it like a snake poised to strike.

You don't need to answer it.

But I did—I'd have to deal with it all sooner or later. Sooner might get me back to my coffee.

"Hello? I'm looking for Knight Air Conditioning?" the voice asked. Honey-dripped Southern accent, more north Mississippi than around here.

Stupid wrong number. But not one I'd ever gotten before. If it's a reversed digit, usually I'll get a call or two on occasion. Someone was really off on their dialing.

"Sorry, this is a private investigation agency," I answered.

"Oh. Can you transfer me to Knight Air Conditioning?"

A gut feeling took over my impolite answer. "Stop playing games, Aimee. Who's the dead body in the morgue?"

Click.

I checked the caller ID. A 404 number.

Atlanta.

A cross check revealed no name. Probably a burner phone, but one bought in the Atlanta area. Either stupid in that it strengthened the Atlanta connection, or arrogant that they thought I'd never catch on. Or deliberate to throw me off and make it seem like Atlanta when it was Biloxi.

The accent had been too thick, someone putting it on instead of being the way they spoke. How she pronounced Knight, the lift on the "i." Nothing big and glaring.

And…just a feeling.

Aimee, or Sally or whoever she was, was checking up on me. Making sure I was here?

Why?

Or was it just a wrong number who hung up on me when I said something that sounded crazy? No, Miss Honey-Accent ditz would have sputtered or gaped or asked me to repeat or again demanded to be connected to the air-conditioning division.

Even if I was right, what did it get me?

We still didn't know if Aimee and Sally were two different women or the same one. If she was alive, she couldn't be dead—well, duh, of course. But there was a woman in the morgue, and whoever it was wore the same clothes and jewelry as the woman in my office.

It was still the same maddening circle. We didn't know who the dead woman was—well, I didn't, although maybe Joanne had worked forensic magic with dental records or DNA and now had a name.

I could call Joanne back and ask. But if I blabbed my suspicions—an Atlanta crime family with a similar name and a gut feeling she'd called me—I doubted she would be impressed.

I didn't need to tell her any of it. I could just call her back.

The phone rang again.

This time I looked at the caller ID.

Karen.

I answered it. I had a few questions for her.

"Hi, Micky—"

"What kind of jewelry was she wearing?"

"What?"

"So-called Sally Brand. What kind of jewelry?"

"What kind of—? I don't remember…it's such a blur."

"C'mon, Karen, you're a high-end Realtor. Can anyone walk into your office and ask to see your properties?"

"Well…what do you mean?"

"If I walked in and said I wanted to buy a Garden District mansion, would you show me houses?"

"You can't afford them."

"How do you know?"

"I mean, well, Cordelia paid the bills and—"

"She did not! We split everything."

"Okay, yeah, but she did your down payment on your current house."

"And I pay the mortgage. Okay, I'm not the best example, you know too much about me. How do you assess your client? Separate the ones who just want to look from those who are serious buyers?"

"Well, it's a bunch of things. Mostly the credit report and their assets. But…yes, there are clues. The cut of the clothes—well-made, tailored or off the rack."

"Jewelry?"

"Yes, but probably not what you think. Big bling is usually meant to put on a show. Old style to indicate an heirloom is better."

"Think about Sally. When you first saw her. What impression did she give?"

Karen was quiet for a moment, then said, "Well, frankly, nouveau."

"New money?"

"Yes, but new money can buy just as well as old money. She was…too friendly, like she was trying to make an impression."

"What was she wearing?"

"High end, but bought, not made. They didn't fit well enough to have been tailored."

"Not everyone can afford a personal tailor."

"But she should have been able to afford to have expensive clothes fitted to her and she didn't. And they were nicely done, but not the latest fashion, colors a few seasons behind. Like she did her shopping in Houston or Dallas but not New York or Paris."

I shopped online for whoever had black or gray T-shirts on sale. But I didn't say that. As I suspected, Karen was observant and could see things I was oblivious to.

"Atlanta?" I asked.

"Yes, that could be it. But she didn't mention Atlanta, said she was from Dallas, newly divorced and wanted to move away. But…"

"What?" I prompted.

"She didn't have a Texas accent. I mentioned it and she seemed taken aback, like I'd insulted her. Claimed she was Texas born and raised. As long as her check cleared, I wasn't going to argue."

"What about her accessories?"

"Shoes—kitten heels, basic style. No brand I could tell. Big leather purse, Versace. Had too much stuff in it, like it was the only purse she used. Jewelry was like she'd gone on a shopping spree in New Mexico. Lots of turquoise. Nice stuff, although not to my taste. But too much, so nothing stood out. You should wear one stunning piece of jewelry, not ten."

"The woman in my office also wore a lot of turquoise pieces."

"You think it's the same woman and she's dead?"

"I think it's the same jewelry. I'm not sure who was wearing it."

"I am not going back to the morgue!"

"I can ask Joanne if she can get us a picture."

That mollified Karen.

"Pictures of the jewelry only, okay?" she stressed.

I assured her again that it would be pictures. I didn't want to return to the morgue again for a long time—indeed, until I was dead and no longer bothered by the smells. Before she could think to start asking questions about "our" case, I claimed I had to go and hung up.

Before I could talk myself out of it, I locked up my office, tramped down the stairs—damn that pumpkin spice smell—and got in my car, blasting the AC to cool it down from sitting in the August sun and also to get rid of the autumn special flavor smell.

Joanne wanted to talk to me. If she wasn't there, I could claim I'd come by as she asked. And cajole some newbie into sending the needed pictures.

She wasn't at her desk; she wasn't in the area.

I sidled up to my prey—newly minted officer Carol Rosenfeld, her name badge said, her uniform still crisp and shiny. She was smart and in about six weeks more I'd never get away with this, was probably on thin ice now, but she was the best option. Besides, she was cute.

"Hey, Carol, I'm helping Joanne with the murder investigation and need—"

"To talk to her directly." From right behind my shoulder.

I whirled around. Joanne.

"I looked for you but couldn't find you."

"I just got in. Thanks, Carol, I'll take it from here." She was sweating enough to prove she hadn't been in air-conditioned comfort. "Let's go to my office and we can sit and chat." She turned away, giving me no choice save to follow. She motioned me into her office, then left me there to sit and wait for about ten minutes before she returned, the sweat wiped off her face and a cold bottle of water in her hands.

"No, I'm not thirsty at all," I said, as the frosty bottle made me realize I was.

"Sorry, budget cuts. We don't have water to give out to everyone who wanders in."

"I didn't wander. You called me and said we needed to talk."

"And you didn't call to see if I was here." She took her coffee mug out of her desk drawer and poured a generous swig of the water in it, then handed it to me.

I took a long gulp, to avoid responding to her statement and because I was thirsty.

"Why were you hitting on my new kids on the block?"

"Not like that. I needed a favor—one you'd do—and she seemed the best one to help."

"Too new to know to avoid you like a swamp full of snakes?"

"No…"

"Yes. So what is it you want?"

"Pictures of the dead woman's jewelry."

"Why?" But her tone had changed, curious and interested instead of bored and snarky.

"I want to see if Karen recognizes it as the same jewelry on the woman who came to my office."

"How will that help?" Joanne asked, but still curious and not a challenge.

"I'm not sure," I admitted. "I'm trying to get as much info as I can. Was it the same woman for both of us? Is she the dead woman? Or was the dead woman made to look like her? If the jewelry is the same, then it's likely to be the same woman."

"Which still doesn't prove she's the woman in the morgue."

"No," I admitted. "But it does prove there is a scam going on. If it's the same woman, why use two different names and two different stories?"

"Maybe she thought both you and Karen are attractive and wanted to get to know you better."

"No, the woman in my office was straight."

"How can you be sure?"

"Trying too hard to look younger than she is or was. Too much makeup for this heat. Too much jewelry. Looking like a woman who needs to look like what a man would find appealing."

Joanne nodded.

She is too good a listener. That's what makes her such an excellent cop.

I told her about the Brande crime family in Atlanta. About the phone calls. She nodded, paid attention, didn't interrupt. Only when I finished she said, "Is it possible? Hell, aliens checking us out is possible."

"But I don't have real evidence," I admitted.

"No. And I have to have real evidence."

"How did she die?"

"Not sure yet. Nothing obvious like a blow to the head or a bullet wound. We're waiting on tox screens." She added, "There are signs of needle marks."

"Overdose?" I remembered her long sleeves even in the heat of the summer.

"Maybe. I'm waiting for the results. I'll get pictures of the jewelry sent to you."

I stood up.

She waved me back down. "Torbin's big drag show?"

"The fund-raiser for CrescentCare?"

"Yes. Are you going?"

"I'd been planning to. Why?"

"Well, Danny was talking about it, so a bunch of us are going."

I knew where this was heading. Into giving me a headache. "You mean Cordelia and her new girlfriend will be there?"

"They were talking about it."

"And you're hinting that I shouldn't go?" I crossed my arms across my chest. The AC in here was chilly.

"No, not at all," Joanne said, just a little too quickly. "I wanted to give you a heads-up."

"Did you pull the short straw or are you the only one who thought I should know?"

"Look, Micky, I know this isn't easy—"

"Not answering my question, are you?"

"There were no straws, and I'm sure everyone else will tell you as well. It just came up last night, and you and I needed to talk about the case anyway."

I got up. "I'm sure you're busy. Send me the photos when you get a chance."

I turned and walked out, pulling my phone out and pretending to be on a call and in a hurry so I could avoid any chitchat.

It was a two-block walk to my car and I made it in record time. Record sweat as well. I was dripping when I finally slammed into my seat.

They had talked about it last night. When they were all together. Except for me. The odd girl out. Not part of a safe, sedate couple. The angsty ex.

Torbin had made a point of telling me about the show. It was a special drag extravaganza, him reprising his greatest hits and new material. It was to be at Rob's bar, my favorite hangout.

"This is my downtown world," I said out loud to my steering wheel. How dare she invade it? This wasn't neutral ground. I knew it had to happen, eventually we'd run into each other. I'd meet the new girlfriend. I'd be polite. She'd be polite.

But not like this, not here, not now. That bar was my home away from home, the kind of old Quarter queer hangout that Uptown doctors did not go to, on the fringes on Rampart Street. I could be there without worrying it would be the place she'd walk into. Yes, most of the rest of the Quarter, I looked over my shoulder, wondering if she'd just finished eating at SoBou or Brennan's. Or was sitting at the Carousel Bar in the Monteleone. The nice parts.

But R&F was mine.

I turned the AC on full blast, the noisy fan matching my mood.

Calm down, I told myself. Then answered, Why? Why should I be the one to calm down? Why should I be the one who made space for them? I didn't want to be the kind of ex who leaned on our mutual friends to choose. They could have parties and invite Cordelia and her partner, they could meet uptown—or in those parts of the French Quarter. Yes, the rules were unspoken, but that didn't mean they didn't exist. I got downtown and she had uptown.

Damn it, damn it, damn it.

I took a deep breath and pulled out cautiously. Driving while pissed off is not a good idea, and I needed to compensate.

It also wasn't fair because they'd all be watching me, how would I behave, how would I react to both Cordelia and her new girlfriend. She had a name and I had looked it up—being a private detective and all that—but I was damned if I was going to waste memory cells on recalling it. My brain was busy enough with New Orleans traffic. A small tin-can car was pretending to be a Maserati and weaving in and out of traffic and was now attempting to jam in front of a minivan from Oklahoma that was a little too close to the car in front for any reasonable person to try.

I backed off. Let the crazies have their crazy space. The minivan sped up enough to block the tin car. Its tiny horn squealed in outrage.

"There are dead people in the morgue and you think you have problems?" I muttered.

I turned onto a side street to avoid as much of the stupidity as I could.

Then another turn and somehow my car ended up going past my favorite po-boy shop. With a parking place calling my name.

A fried shrimp po-boy and, yes, bread pudding for dessert, and I headed back to my office.

As if to mollify me, when I arrived, Joanne already had emailed pictures of the dead woman's jewelry.

I shut down my email. Lunch was more important.

And then a bathroom break. Then making more coffee. Which I iced down because even I'm not enough of a caffeine junkie to serve it hot on a hot August afternoon. Especially with the heat of digesting bread pudding.

I opened the email again.

Stared at the pictures.

I remembered an impression of the jewelry. A lot of it, several rings on both hands, big earrings, heavy necklace, silver and turquoise. Was this the same? Probably. Maybe.

I sighed. I could just email Karen the pictures.

And sighed again. I couldn't just email Karen the pictures. She knew her bangles; I knew the questions to ask, and for that to happen, I had to be sitting in front of her when I showed them to her.

I sighed again. Burped fried shrimp and bread pudding.

I picked up my phone and dialed her number.

"Where are you?" I asked, when she picked up.

"Why do you want to know?"

"I have the pictures of the dead woman's jewelry. I need to show them to you."

"Um, okay. I'm at home. No bodies, just the stuff, right?"

"Rings and things on a brown paper bag background. Not even the pudgy finger of an evidence room officer intruding."

She agreed, telling me she lived at the same Garden District home I'd been to before. I still asked for the address. It had been a long time since I'd been there.

One of my least favorite things to do in the world is get in and out of hot cars, especially during the August steam bath. Between going to see Joanne, the po-boy stop, and now this, I was over the limit for in and out of the heat. I pointed both blowers at my face, but even so it took most of the trip up there before my car had cooled down to a comfortable temperature.

I skipped the parking place right in front and instead drove past looking for a shady place. It took doing the entire block to know that everyone else had the same idea and my choices were close and in the sun and not so close and in the sun. Close—and hot—it was.

Karen's house wasn't one of the Garden District monsters, but it was still way out of my price range, a perfectly manicured lawn, with dots of color from a profusion of flowers, mainly pinks, reds, and yellows, a few deep blue irises in the shade. A large oak dominated the side yard, with a mature magnolia in the front, close enough to the house to offer it shade, leaving the street in the sun. The house itself was two stories, a wide porch on at least two sides, with a balcony on the second floor. The white paint gleamed, a sky blue door, the same hue echoed in the woodwork ornamentation, crafts from a bygone era.

Even though it didn't rival the houses on St. Charles Avenue, it still seemed too large for one person. My opinion, of course. Karen liked to entertain, parties of people spilling onto the porch and yard. I'd been to enough of them when Cordelia and I were together. She did charity events, opening her house—and even her wallet—for various causes from battered women's shelters to queer youth. But non-charity events as well. I'd hate to have to clean all that space. Oh, wait, she had a maid. Maybe a lot of room let you keep part of it company ready and then live in the parts people didn't see. I always had to clean up if I wanted company over.

I climbed the stairs to the porch, wiped the sweat from my brow, and rang the doorbell.

And waited. I gave it an additional slow count to ten, then rang again. She could be in the bathroom.

I decided the doorbell didn't work and raised my fist to knock when the door opened. I again wiped the sweat off my face; it had returned in the interval I had waited.

"Come in," Karen greeted me. She was dressed in off-white linen pants and a light pink sleeveless cotton top. No shoes. She looked all too cool and comfortable.

I brushed past her, again wiping off more sweat while she closed the door.

"Come on to the back, we're having homemade lemonade."

I hesitated. We? "I don't mean to disturb you."

"No problem." Karen kept on walking. Reluctantly, I followed her, bracing for who the "we" might be. Karen's was also on the list of places I didn't want to run into Cordelia.

It would be like Karen to throw us together and watch the fun. They were Southern cousins, so of course saw each other at family gatherings, and being the queer kids of an old New Orleans family had given them a bond, but their lives had taken different paths—Cordelia to medical school and being a do-gooder and Karen to the family tradition of not worrying too much about the little people except at Christmas bonus time. I, of course, had been firmly on Cordelia's side, disdaining Karen's choices with the best of them. For payback, Karen brought up our brief (very brief!) affair before I'd met Cordelia as often as she could and flirted with me when she thought she could get away with it—and when Cordelia was watching.

Since Cordelia and I had broken up, those occasional meetings had ceased. I was no longer part of the family.

Karen led me through her kitchen, updated since I'd last seen it, with new trendy gunmetal appliances, a spotless counter in a shade of charcoal-veined granite with the long counters filled with all kinds of appliances, espresso maker, stand mixer, pizza oven. But it looked more like a show kitchen than a used kitchen. I'd take mine with flour dusting the countertop from the last time I made bread, I told myself, with a last glance at her six-burner stove.

She led me into the back plant room, mercifully still in the air-conditioned confines of the house proper. It was filled with light from the three walls of windows, shimmering off the profusion of green from the plants everywhere they could fit around the white wicker seating, a love seat and several lounge chairs.

I braced myself as I entered. Cool, nonchalant, here only on business.

The woman in the room wasn't Cordelia. I'd never seen her before. I would have noticed her. Tall, maybe five eight or nine, wavy chestnut hair, the kind of deep brown eyes a camera would love, full lips, high cheekbones, and either good genes or a great plastic surgeon, with a perfect nose, a little delicate for her face, but it led back to her arresting eyes.

"Holly, this is Micky," Karen said.

Ah, Holly, the girlfriend. I tried not to look as relieved as I felt. It wasn't Cordelia, and I wouldn't have to worry about Karen flirting—I didn't know if she meant it or just did it to make us—me now—uncomfortable.

"Hello," I said.

"So this is the Micky you've told me about?" she said to Karen, but arching an eyebrow in my direction.

Well, I wouldn't have picked you as a social worker. I had the sense to only think it. Politely, I said, "I'm just here to look at the pictures. I'd like to get back to Joanne as soon as I can." A not subtle reminder to Karen that what transpired here would be related to others.

Karen was not stupid. If I told Joanne, Joanne would tell her partner Alex, and Alex and Cordelia had been close since high school. That was one of the tensions in their relationship, Cordelia and her friends' disapproval of Karen's choices. Karen, for reasons I didn't understand, wanted their approval. "Would you like some lemonade? I just made it, fresh."

"It's good, unless you like it sweet," Holly seconded.

I said yes, mainly because I'd already sweated out every ounce of liquid I'd taken in and I still had the sweltering car ride back. It was already made and sitting on the table. With, I noticed, enough glasses for all of us. Well, Karen did know I was coming—I had called.

I had printed out the pictures, large color prints, better than on my phone. Holly was on one of two paired lounge chairs, with a wrought iron table between them. I sat on the love seat—it was that or next to her, presumably where Karen had been sitting. Or the far side of the room under a plant that needed to be cut back.

I pulled the photos out of the folder I had put them in and spread the first few on the table.

Karen handed me a glass, then sat beside me to look at them.

I took a sip. I noticed that Holly was watching me while trying to make it look like she wasn't watching me.

I took another sip. She was good looking; Karen was rich. Story older than time, in the new lesbian version. But to be honest, Karen was also attractive, a well-honed gym body, hair that was a rich shade of wheat blond or expertly enough dyed to look natural. Same blue eyes that Cordelia had, probably their most noticeable family resemblance. Bone structure that would be kind to her as she got older. Karen was in her mid-thirties, starting the slide to forty. Holly was at most late twenties, but I'd bet twenty-eight was stretching it.

And maybe they really cared for each other. In any case, it didn't matter. This would be over soon, and in all likelihood I might run across Karen at some future Mardi Gras as we passed in the street and that would be it.

Karen stared at the pictures. Holly stared at me sitting next to her on the couch.

I drank my lemonade.

Being a private detective is so glamorous.

"What do you think?" I asked as I put down my half-empty glass. "Are they the same?"

Karen shuffled through the photos, then said, "Some are. That cheap ring is the same. I remember looking at it and thinking I hoped she didn't pay more than ten dollars for it." She pointed to its picture.

"Why do you think it's cheap?"

"How thin the metal is, the slight tarnish on one edge. The turquoise looks like mismatched chips, the leftover stuff jammed into another ring to sell to the tourists."

"Okay, so you believe she was wearing this? The woman you saw?"

"This ring, yes. But she also had on an expensive necklace, beautiful artistry, sapphires and a nicely done rose gold filigree. I don't see that here."

I looked through the pictures but didn't see the necklace Karen described. I closed my eyes trying to picture the woman I'd seen. A lot of jewelry—what was on her neck?

I'm going to install a camera in my office and take pictures of all my clients, I vowed, as I struggled to remember and not let Karen's description guide me.

Something blue, but delicate, probably didn't fit with her other pieces, but I didn't pay attention to things like that. It could be the same one Karen mentioned.

"It's not here," Karen said after another look through the photos.

"If it was the best piece, maybe it was stolen."

"But why leave everything else?" she asked. "If you're a junkie looking for drug money, why not take everything?"

"I don't know," I admitted. "Maybe he was interrupted. Or maybe it was someone after that specific piece."

"It was nice," Karen said. "But most likely a family heirloom, their best piece from the old country. Not worth more than a thousand or so."

"That's a lot of money to some people."

"Not a jewel thief. Anyone who knows their stuff wouldn't bother. They have to sell it underground, and that clips the value."

"The other possibility is someone put enough of the jewelry on the dead woman to make it look like the person we saw, but they didn't want to give up the good stuff, so they kept it," I said.

"But why?" Karen asked.

It was the question I was asking as well.

"It makes no sense," Holly said. "Maybe it's a stupid prank."

"Yeah, but with real money involved," I pointed out. "I think it has to be some sort of con, but I can't work out for what."

"Maybe. It still sounds stupid to me." She got up, came around to perch on the armrest next to Karen, and put her arm around her. Claiming her territory. Karen and I had been sitting next to each other on the sofa to look at the pictures.

I stood up as well.

"We haven't gotten any closer to solving this," Karen said.

"No, but we have more information. At some point the information will add up." I put the pictures back in the folder, noticing a still-damp area where it had been tucked under my sweaty arm. I picked up my glass for one final swig of the lemonade. I would sweat it out before I got back to the office. "Thanks for seeing these on such short notice."

"No problem," Karen said. "I'm stuck in this, too." She stood up, awkwardly, with Holly's arm still around her shoulders. "I'll see you out."

I led. I could find my way back to her front door. Holly came with us, as if our good-bye needed a chaperone. The few yards to the door was the usual chitchat, the lemonade was good, I'd be in touch if anything came up, yadda-yadda.

I headed down the stairs, Karen still at the open door. I heard it shut only after I'd passed the magnolia tree.

Yep, my car was hot. I opened all the windows and turned the AC to full, trying to get at least part of the hottest air out. But I didn't linger. Karen was probably watching at the window. I wondered what she was saying to Holly. And what she had told her about me.

As I expected, my car only cooled to reasonably comfortable when I was about five blocks from my house. It was midafternoon. My choice was to call it a day and go home, or to go back to my office, stare at my computer screen, and pretend I was working.

A third option beckoned. With the holy grail of a parking space right by it. I pulled in, half a block from R&F. I could check on how the installation of the security system was going, hang out and observe in the afternoon and call it work.

I caught Lisa and Valerie of the Electric Girls just as they were finishing up.

"Hey, Mick, perfect timing. Let us show you what we have."

Lisa led me back to the small office in the back. On one side was a desk piled high with paper, but the other side was a fancy new monitoring system. As we had asked, there were no cameras inside, but the outside was covered, the back alley and the street outside it as well as two angles on the sidewalk out front, so you could see people coming from both directions. In color, even. The picture quality was good. They showed me how the paging system worked. The phones—one in the office, two behind the bar at either end—could be used as a loudspeaker, in case someone needed to broadcast a warning. For example, someone with a gun out on the street.

Under the bar they had installed both an automatic lock on the doors and a panic button.

"It calls the police," Lisa warned me, "so only hit it when that's what you want to happen."

I admired their handiwork and told them I appreciated how they had fit it into their schedule as we walked back outside to their truck.

"Hey, it's for the community—can't do it for free, but can do it more quickly," Lisa said. "We going to see you at Torbin's performance?"

I managed a smile and said probably, but work was crazy so I couldn't be one hundred percent sure. I changed the subject by offering to hang out and train Rob and his staff on the new system.

They didn't argue. Lisa got on her motorcycle, leaving Valerie to drive the equipment truck. I'd be happy with the air-conditioned truck myself, but different tastes.

A quick wave good-bye and I headed back to the bar and its high-octane air-conditioning.

And a nice frosty beer.

Chapter Seven

I was good, just one beer. With a bottle of water to go with it. When it's this humid, you have to remind yourself, the moisture in the air doesn't mean moisture in the body. You still have to suck in the H2O.

I had just finished instructing Mary on the system when Rob arrived and I went over it all again.

Not a problem, I got to call it working, without having to get my brain out of second gear.

Rob bought the second beer.

I didn't say no.

Nor did I turn down the third, although I opted to get my usual burger and sweet potato fries to go with it. I ate sitting in the office, watching the people go by on the camera monitors. Working, right?

I would eat salad tomorrow.

It was the usual flotsam and jetsam, tourists who looked lost, tourists who looked like they were looking for what Rampart Street offered, bartenders and waiters coming to or leaving work. Given the lingering heat and humidity, it was hard to tell which; a two-block walk could take the starch right out of the white waiter's shirt. Clumps of the young out for an adventure.

I took another bite.

A woman alone. Familiar.

But you're dead, I thought. I hit the control that could take a still picture. Then my beer-befuddled brain woke up. I put down my almost finished last bite of burger, got to my feet, and rushed through the bar, slaloming around patrons and raised glasses.

When I finally got outside, she was gone; a group of giggling young girls blocked the sidewalk, like no one else could possibly expect to walk on it.

I pushed past them.

Empty.

I kept going, checked the next block. A few people hanging out on their doorstep about halfway down, but no woman alone.

I trudged back to the bar. What had I really seen? I knew better than to drink when working, but I had done a wink and nod and pretended it wasn't really work.

A middle-aged woman with the same kind of haircut.

I went back to the office to review the video, getting another bottle of water from Mary at the bar.

Yes, I finished the postponed final bite.

It took me a while to figure out the controls of this new system, how to review one tape while still recording what was going on.

Was it her?

Yeah. Maybe. No. Enough of a resemblance to not say no, but also too little detail to say yes.

She was catching up to and then walking through the gaggle of sidewalk hogs I'd seen earlier. They blocked getting a good look at her until she was just walking under the camera. At that precise moment, she moved into the overhead light from the bar door, and it both changed the shadows on her face and washed it out, as the camera was set for the ambient light in most of its range.

I kept looking at the still shot and the video. It was just a few seconds. Her bobbing at the back of the sidewalk group, weaving through them, then briefly in front before leaving that camera range. On the camera facing the other way, it was a brief second of her back, then the group came into the picture and blotted her out.

"Damn, damn, damn," I muttered.

A ghost in the night. Most likely a random woman that my brain decided resembled the putatively dead woman because I was thinking about her so much.

I finally gave up, emailed a copy of the snippet of video and the still shot to myself. I'd look at it in the sober daylight.

With that I decided I was off work and had another beer.

But my mind didn't relax into the buzz. Instead it started going in agitated circles.

Was Karen behind this? She was devious and manipulative. But her revulsion at the dead body was real. I could see her as a con artist, but not a murderer. Or had she gotten in over her head and involved me as some sort of bizarre cry for help? But could she possibly be this good an actor to keep playing a believable victim? With me watching? I had once been fooled by her blue-eyed good looks, but that was a long time ago.

If it wasn't somehow connected to Karen, why would anyone pick the two of us? Maybe it was just random, but I didn't believe in those kinds of coincidences. If it wasn't random, it made no sense. We weren't friends or connected in business. We weren't close enough that if someone wanted to get one of us, they'd pick the other. Maybe a vendetta against the lesbian community—but again, the two of us didn't make sense. I was out, but not a big activist. Karen less so, at most discreet donations to a few organizations.

It was time to go home. I was two blocks away when I remembered I'd parked here. I kept walking. I wasn't as sober as I'd like to be when driving, and it was late enough in the evening that most of the street parking around me was taken by people heading to the French Quarter. I could get my car tomorrow.

Plus I was hoping the walk might clear my head.

It did not. I was hot and bothered, and not in a fun way, by the time I got home. Made more hot and bothered by the shaking of the shrubs outside my front steps. I bolted back to the street, only to have a small sparrow flit out.

Damn snake.

I stuck my head in the freezer door for a minute, then filled a glass with ice, leaving only a little room for the water. I guzzled half the glass before flopping down on the living room couch. I sat for about half a second, then got up again and went to the back where my office/reading/hide stuff for parties room was.

I started writing things down. Aimee Smyth hired me to find her sister Sally Brand. Sally Brand went to Karen to buy a house—an expensive house at that, at least over 500k to be in the property Karen's firm showed. Hadn't she said just over a million? Who has that kind of money only to flake out?

I can be a Jill of all PI trades but tend to do missing people and security. Places like Rob's bar, nonprofits in the Lower Ninth, not the high-end stuff. There should be very little overlap between the people buying homes from Karen and those seeking my services. Occasionally a well-to-do gay guy or lesbian came my way so they could be open about who slept in what bed when we were going through their house to install a system.

But I wouldn't send my clients to Karen to buy a house—assuming I'd even known she was doing real estate. Nor would she be likely to send anyone down to my scruffy (albeit gentrifying) Bywater office.

I took out a new piece of paper. I drew a big circle. Karen and I were at opposite ends.

In the center was the dead woman in the morgue. She needed a name and someone to mourn her. But was she Sally or Aimee? Or neither of them?

I put Aimee on my side; Sally on Karen's, with lines connecting them to us. Then dashed lines from them to the dead woman.

I stared at the page. Scribbled notes on my side about the possible phone call and possible sighting. But I couldn't draw any lines connecting them to anything. In frustration, I drew a brain with question marks around it—the pictorial depiction of my fevered brain—and put the dashed lines between it and them.

Then I got up and got another beer.

I sat back down and stared at my scribbling some more. No enlightenment.

I looked up flights to Atlanta.

It was cheapest if I left on Saturday and came back on Tuesday. Dirt cheap, in fact, which meant they were hauling people in for some convention and wanted to do whatever they could to fill those leaving seats.

If I left on Saturday, I'd be out of town for Torbin's show. I could miss it and say I had to work. No one needed to know that work was a wild-ass goose chase after a chimera of a woman.

I reminded myself no one was paying me for this. Then reminded myself Aimee's check had cleared. It would about cover a trip to Atlanta with enough left over to buy a cup of coffee—if I didn't go to the fancy place that rented my downstairs.

I finished the beer.

I could just let this go, let the cops with their greater resources hunt down who the woman was and why she died.

I got up and got another beer. I'd need to buy more next time I went to the grocery store.

I sat back down at my desk, still staring at the pages. Sober hadn't worked; maybe being drunk would jar something loose.

The beer helped, but only in mellowing out my mood. Everything else stayed the same, with nothing making sense. Except even if the police did solve the murder, that didn't mean they'd find out why Karen and I were involved. Someone went to time and trouble—and spent money—to weave us into this. I wanted to know why.

No, I needed to know why. One woman was dead. Whatever the game, the stakes were high. Right now, I didn't even know if it was poker or chess. Or some new video game, to stretch the metaphor. If I was going to protect myself—okay, and Karen, too, I supposed—I couldn't wait for them to make their next move. I had to be moving as well.

I had to hope it wasn't in the wrong direction.

I booked the flight to Atlanta.

In the morning nothing had changed except my level of sobriety. Sleeping on it hadn't helped.

You don't have enough information yet, I told myself. *Only Miss Marple could solve this as it currently stands.* And she could only do it because she had a writer making sure she found the right clues.

I did rounds for places I've put in security systems, checking to see how things were, good business practice to be attentive, but I mostly did it because it kept me in motion and distracted by New Orleans drivers and the heat. I spent most of the time cursing either one or the other and not obsessing around the case.

I went back to Rob's in the evening, watching the monitors, but I only saw the usual suspects, tourists, the bar locals, waiters. No one who resembled the dead woman. Or even the live woman I'd briefly glimpsed.

The next few days passed, slow at the office—I did get the filing and invoices done—checking the monitors at Rob's in the evening. But nothing. A big fat nothing. As much as my brain was on overload—or melting in the heat—it still made no sense.

CHAPTER EIGHT

What the hell are you doing? I asked myself as I stood in the slow-moving security line. Going on a stupid trip to a city that can be best described as Los Angles with humidity and no beaches. If you live in New Orleans, you pretty much have to fly through Atlanta. That or Houston, another traffic-jammed city with high humidity.

Sobering up had made me question this decision every time I thought about it, but even stone cold sober, I couldn't come up with anything else that might lead to useful information. I wanted to find out if Sally could be part of the Brande crime family. Maybe they were branching out to New Orleans. If she was, it might help ID the body. If she wasn't, at least I could close this door.

Finally through the checkpoint, I made my way to the gate. I found a seat off in the corner. I had to make some phone calls.

I chose the one I wanted to do the least first.

"Hey, Torbin," I said as he answered. "Sorry to do this, but work is going to make me miss your show tonight." As if on cue, a flight announcement blared loud enough that he had to hear it.

"Wait, where are you?" he said.

"At the airport," I said.

"Why?"

"Work."

"What work?"

"Confidential," I answered.

"Where are you going?"

"Confidential."

"Really? Since when have you refused to at least let me know where you're off to?"

I sighed. "Since my client told me to tell no one." He didn't need to know the client was me.

"Okay…" He yawned. Torbin was not a morning person.

Which made me yawn. I wasn't a morning person either, but the airline schedule didn't seem to care about that.

Before I finished yawning, he continued, "We'll miss you. I even put in the 'what Lola-Nola wants' number for you."

"Others will enjoy it as well," I said. "Besides, I'm sure you'll have a crowd."

Torbin knows me too well. I thought my voice was neutral, he knew it wasn't. "Ah, so you heard."

"Yes, Joanne bothered to tell me."

"I know. She told me. Which is why I didn't tell you. Is this trip just to avoid running into her?"

"If I wanted to avoid anyone, I could stay at home and do that," I answered. I had been planning on this being one of the fake polite calls. I'd say I couldn't make it; we'd say we'd catch up later and ring off and be done with it. He'd know and I'd know and we'd never discuss it. It's the way of all Southern families.

"Look, I'm sorry I'm out of town. I would be there otherwise. Our paths will cross; it will be okay. You don't need to choose." There, nice and adult of me, I thought.

"I thought it was kind of shitty myself. But Danny and Alex were talking about it in Danny's kitchen, girlfriend overhead and thought it would be great fun to go. I couldn't exactly say no, that's not your part of New Orleans and I'm doing a special number that will embarrass the hell out of my dear cousin Micky and it's not going to be nearly as much fun with you there."

"You didn't invite them?"

"Not on our dear grandmother's grave!"

I hazarded a guess. "You don't like her, do you?"

Torbin sighed. "We need to talk when you get back."

"What, you can't admit that over the phone?"

"More important things. Girlfriend doesn't think it's fair you got the house and they're living in an uptown condo."

"But—" And I couldn't think of anything to say.

Another flight announcement; this time mine. They were about to start boarding.

"We'll talk when you get back."

"Yeah, we'll do that. Break a leg. Or a wig. Or whatever."

I clicked off the phone, then dialed another number. I needed to get through my calls. I had also been putting this one off, dithering about whether or not to bother.

"Karen," I said, not sure if I was talking to her or a machine. "I'm going to send you a picture. I want you to see if you recognize it."

"Oh, okay," she said.

"I'm traveling, but I'll call when I get back and you can tell me what you think." I hung up. I'd said what I needed to say. I sent her the picture, then got in line to board.

Like I needed any more complications in my life. Okay, so Cordelia and I hadn't exactly worked things out. But…But she'd left. First to Houston for treatment for her cancer. I went there when I could. Just…not enough. Not enough for someone who was ill and scared. My fault. I couldn't rationalize myself out of that. I hadn't been there when she needed me, too afraid I'd lose everything, if I locked my office for a few months, turned away all clients. At the time I thought I had done what I could, getting to Houston most weekends. But then she left without telling me, going to the Northeast where her mother's family was. With someone new, the nurse who had been at her side every day.

That was it. I kept living in the house we'd lived in.

Paying the entire mortgage. What? Almost two years now. She couldn't just barge back into my life and tell me to give her the house back.

Could she?

I'm not a lawyer. But even I knew I didn't have the strongest of legal cases. She's a doctor from a well-to-do family. She had the money for the down payment. We'd split the costs after that. I was stubborn that way, too proud to not pay my way. It wasn't always easy or always the best choice, but at least I had that. Plus, I'd done more of the work that needed to be done, arranged my schedule for the plumber, painted a good part of the interior, stuff like that. I had the more flexible schedule.

I found my seat, going halfway to the back in hopes that at least the middle seat would stay open.

Torbin had dropped a bombshell on an already hazardous path. Sitting next to Chatty Cathy might drive me over the edge.

We'd been together for over a decade, bought the house after three years together. She'd paid half the mortgage for seven years; I'd paid it all for two. Even if we agreed on it being the same price we'd paid, that would still be a chunk of change for me to come up with. We'd bought in the Treme section of town, just a few blocks out of the French Quarter, back when it was considered a "bad" part of town (mostly meaning the black people outnumbered the white people). Since then the area had gentrified and our house was worth a lot more.

If she wanted what it was worth now…I couldn't cover that. It would probably be more than our original note.

I watched the passengers slide by, desperately searching for overhead space.

I'd have to sell. We could split the proceeds. That was the only way.

Or she could buy me out. And she and her new partner could live there. I would drive by every time I went to visit Torbin.

Why was I saving Karen, her cousin, again?

Oh, right, only because I'm also involved.

Maybe it was just talk. Maybe it wouldn't happen.

"Thanks, Torbin, like I needed to know this," I muttered.

The plane was filling up. The flight attendant announced it would be a full flight. A dude eyed the middle seat, then decided he could do better than being stuck between a middle-aged woman and an old guy in a suit.

An old woman with a hat—a frumpy hat—threw a small bag in the overhead and swung into the middle seat.

Great. Now I was going to have to spend the entire flight looking at pictures of her grandkids. Or her cats.

Politely, I handed her the seat belt that had fallen between our seats.

She took it, gave me a quick look, then said, "Thanks. Hope you're not the talkative type. I hate chatting over the noise of a plane." She buckled herself in, took a book out of her purse, and pointedly ignored me. I glanced at the title. *Treme Tango* by Greg Herren. Never heard of him. Probably some Yankee who didn't know anything about New Orleans, let alone Treme.

I didn't want to talk to you, either. Rejected by both the young and the old.

I took a book out as well.

One of the biggest mercies of flying to Atlanta is that it's short. They now list it as about an hour and a half, but I can remember when they didn't pad the flight time and, crossing back into the New Orleans time zone, you left at the same time you arrived.

I managed fifty pages in the book by the time we landed.

It was the usual mess getting off. People pushing into the aisle and other people deciding they didn't need to get their overhead baggage until they were standing up and blocking the aisle. I had my bag already in hand and sprinted down the aisle the first chance I got.

I had checked baggage. I brought several changes of clothing, really costume. I couldn't very well knock on the Brande door and say I was a private detective and wanted to know if any of their female relatives might either be dead or pulling a scam on me. Did I want to be frilly pink (yes, on occasion I have) or professional suit or all black? Also, it was summer, and summer in Atlanta isn't much cooler than summer in New Orleans. I'd already sweated enough that I wanted to change clothes after I got to the hotel.

Once I got my bag, I went to the car rental area. I'd need a car. I'd thought about driving; it's only about six hours or so. But I decided it was safer to have an anonymous vehicle, with plates that didn't lead anyone directly to my address. Yes, I was using credit cards, and those could be traced, but that's mostly the realm of law enforcement, and I was planning to avoid that. I didn't want the Brandes to be able to recognize my car.

It was a tin-can compact, but navy blue and generic enough not to stand out. Cousin Torbin drives a red Mini. Cute and fun to drive, but not a ride for a PI.

I plugged in my phone and turned on the navigation. Atlanta is a great big freeway.

One city got burned down in the Civil War and one city didn't. I've always said if you told someone no more than that and then dropped them into Atlanta and New Orleans for a five-minute look around, they would know which was which. The old homes and aged oaks of New Orleans and the big freeways, new buildings of Atlanta.

The change has been around for so long it feels like forever, but the scars linger. It changed things. Maybe like Katrina, eventually, it would be better for New Orleans, as Atlanta had built back after the

Civil War into something different with a changed future. Maybe. Even so, those caught in the maelstrom lost. Their lives. Their homes. Better would never arrive for those caught in the change.

I took the beltway around the city. The Brandes weren't in downtown Atlanta but the tony northern suburbs.

I found an exit that would suit my needs. A few reasonably priced hotels, a choice of places to eat in addition to the usual McBurger Things. A seemingly random stop. A businesswoman in a rental car at a hotel that wasn't a destination, only a stop on the way.

I wasn't sure if I was being too cautious or not cautious enough. A lot of traffic, travel, and people in this area. Not that anyone was looking for me, but if they were, this was not where they would look.

After checking in and unpacking, and changing into non-sweaty clothes, I left again, driving to the address I'd found for the Brandes.

Yep, a McMansion. Boring and tasteless. Worse, there were several strung together, a family compound. All equally boring and tasteless. Of course, I'm from New Orleans, it's hard for anything to compete with the Garden District for beautiful, lavish homes. But then, ours didn't get burned down.

I drove around in a long loop, getting lost for about ten minutes in the winding roads that signaled "we're too rich to drive in a straight line." I found a place to pull over as close as I could to the entrance—a cheap wrought iron gate that badly needed a new coat of paint—and pretended to talk on my phone for as long as I reasonably could. A righteous citizen not driving while on the cell phone.

Except for the leaves fluttering in the breeze, nothing visible was happening.

I drove away, did another loop around the area, scoping it out. Then I headed back to my hotel. It was late afternoon; I was tired and hungry. I stopped at what looked to be a non-chain sandwich place and got two, one for now, one for later. There was a liquor store across the way. I debated for a moment, then went in and got a small bottle of vodka and some tonic water.

Well, this is exciting, I thought as I finished my sandwich while watching a home buying show on TV that I suspected I'd seen before, but there really wasn't anything else on and I couldn't remember which one they picked, so I stayed with it.

I left the vodka unopened.

After dark, I headed back out to cruise around the Brandes'.

It was Saturday night and they were having a party. Most of the driveway was parked up. I found a street spot that could reasonably be for someone going to the party. After about half an hour, I could see why they weren't well liked by the neighbors. The music was way too loud; it was vibrating my car seat, and not in a fun way. People in and out, cars parked everywhere. A large and growing clump of smokers out by the gate, throwing their butts into the road. I could smell the smoke from where I was.

Another half hour and one of the smokers threw a punch at another of them—both men, of course. They were quickly pulled apart. But much unsuitable language was unleashed.

I got out of my car and strolled, as if a neighbor taking a leisurely walk. This was a public right of way, and I had the right to be here.

As I got to the group, I picked the person who looked the most approachable, an older man puffing on a cigar, who seemed to be enjoying the show. He was well onto the sidewalk and I'd have to walk around him anyway.

"Wow, nice party," I commented.

He looked at me. First, a who the hell are you look, then realizing I was female and a good twenty years younger than he was, a more friendly smile.

"The Brandes know how to have a good time," he answered. He followed up with, "You from around here?"

"Not really," I answered. "House-sitting down the road for some friends off in Europe. Have to have my air-conditioning redone and they offered to let me stay. Just have to water a few plants." I smiled.

"So what are you doing down here?"

"I got lonely and decided to take a walk. This seems a safe enough neighborhood."

"Indeed, it's very safe," he said. "Especially with all these people in the streets. Alas, the neighbors don't always think so."

"They complain about the noise?" I asked.

"They complain about whatever strikes their fancy to moan about, like they want to live in mausoleums."

"Yeah, this seems like an uptight neighborhood. I mean, my friends are great, but they prefer museums to going out dancing."

"Ah, and you prefer dancing?"

"I like both. I'll save some energy from museums to go out in the evening. See both worlds." He was flirting with me, I recognized, but it didn't feel threatening, instead probing, to see what was possible. Or a pleasant way to pass the time. Maybe he had a wife—presumably, at his age—but still enjoyed the company of women and a little verbal back-and-forth was as far as he would go. Or maybe not, but he was a rotund man, puffing on his cigar. I could easily outrun him. Or take him down. I was probably as safe here as I could be, considering I was surveying a crime family.

"Indeed, museums hold many wonderful things, for the mind and eye, but dancing is a pleasure of the body."

"Are you one of the Brandes?" I asked.

"Me? No, an uncle in the sense I've been a longtime family friend."

"This is a very nice house. Would I be nosy if I asked what the Brandes do to get it?"

He laughed. "So many things I can't keep track of. Import and export, finance. They've been at it a few generations."

"That seems reasonable," I said.

"Would you like to see the inside?"

"I wasn't invited to the party. And I dressed for a walk, I'm not very presentable." I was in nondescript PI gear, black jeans, but lightweight for the summer, and a gray cotton V-neck shirt. More for skulking around bushes than hot time on the old town. Of course I wanted to get in, but I needed to make it his idea, not mine.

"The Brandes welcome all types. You just have to like to dance." He crooked his arm, an invitation.

I hesitated for the briefest of seconds, then decided not to look a gift horse this big in the mouth. A little more mild flirting, and then an excuse to leave—a migraine, a phone call from my husband on a business trip in Australia, so this is the only time he could call.

I slipped my arm through his and we headed up the driveway to the party.

Chapter Nine

Dictator chic. No, tasteless dictator chic on a budget. Gold (brass really) and mirrors everyone, more bling per square inch than any zoning code should permit. Marble floors that showed a few wine stains. All the hard edges made the music and the voices take on a strident pitch, almost impossible to hear anything or anyone over.

"Wow, this is something," I said. I had to lean in closer than I would have liked to make that comment.

"Let's find the bar," my escort said.

I didn't attempt to fight the noise, just nodded agreement. He led the way to the back, through the kitchen into a large back room. All the carpet was here, lush red shag pile. Bordello in Meridian, Mississippi, style.

He knew exactly where the bar was. He cut around a clump of people either in a sloppy line or wanting to block the bar so they could easily get their refills.

One person looked like he was going to complain, but my escort gave him a stare and he backed off.

"Vodka and tonic," I asked when we got to the bar.

Mercifully, the carpet and flocked (red!) wallpaper muffled the noise, and I didn't need to shout.

He got bourbon neat.

"I'm sorry," I said as we moved away to a less trafficked area. "I don't even know your name."

"Don. Donald. A few people call me Uncle Donnie. And you?"

Scramble brain. Who was I? If I lied, I'd need to keep track of my lie. I decided to go for the soft truth. "I'm Michele." He hadn't given a last name, so I wasn't going to either. "And I won't be one of the people calling you Uncle Donnie. I don't think you're old enough to be my uncle."

He laughed happily at that, which distracted him from names. As I'd intended.

"Are you a longtime Atlanta person?" I asked. My goal was to ask him questions and keep him talking. Most of it would be mindless chitchat, but I hoped to mix in a few queries that would help me get the answers I was looking for.

"Came here as a young man," he said. He then launched into the story of coming from a small town in Alabama, knowing no one here, sleeping in a fleabag motel hoping for a job before his small amount of money ran out, and then being hired by Elliot Brande, God rest his soul, now passed for over ten years, and his being willing to work at anything, from sweeping the floors to driving trucks through the night. Elliot's son Ellis had taken over a few years ago and recognized Donnie's hard work. And so on and so on and so on.

I had to remind myself to slowly sip my drink. It had more vodka than tonic. That would explain the time line. Patriarch dies and a feud to take over erupts. Eventually Ellis is the winner.

I nodded as appropriate, murmured a few "wows" or "that must have been hard" as seemed to be needed. While looking at him, I took in the background, the people swirling around him. My goal was simple, see enough of the Brandes to know if there was a resemblance to the woman in my office. After that it was a fishing expedition. Yeah, well-thought-out plan.

Getting into the house was a stroke of luck—one I hoped not to regret. I wondered if all the drinks were strong or if Uncle Donnie had an agreement with the bartender to make those for his lady friends especially potent. But there were so many people here there was no way to see who was Brande and who was a guest.

Until a woman walked into the far end of the room. No, not Aimee/Sally. Her face was harder and sharper, her body willed into the curves of a young woman, which she no longer was. She was probably late thirties. Fighting middle age as if her life depended on it. In this family of buxom blond wives, it probably did. But the hair was the same, waves that fought being tamed, the same shade of dark brown, almost black. The same nose and eyebrow.

Don noticed my attention had wandered from his riveting story. He glanced over his shoulder to see what I was looking at.

"That woman who just came in the room, the one in the white dress," I said. "Who is she? I swear I've seen her before."

"Really?" he said with a lazy look between me and her. "She your type?"

I played dumb. "Type? No, just looks familiar and I'm trying to place her."

He nodded. "That is Miss Brande." A little too much emphasis on the Miss, as if he hadn't been clear enough with his earlier comment.

"Do you know her first name?"

"Where did you say you were from?" he asked.

"Oh, I don't think I did," I answered, now turning my attention back to him. He didn't like me looking at another woman, especially one who might look back. "Like you, small town, but Louisiana, not Alabama. Moved to New Orleans after college."

"You stayed after Katrina? Must have been crazy."

"Yes, I did. I thought about moving on, but my house was okay and a number of my friends came back. It still felt like home."

"Anna-Marie. Calls herself Anmar. Brandes are an old Irish family."

I shook my head. "No, that's not ringing a bell. Maybe someone who looks like her. They say everyone has someone who looks just like them. You were telling me a fascinating tale about how you came to know the Brande family, how kind they were to you."

I didn't bat my eyelashes at him but gave my full female attention, listening to his words, praising him when it seemed like it would fit. Just when he got to the logging story and having to fight a bear with his bare hands (yes, I laughed as I was expected to) several young women shouted across the room, "Uncle Donnie! There you are."

A flicker of annoyance crossed his face, then he turned with a beaming smile to them.

Younger Brandes, I guessed. Their genes combined the dark coloring of their Brande fathers—dark brown eyes, wavy hair—with the blond curves of their mothers. Or they'd all had boob jobs and dyed their tresses blond by the time they were eighteen.

"Uncle Donnie! You have to come! Jared is about to have a fight in the pool room! You have to talk some sense into him!" Either the oldest or the one wearing the tallest high heels. She did speak only in exclamation points. Or maybe Jared in the pool hall with a cue stick was worthy of such emphasis.

"On my way," Donald sighed. In a courtly gesture, he took my hand and kissed it. "I hope we meet again," he told me, before being dragged off by the blond squad.

Saved by the bimbos.

I put my drink down where a number of them seemed to be parked. I wasn't going to push my luck and go where I didn't belong, but I could wander around all the party areas—excluding the pool room. I wanted to see if I could get a closer look at Anmar, make sure the resemblance was really there and not features across the room that only passed at that distance. I also wanted to be long gone before Uncle Donnie came looking for me. Given what I knew of the Brande family, he was one of their fixers; the trucks he drove probably were loaded with illegal booze or cigarettes, the logs stolen without permits. I didn't want him asking any more questions about Michele from New Orleans.

The house was huge. The big marble entrance, enough space for a small ballroom, had a double height ceiling. To get to the bordello room, as I thought of it, you could go through their kitchen, with its faux French country cabinets, a stainless steel refrigerator you could hide a body in, and a stove with enough burners you could cook the body as well. Or else go through the media room, with a wall of at least eight large screen TVs, set to different sports channels with a line of leather recliners facing them and a built-in bar and popcorn machine behind them.

I didn't linger there. The cacophony of the TVs was worse than the bass beat in the marble room. I went back through the bordello room, got another drink, still vodka and tonic, but I asked the bartender to go easy on the booze.

Then I wandered out to the back patio. It was still hot enough that most people stayed inside. Two men conversed in hushed tones that made me veer away, and there was another couple under a tree not doing any talking. I headed away from them as well. Given what was currently going on, they'd be naked any minute.

The patio was huge, outdoor kitchen, several seating areas, fire pit, goldfish pond. It was several steps up from the lawn. Lighted paths led off to the other houses in the compound. The yard itself was small, sacrificed to the large rooms of the mansion, and half of that was taken up by a swimming pool, a rock arrangement so fake it didn't look real even in the dark. A lone pink flamingo swim toy floated on its glassy surface.

What did they have to do to earn the money to buy this monstrosity?

I turned to look back at the house, leaving the amorous couple well out of my sight line. Lights gleamed from most windows. A few bedrooms were dark. Which didn't mean they were empty.

The woman in white appeared at the patio door.

I stepped closer to the hedge by the pool, sliding into its shadow so I could watch her without being obvious.

The resemblance was there; I wasn't just making it up. The planes of the face—Aimee's were softer, sliding into middle age, covered by makeup instead of hours at the gym, but they were the same. Eyebrows the same line, Aimee's plucked more harshly, but the same arch.

But even so, what did it mean? Weird coincidence, some grandmother coming down to two divergent lines of the family? Even if Aimee was part of the Brande family, it only confirmed what I already knew, Karen and I were involved in a con. But how and why—and to what extent—pawns now dispensed with, or was there more to come?

The woman scanned the patio as if looking for someone, first a quick sweep of her head, then a slow inspection. The lawn wasn't truly dark, not with the candle watts the Brandes liked, even in their path lights. She would see me if she looked in this way.

She looked right at me and started walking in my direction.

In her thirties, probably late thirties, I guessed. Younger than I was, but with hard and wary eyes. The white dress was simple and, an anomaly, tasteful. A reasonable amount of cleavage, but nothing too flashy. A flare to the skirt that gave it animation as she walked.

She planted herself in front of me and said, "Who are you?"

"Who are you?" I returned.

"One of the people who owns this property."

"Well, I'm not," I admitted.

"Uncle Donnie said you asked about me."

Thanks, Uncle Donnie. "I thought you looked familiar. From across the room. My mistake."

"Okay, what's my twin been up to now?"

"Wait—what? You have a twin?" That was a bombshell—one I had to keep from showing on my face.

"Don't act stupid."

"I'm not acting stupid." Then not liking the connotations of that, continued, "I'm from New Orleans. I thought I saw someone who looks a lot like you down there. Maybe it's your twin. But it could just as well be someone who looks like you and is no relation."

"Are you trying to come on to me?" She gave me a look up and down, openly appraising. Unlike with Aimee, the gaydar was going off.

"I haven't even met you," I said.

"A lot of women come on to me," she said. "It gets boring."

"I don't want to bore you." She was a good-looking woman, but her expression was hard, shading to bitter. What was the dyke daughter doing still here in this family? Uncle Donnie had been clear about his disapproval, and he was good at toeing the party line.

"I know what you're thinking. I don't break mirrors and I have a lot of money. That seems to be enough to attract women."

"Probably men, too," I said. "But I'm not one of them."

"Okay, you're an angel in disguise," she said, crossing her arms.

"Nope, not that either. Not after women for their money or their body. Neither says much about the person."

She scowled, as if she didn't believe me. "Where did you see this woman who looks like me?"

"In New Orleans," I said.

"Where in New Orleans?"

"The French Quarter." That was safe enough. Everyone went to the French Quarter in New Orleans.

"You just saw her passing down the street and she was so memorable that you noticed her enough to notice we looked alike?"

"There was a cat sleeping in a store window, we both stopped to look. We started chatting."

"About cats?"

"It was a cute cat. I asked if she liked the artwork, she mentioned another gallery she had passed. She asked me for places to eat."

"Two strangers started chatting?"

"It's New Orleans, cher, we do that sort of thing." Not a great story, but I wasn't going to admit I was a private eye hired by someone who could be her sister to find her sister.

"So if you don't want women for their money or their looks, what do you want them for?" She was probing, pushing me for a weak point—or one she'd consider weak.

"Their brains. The same thing I look for in a man. Brains, compassion. A sense of humor."

"Really? Men and women? You swing both ways?"

"Not swinging tonight," I countered. I wasn't going to out myself here. Playing on the edges was one thing. We both understood neither of us was the frilly pink hetero girl. But how far beyond the line? Safer to leave it vague. Uncle Donnie was an old-fashioned gentleman—one who took care of the good women and took his rage out on the not good women. Even if Anmar Brande was gay, she wasn't the power in the family. I'd find no alliance with her for admitting my sexuality.

"Then why come to this party?"

"Why are you here?"

"I live here, remember?"

"Doesn't mean you have to appear. You could stay in your room and read a book."

She laughed, but with no joy, as if I was suggesting something outrageously impossible. "My dad burned all my books when I finished high school. Said girls shouldn't read, it made their eyes squint, and men didn't like squinty-eyed girls."

A piece of where she'd been broken slipped out. Then her face hardened again. "I'm required to attend the public events. One big, happy family."

"Atlanta has a big airport. Why not fly away?"

"And do what? High school education. No job experience. At least nothing I can put on a résumé. Serve burgers and live in a double-wide?"

"You'd be free."

"Free? Poverty has its shackles. Besides, it's not as easy as you think it is."

"I don't think it would be easy. I'm just pointing out there are options."

She leaned in closer to me and said in a harsh whisper, "You don't understand. Women don't leave the Brande family. If you're not loyal, you're worth nothing. If you're a woman, you're not worth much. A disloyal woman? We swim with the fishes."

I kept my face as blank as I could. I knew the Brandes were a crime family, but I wasn't supposed to know they were, not as the innocent house-sitter who just wandered by. "That sounds…"

"Crazy?"

"Well…extreme."

"Two of my aunts disappeared. One married the wrong man. A cop. They both vanished. I asked Uncle Donnie about her once when I was young. He looked at me and said, 'Don't be like her.' I got the message."

"You are accusing your family of…murder?" I kept to my naïve house-sitter persona. Tried to, at least. And hoped the shadows covered for me.

"Two aunts I know of. Some great-aunts no one talks about. No one visits their graves. Or even knows where they are. Disloyal women are worth nothing. Now my twin is missing."

"Was she—is she 'disloyal'?" I asked.

"No more than I am. But she…she didn't do a good enough job of playing one big happy family. Maybe that was enough."

"That's horrible," I said.

She nodded, then looked away from me, as if she'd crossed lines she shouldn't cross. And she had, if I'd been that house-sitter. There was a dead woman in New Orleans. And a family of men who disappeared their disloyal women. Chilling. I had no evidence of any of this, but it might be time for me to leave, dump this on Joanne and pretend I'd never been here. Anmar was broken—and scared, but I couldn't do anything about that. I added, in a soft undertone, "I'm really sorry. I'm not going to…do anything that would make it worse for you. What you've said here—"

"No one will believe," she said bluntly. We both knew she was right. Then she added, "I'd like to find my sister. If I come to New Orleans, would you take me to where you saw her?"

Oh, hell, no, my brain screamed. First, it was a lie. Second, the last thing I wanted was her coming to New Orleans, trailing her crime family behind her, especially since they had likely already killed her sister. And third…I was a coward. I didn't want to deal with this broken woman, didn't want to have to consider if I could help her; if I should help her.

Instead I said, "But can you travel?"

"Oh, yes. As long as I have a return ticket."

"I can take you, but it was a random encounter. Millions of people traipse through the French Quarter every year."

"It's the only clue I have."

"And it might not be her. I could be wrong."

"You don't strike me as a woman who's often that wrong."

The wide French doors to the patio opened. Light flared our way.

"Anna-Marie! Your dad wants to speak to you." A man who looked vaguely like all the other Brande men called to her. He waited at the door, staring in our direction.

She turned away without saying another word and followed him into her prison.

I took a breath, then another. Then counted out a full minute before reentering the house. The yard had a high wall around it, and I could see no way to get out save through the front entrance. The Brandes didn't build a wall that could be easily scaled. A glint from the lights showed glass shards embedded in the top.

Not wanting to appear like I was anything other than a party guest, I didn't hurry. Stopped at the bar for another drink that would only be a prop. I also wanted to scan each room before fully entering. Better to avoid both Uncle Donnie and Anmar.

The media room still had sports blaring from every screen—all men's, of course—and the testosterone seemed to leech from the TVs into the room as two groups of men were arguing, now shoving and on the verge of a fight.

I backtracked through the kitchen, mostly filled with the catering staff, who seemed to know something was off here and were seeking strength in numbers. I smiled at them, silently wishing them luck, and hoped they weren't disloyal caterers. And that the shrimp dip had passed muster.

At least the yard here was too small for many bodies to be buried.

The grand marble foyer was still loud, made louder by another group of men arguing, but they were surrounded by the big-chested blond women, so it felt more for show than the edge of violence in the media room.

Wrong call. A woman shouted, "Jared! Jared, don't be stupid."

Presumably the person who was Jared threw a sloppy punch that only pissed off his opponent, who punched back, not at all sloppy, and Jared went down, saved from bashing his head on the marble by falling into three of the women, who went down with him. *Oh, Jared, you had to be stupid.*

As gracefully—and quickly—as I could, I sidled through the crowd, taking the long way to get around the back of them. I was at the door.

It was flung open. Three men, with three women draped on each, pushed through, expecting everyone to move away from them. I let them pass. This was not the time nor place to take on how men sucked up space.

I zoomed out of the door before someone else came through.

Drink still in hand as I hadn't found a place to ditch it, I sauntered down the lawn, keeping my pace to that of the other partygoers out in the humid air.

"Leaving so soon?"

Shit. Uncle Donnie.

I held up the drink in my hand as if proof that I was still in party mode and said, "No, just getting some fresh air. It's a beautiful night."

"I heard you were talking to Mr. Brande's daughter, Anna-Marie. She's a special girl; we like to take care of her."

"She came and talked to me, said you told her I thought she looked familiar." He was there, he should remember that.

"Really? And what did you talk about?"

"That I saw someone in New Orleans who looked like her, but it wasn't her, just an odd resemblance. I was mistaken in thinking I'd even seen her before."

"Michele. I didn't get your last name," he said taking a cigar from his jacket pocket. He was dressed for the cool indoors, not the muggy outside, a dark suit, open-necked blue shirt, all expensive and well made. I couldn't detect the bulge of a gun, but I was sure it was there.

"Meraux." I had to spell it for him. I had a business card for Michele Meraux, editor, in my wallet. Meraux is a small town downriver from New Orleans. It's odd enough that people think it can't be fake.

"And the friends you're staying with?"

I was expecting that one. "The Silversteins. About eight blocks that way." I pointed in the direction I had walked from. I kept my tone pleasant and light, not letting on that I knew this was an interrogation.

"How long are you staying?"

"About a week, less if my AC gets fixed sooner. Parts. They claim they're waiting on parts."

"So, what did Anna-Marie say to you?"

"Not much, just asked why I thought she looked familiar. I described chatting with a woman in the French Quarter about a cat in a shop window who looked like her, at least from across the room."

"Looked like her how?"

"Up close, not so much, but from across the room, about the same height, similar hair color, slim build."

"When did you see this woman?"

"I don't know, a couple of weeks ago."

"Where did you say you saw her?"

He was repeating his questions. Trying to catch me in discrepancies or to add more details. I had to be careful to keep my lies straight. "In the French Quarter section of New Orleans."

"You live around there?"

"No, I work in the CBD—Central Business District—and I often walk there around lunch or after work."

"What made you think she looked like Anna-Marie?"

Past tense. He didn't seem aware. "I didn't think she looked like Anna-Marie. I merely thought Anna-Marie looked like her from across the room. Up close, she and the other woman didn't look as much alike." Before he could ask another question, I continued, "Why all this interest in a random stranger who looks like Anna-Marie?" I wanted him to be answering now—and to put him on notice that his questions were odd. At least to someone like I was purported to be.

Donnie sighed, then lit his cigar and puffed on it. Sweat was forming on his brow. I thought he wouldn't answer.

"Anna-Marie has a twin sister. We are trying to find her."

"You think she might be in New Orleans?"

"We don't know. It's possible."

"How long has she been missing?"

"Long enough for us to be worried."

He was good at evading exact answers.

"What do the police say?"

He looked at me. "The police?"

"You've reported her missing, right?"

Going to the police was not something the Brande family did. He took another puff on the cigar. "She's an adult. The police don't care." He didn't look at me as he said it. Not as good a liar as he thought he was.

"I'm so sorry to hear that. You must be worried. But I'm pretty sure the woman I saw in New Orleans only has a superficial resemblance to Anna-Marie, not close enough to be her twin." I added, "I'm sorry, I can see you were hoping it was." As if they were really looking for her and concerned about her well-being.

He gave a smile that was only movement of the muscles around his mouth. "I'm sure she'll turn up; she always does."

"I certainly hope so. That has to be a scary thing for a family. How long is she usually gone for?"

"Donald." A low croak of a voice, an old man who had smoked many cigars. I hadn't heard his approach. That worried me. "Don't bore our guests with tiresome family stories."

I turned to him. The look on Donnie's face told me this was the head of the Brande family. He was in his seventies, maybe upper sixties, the years of wafting smoke and boozy nights aging his face. He was tall with broad shoulders, but they now slumped into age and a body that spent more time smoking and drinking than moving.

What scared me the most was the anger in his eyes. It was well hidden from his facial muscles, a contained fury.

"Ellis," Donald said. "It's late for you."

"You think because I'm an old man, I should be in bed with hot milk?" he snapped. "I can keep up with the young ones. The most beautiful women come to me."

"Of course they do." Donnie placated him. "They recognize a truly strong man."

Strong because he had money and power. How long would he hold on to that? How many younger Brande men were waiting for him to stumble and fall? His anger wasn't just at Donnie speaking too freely but a world that was slipping from his control, his body aging, irrevocably taking from him all he cared about.

"I should probably go," I said.

He gripped my elbow, deliberately too tight, grinding his fingers into my arm. "Yes, you should go. Donnie and I need to talk."

"Ellis, it's okay," Donnie said. "I'll walk her back to where she's staying."

"That's not necessary. This is a safe enough neighborhood," I said. I wanted no escorts.

"I'll have one of the boys walk her. You and I need to talk."

He let go of my elbow. I felt my blood flow return. He put a hand on Donnie's shoulder, control. But also weakness, to help balance and steady him. It only added to the fury in his eyes.

"Wait here," Donnie told me. "Someone will be with you shortly."

I nodded like the good girl I was supposed to be, then watched through the corner of my eye as they entered the house, going around the side to a hidden entrance.

As if she had been watching, Anna-Marie came from the main door. She looked at the people out here, checking them out, then crossed to me. With one final look over her shoulder she looked at me, then handed me a card and said, "Call me." She quickly turned and walked away.

This is all too bizarre. I put my drink on the ground—no other place to set it—and headed down the driveway. I got about ten feet before I heard footsteps behind me.

A hand on my shoulder. One of the boys. "I got to walk you to your house."

He was probably what Ellis looked like in his twenties. Strong, confident his strength could take on the world. Dark brown hair, hazel eyes, the look I was recognizing as Brande family.

I stepped away from his hand. "That's not really necessary," I said.

"It's dark. Never know what might happen in the dark." He smirked. He was the kind of person who made bad things happen in the dark.

"Fine, but it's a bit of a hike," I said, heading down the driveway to the street, taking long steps at a fast pace.

"Whatever you say," he answered, keeping pace. Even if he wasn't a gym rat—and his muscles proved he worked out with weights, if not cardio—he was young and I wasn't.

The earlier crowd out here was gone, only a few straggling

smokers and one couple that thought they were better hidden by the trees than they were. My escort sniggered at them.

Try to chat him up, make him think you're harmless. "Why did you get stuck with making sure the old ladies get home safe?" I asked, keeping my tone light and friendly.

"I do what I'm told."

"It looks like a fun party."

I walked past my rental car, alas on the other side of the road, otherwise I might have stumbled into it and hit the alarm on the key fob at the same time as a distraction.

"Yeah, it's a fun party," he said. "I was about to get my dick sucked down in the basement."

Oh. So that's how this is going to be. You're going to do your best to shock me and make sure I'm aware of what a manly man you are. He was also drunk enough to loosen every inhibition he might have had.

"Perhaps that's what you should do, then," I said, as if talking about the weather. "You really don't need to follow me home."

"This isn't about what you need," he retorted. I hadn't been upset enough for him, so he was getting angry.

I stopped at the corner. "In fact, I'd prefer you not."

He still smirked but with a sheen of resentment behind it. "Your preferences don't count."

I headed up the steepest of the streets, pushing the pace as much as I could. Halfway up, I heard his heavy breathing.

Of course, I was also feeling the strain. New Orleans isn't known for its hills, and even a good workout on the elliptical at the gym doesn't prepare you for this.

"How far we got to go?" he demanded.

"Another eight blocks."

"Fuck this," he muttered.

I stopped again. "Then go back. You say you walked me home. I'm not going to tell anyone otherwise."

"Don't tell me what to do."

"I'm not. It was a suggestion." I strode uphill, trying to keep a few feet between us.

Another two blocks. He was cursing under his breath.

"We'd better be close, bitch," he said as we passed another corner.

"About another six blocks," I said.

"How fucking far is that?"

The blocks were long and windy here. "About another mile."

"You walked it?"

"Indeed. I like walking."

"Fuck this." He lunged at me, grabbing my upper arm. "End of the road, bitch."

I had been expecting this, so as much as possible, I was prepared. Clearly his job wasn't seeing me safely home but to take care of me and make sure I got the message not to talk about the Brandes. He got to choose how to deliver it.

I fell back as if pushed by him, enough that he had to overbalance to keep his hand on me. He was not expecting a judo move from an old lady like me. I jerked him further off-balance, planted a foot on his stomach at the same time I went down (veering enough to land on the grass and not the sidewalk). My momentum and his, with my leg in his stomach also thrusting up, sent him flying through the air and landing hard on his back.

I scrambled up as quickly as I could. I had surprise and intelligence on my side; he had brute strength and anger on his. I had to make sure he didn't have a chance to use them. On my feet, I aimed one kick to his groin and another to his sternum.

This old lady had a brown belt in karate.

He let out a huffing grunt, then curled into a ball.

"End of the road, bitch," I said as I took off running, going downhill.

I kept running for at least three corners and four blocks; only then did I look for a hiding place, up a random driveway and into the bushes of a darkened house. I hoped everyone was asleep and would not be woken any time tonight.

I slid down to the ground, catching my breath. Sweat was rolling off me—fear and heat. At least I was watering the plants. Once the blood ceased pounding in my ears, I strained to listen to the night.

Far-off traffic. A distant TV. The rustling of a breeze, then still again. The buzz of insects.

A car.

I scrunched against the hedge so no part of me would be visible as a shadow outside its outlines.

A slow car.

No, two, traveling as a pack. Two large, dark SUVs. Slowly trolling the streets.

I held my breath as if that would help conceal me.

But I had hidden myself well, far enough off the road to be well beyond anything but a direct beam of light, hidden behind a dense hedge well into the yard. Totally trespassing, but that wasn't my biggest worry.

They prowled past me.

Once I could no longer hear them, I chanced a look at my watch. Almost two a.m.

These were not patient men.

I stayed where I was for another forty-five minutes, silently swatting insects off me, out of the matted sweat in my hair.

But the mosquitoes were driving me crazy and I couldn't stay here all night. For all I knew, I'd picked the house of a baker and he—or she—would be up very early.

I stifled a groan as I stood from my cramped position.

Slowly, carefully, I made my way back down the road, listening for any cars, hiding in dark patches at the first glint of headlights. But the few cars that passed were single and traveling as if intent on getting where they were going and not looking for someone.

After a few blocks I had to pull out my phone to look at a map to find out where I was. I had taken off haphazardly and didn't pause to read the street signs. The brief flash of light from my phone was a risk, but I needed to know where I was to know where I had to go.

It was a gamble to go back to my rental car, but it was also a risk to call a taxi. For all I knew, the Brandes had a finger in every taxi company in the area. It might be even more dangerous to wait until the next day to retrieve it. A rental car still there in the daylight would be all too obvious.

I was slow and careful. Didn't come back the way I'd left. Once I got close, I waited in a dark area to watch the street for several minutes. I told myself give it ten, but the mosquitoes pushed that to eight and a half minutes. The street was quiet, still a few cars parked around, the lights still on at the Brande house.

The party still going.

I hugged the shadows as I headed to the car, alert for any prowling headlights.

The street remained quiet.

I quickly got in, then shut the door as silently as I could.

It was muggy in the car, the still hot night uncomfortable in this small space. I didn't turn the car on yet.

I grabbed the small duffle I carried with me. You never know when you might need binoculars or a long distance camera. Or a disguise. I pulled out an old ball cap and a pair of glasses, fake ones with just glass in them. That would have to do. I also slid down in my seat to make myself look shorter.

I turned on the car.

The street was narrow enough that it would be hard to make a U-turn, so I drove slowly and steadily past the Brande compound, as if just someone going home and not a person worrying about being killed.

The music kept playing. None of the smokers glanced my way.

I kept driving, taking the side streets, a meandering return to my hotel, making sure no one was following. It was late enough at night that few cars were out, especially in these back lanes.

I couldn't trust it, but I doubted Junior Boy told Big Daddy Ellis Brande that I gave him the slip by beating the crap out of him. Junior Boy was stupid enough to think his ego was more important than admitting what had happened long enough to wonder how a middle-aged lady like me knew how to fight. If so, those two SUVs had looked long enough for him and his pals to get bored, and that would be it. Ellis, even Donnie might be more worried. Clearly there was something going on with the women in the Brande family they didn't want outsiders to see.

I got back to my hotel room around four a.m. I stayed awake only long enough to take the briefest of showers, then collapsed into slumber. After putting the chair in front of the door.

CHAPTER TEN

Tired as I was, I woke shortly after eight a.m. I turned over to go back to sleep, then heard a noise outside my door. A moment of listening told me it was another guest leaving their room and not caring if the door slammed.

But I was awake. And I needed to be awake.

After lousy hotel coffee and a crushed granola bar scrounged from my luggage, the first thing I did was take the rental car in to exchange for another. I lied and said it was making a weird noise. I made sure to get a different color and make.

If I was wrong about Junior Boy telling Big Daddy, the latter might have had enough smarts to photograph all the cars in the area. Or he might do that anyway for security. I didn't want to be driving the same car. I hadn't seen cameras, but this was their area and they had a long time to hide them.

Next I had a real breakfast, eggs, toast, grits. And a lot of coffee. Caffeine would have to make up for sleep.

Then I found a phone place and got a burner phone. I turned off my real phone, and it would stay that way until I was back in New Orleans. Maybe a few months after.

And next—was a quandary.

Smart would be to get on the next plane back to New Orleans and forget I'd ever been here. Drop this case like the big stinking piece of turd it was.

But…I had learned things I couldn't unlearn. The dead woman looked enough like Anna-Marie Brande to be related to her. No proof.

It could be an odd coincidence. Save for how interested all the Brandes were in whether I'd seen someone who looked like her in New Orleans. Donnie had been clumsy in his interrogation, too intent on getting information from me to realize what his questions were revealing.

I drove around a bit, then found a shopping mall—not that I needed to shop, but it was a place with a purpose and to look like what I was pretending to be, someone just visiting Atlanta. People enjoy shopping malls, I've heard. It's a place to be anonymous and alone without calling attention to yourself. I could think while I wandered the mall, pausing at shop windows, letting people behind me pass to make sure I wasn't being followed.

Paranoid?

Probably.

The Brandes' misogyny was to my advantage. Donnie clearly took me as what I presented—a harmless woman, someone he could manipulate. Even Ellis thought a few snarls from Junior Boy would keep me in line. It wasn't likely they'd consider I might be a top-notch private eye.

Unless they already knew.

Someone had involved both me and Karen. Was it the Brande women trying to escape? Or the Brande men trying to capture them? But if they knew, would Ellis have so easily dismissed me with the second tier? I'd like to think not, but men who hated women the way they did, didn't respect them. Maybe he thought the male part of Junior Boy outweighed anything a woman—one over forty—could counter with.

Maddeningly, I had what I knew—the Brandes were involved and the dead woman might well be Anna-Marie's sister—but nothing resembling proof I could dump on Joanne's desk and leave it to her and the resources of the police.

I bought a pair of socks with cats and books on them. And a bag of high-end popcorn.

The expenses on this case were mounting.

I headed back to the car.

The next step was the obvious one. One I didn't want to take.

Call Anna-Marie.

Maybe it was a trap, and she was more loyal to the family she knew than her desperate loneliness. But I had seen it in her eyes, the way she looked at me. She wanted out of the cage, as much as she was afraid of leaving. I was an independent woman, maybe a dalliance, a long night of bodies touching, taking her away. Maybe someone who could show her how to be free.

If I called her, I would be using that despair for my own ends. It was a fire that might burn us both.

I drove back to the hotel, packed, and checked out, claiming I had to leave due to a business emergency.

I headed for the crowded convention hotels in the downtown area, parking the car at a lot a few blocks away—expensive, but far cheaper than big hotel parking.

Again, an anonymous space, hundreds of people in and out. One with far better security than my hotel on the beltway. In my room, I took another shower, a long lingering one, to wash off all traces of the heat and sweat of yesterday, the grip of Ellis on my arm, Donnie on my shoulder, Junior Boy's clumsy attack.

With as many of my sins washed away as water could, I dressed, comfortable lightweight gray pants, a decent button-down shirt. Not to stand out, but not to look like I didn't belong.

Then I dialed Anna-Marie's number, reading it carefully off the card she had given me.

Voice mail.

"Hi, you asked me to call. I'm calling," was the message I left.

Five minutes later, my burner phone rang.

"Sorry, I had to get somewhere private." Her voice had an edge, doing something she shouldn't. Something she could get punished for. If this was a trap, she was a phenomenal actor. She added, "You called. I didn't think you would."

"I wasn't sure I would either," I admitted, as close to honest as I could be. "You don't seem like a nice, safe suburban girl."

She laughed, a harsh one. My comment wasn't funny but absurd.

"But," I continued, "I'm curious."

"About?"

"About you. It would be interesting to talk."

"Talk? We both know what this is about."

"Do we?" I countered. "Is just sex all you want?"

She was silent.

Long enough for me to prompt, "Anmar, are you there?"

"Maybe." Then softly, "I don't know." Her voice almost broke.

"Why don't we get together and talk?"

"Okay," she said. "Where?"

I suggested the hotel bar—at a different hotel than the one I was staying in. Much as I didn't think this was a trap—or if so, one she was caught in as well—better to be safe. We agreed to meet in a few hours.

I walked for a while, but it was too hot on the concrete streets. There was a small mall attached to the hotel though a walkway, but I was malled out for the day. I went in only to get cool and look for something to eat. I wasn't really hungry, but I didn't want to meet Anmar for drinks on an empty stomach.

Then I went back to my room, nibbled a little, then set my phone alarm, carefully laid my clothes over the desk chair, and took a nap. I could be full and alert for meeting Anmar.

I woke well before our meeting, giving myself plenty of time to get dressed, snack some more, and even brush my teeth afterward.

I took a roundabout way to the other hotel, a slow saunter down a long block before taking a corner and heading back in its direction. It wasn't just caution; it also gave me time to think. And there is always the dumb luck quotient—I could run into Junior Boy running errands to Big Daddy's favorite cigar shop.

My luck held, only passing strangers, all of us safely anonymous.

Anna-Marie Brande was a dangerous woman. Not with malice and intention, but because of who she was and what she needed, the fearful pull in her made her unpredictable.

If I was young, I would have been wildly attracted to her, the perfect damsel in distress. Caught in the surety of youth that the world could be made better; that we could fix the broken hearts. Even our own. Still innocent of how fragile life was and how quickly the irrevocable could catch us, haunting us for the eternity left in our short lives.

But I wasn't young anymore. I could not save Anna-Marie Brande. Maybe she could. Maybe nothing could.

My goal was simple and brutal: to get information from her while hiding who I was and what I wanted. Would I sleep with her?

That wouldn't be wise.

But I wasn't always wise.

I entered the hotel and found the bar. I was early, enough that I picked the table, one in back, with my seat facing the door.

I almost ordered my usual Scotch and at the last minute switched to a dirty martini. Scotch was too much the real me to risk.

Anmar arrived just as my drink did. She seemed younger, or maybe it was the light. Or being away from the contempt of the Brande men. Yes, my younger self would have been smitten. Wearing a sleeveless silk top of light lavender and sun-washed jeans that were just loose enough to look comfortable and tight enough to show her gym-worked body, her hair was long and loose, catching the light as she headed to my table, glints of auburn and chestnut in the dark coffee color. Still a family resemblance to the woman who had been in my office—and the morgue—but Anmar wasn't hiding behind a façade like that woman.

"Hi," she said, standing before my table.

I stood, greeted her as if I knew her, with a quick hug and a kiss on the cheek.

Then she sat down, perused the drink menu, but ordered the first one when the waiter asked what she wanted.

I started. It was my game. "Your family is kind of unusual."

She looked at me. "You think?"

"Old-fashioned ideas about women."

"The power of money. It buys a lot of things."

"Really? What's it bought you?"

"Only for those who have it."

"You don't?"

"The old-fashioned family controls the money very tightly. I'm like everyone else; I get my small share for my loyalty."

"The men control it all?"

"The man controls it all," she answered.

"Ellis?" I guessed. Adding, "He thought Donnie was talking too much to me. I got a brief introduction."

She nodded. "Ellis. My beloved grandfather. He thinks my father is useless, a toady. And he's right. A useful useless man. Willing to be second place as long as it's safe." She reached across the table for my drink as if to wash the taste of it from her mouth. "I didn't guess you to be a martini girl."

"It depends on my mood. Some days it's a dirty martini mood."

She took another sip. The more gin she took, the less for me. Probably a good idea.

"What happens when Ellis goes?" I asked. "Will you have a kinder benefactor?"

"There are no benefactors in the family. It's all transactional. It'll be worse when he's gone."

"Why?"

"A bloodbath."

I raised my eyebrows.

"Not literally," she continued, then added softly, "I hope." Another sip of my drink. "No, when he goes there will be two generations of men fighting to take over—his sons and nephews who are waiting their turn and the next generation who don't want to wait."

"Doesn't he have a will or successions?"

She laughed her dry, bitter laugh. "We're not that kind of a family. Survival of the strongest—and most ruthless." She finished my drink. Hers arrived. She signaled the waiter to get me another. "So whoever takes over will be even more ruthless than Ellis."

"That doesn't sound like a happy family," I commented. "What do the discontented ones do?"

"We're all loyal. There is no discontent," she said sarcastically.

"Right. You don't seem very content."

"But I'm just a woman. Our contentment doesn't count very much."

"If you really thought that you wouldn't be here with me."

She took a sip of her drink. "Oh, but this is allowed. A discreet affair. A hotel room. We spend the night together and no one knows."

"We'd know. And what if you want something more? What if you fall in love? Want a life of your own?"

She took another swallow. My second drink arrived.

"No one breaks away?" I pushed. "Runs for the door to see what's on the other side?"

She picked up her drink again, then put it down. Softly she said, "I think my sister Andrea did. I think she's dead."

I reached out and took her hand. It wasn't wise, but it was kind. "I'm sorry. She hasn't been gone long. How can you think that?"

She took a long sip of her drink but didn't let go of my hand. "Something I overheard. They forgot that women listen. Ellis was saying 'no one gets away with this; the lesson this time will be harsh.'"

"He said this in reference to your sister?"

"No, but who else could he mean?"

"Any of the young bucks trying to take what he doesn't want to give. Donnie being stupid chatting up a woman he doesn't know."

She took a wavering breath. Then let go of my hand. "Too public," she said as she took another drink. "Maybe," she added. "I'd like to think that."

I kept my face neutral, I'd meant to be honest and kind—Ellis's words could have meant anyone else—but there was a woman who resembled Anna-Marie in a morgue in New Orleans.

Maybe I could come up with a way to tip off Joanne to pull the dental records without admitting my foolish adventure into a crime family. Know for sure before Anna-Marie learned about the body that looked like her. Could it be her twin? Yes. No. Maybe.

"How many in your family? Who is mostly likely to piss Ellis off?" I said.

"Ellis was one of five boys," she said.

"And how many girls?"

"Two. Outnumbered their whole life. Probably why they weren't good at fighting back. And he had five sons. Three daughters. I'm the daughter of the favored son."

"That sounds like a large family. You the only queer member?"

"It is large. No, Andrea also. Identical twins. Some of the boys, but they disappear—San Francisco if they're smart. A beating in the back street and a bus as far as they can go if they're not. A niece—cousin really, but her mother is my age, so she calls me Aunt. But she's young and knows how to flatter the men, and at the moment, she's useful to them, so she gets away with it. At least for now."

"All here in Atlanta? Living in the compound?"

"No, some spread out in the area. We have operations through most of Georgia, into Birmingham and Huntsville, the Gulf Coast. Ellis sends out the sons he wants to test. Or punish."

"Sons only?"

"Their wives and families."

"The women suffer with the men?"

She took another sip. "The women suffer. Sometimes with the men. Sometimes alone."

Her phone rang. She frowned, looking at the number. But answered it. A pause, then she said, "No, I'm here in Atlanta. Downtown. Meeting a friend for a drink." Another pause. "Why? Is something the matter?"

I took a sip of my martini, looking at my phone screen to pretend I wasn't listening in.

She put the phone down. "That was odd."

I cocked an eyebrow at her.

"Checking up on where I am. That hasn't happened in a while."

"They don't follow the GPS on your phone?"

She looked at her phone, then shrugged. "Probably. But if they do, they'll see I'm where I said I am." She again picked up her drink, but paused. "Maybe she got away. If she's dead they wouldn't worry about where I am." The lines in her face deepened, sorrow and longing. She finished her drink.

"But that would mean she's alive," I said.

"Yes. And she left me behind." She lifted the glass, but there was nothing in it. She looked at me, the pain still there as if she was tired of hiding it. "I know. Crazy. I don't want her dead, but at least I'd know she hadn't left me behind, made her escape without me. When we were young, that's what we plotted to do; wild adventures to faraway places."

"What happened?"

"We got older. The dreams got lost." She signaled for another round, although I'd barely touched mine. "I just thought...no matter what happened, we'd be in this life together."

I had what I needed—enough to identify the body. And more than I wanted—a glimpse into Anna-Marie Brande's soul.

"Did she contact you? Tell you anything before she left?"

"Breezy, told me she was going away for a few days. Made it seem like—well, like this. Met someone, was going to spend a few days, maybe a week in carnal pursuits. Nothing different than other times."

"And how long has she been gone?"

"Just over a week now. Long enough I should have heard. She never goes more than a few days without at least texting me."

"You've tried to contact her?"

"Every day. Nothing. No response."

"Maybe she's worried they could trace her through your phone," I suggested.

Anmar looked at her device. "I didn't think of that. Maybe. Ellis owns a phone store. He gives us all the latest and greatest, a new phone every year. Whether we want it or not."

"If it's his plan, he's in control. He can read your text messages," I told her.

She picked up her phone and put it down again in disgust. What might have been in some of those text messages flitted across her face. "You think I'm an idiot, don't you?"

"I think you've lived here long enough you've forgotten to ask hard questions."

"Questions can get a girl killed."

"Or they can let her escape." I wasn't arguing for Andrea Brande—she was likely in a morgue. But Anna-Marie Brande didn't need to live this way.

Once the name Andrea Brande was attached to that body, the wheels of law would grind into action. Turning a blind eye to criminal acts—she was guilty of that at the least—would take her down with them. Unless she was somewhere far away.

"Okay, so how do I get a safe phone?"

"There have to be half a dozen stores within ten blocks of here," I said.

"And buy it with my father's credit card?"

"Cash still buys things," I pointed out.

"I don't have enough."

"Take a few advances on those credit cards, say you needed to buy makeup or cover your half of dinner with a friend. Get enough cash to buy a cheap phone for a month."

She shook her head but was listening.

"Or is that too much work to try to contact your sister?"

The eyes flashed at me. "It's not too much damn work," she retorted. "It's just—if I get caught."

"Bat your eyelashes at them and say you get tired of the idea of Junior Boy reading your text messages."

She laughed. Almost a real laugh.

Our next round of drinks arrived. Anna-Marie pulled out a credit card and handed it to the waiter. She took a long gulp of hers. "Liquid courage."

I took a sip.

She reached over, grabbed my hand, and squeezed it. "Let's do this," she said. Then smiled.

I got a glimpse of someone Anna-Marie Brande could have been.

Should have been. Happy, not looking over her shoulder as if someone was always there to drag her back with a blow or disparaging cut.

"Planning," I said, pulling up the map on my phone. It wasn't as smart as my real phone, but it would do. I found the closest store still open. "This isn't one of Ellis's, is it?" I showed her the location.

She looked at it. "No."

I took another sip of my drink.

She finished hers.

I didn't finish mine.

The waiter returned her credit card.

We stopped at two ATMs on the way.

In the store I told the male clerk we were just looking. I waited for the woman. I hinted that Anmar needed to use cash to avoid a crazy ex. The woman nodded, like she'd had enough crazy men in her life. She didn't blink an eye at the anonymous bills.

Half an hour later, Anna-Marie had a brand-new phone, one no one in the Brande family knew about.

Once outside the store, she immediately sent a text message to a number she clearly knew by heart.

I finally put a hand on her shoulder as she stared at the phone. "It may be a while," I said gently. "She may have turned that phone off and only occasionally checks it."

Anmar nodded, then reluctantly put the phone away in her purse.

"I've waited this long, I can wait a little longer," she said. Then her phone rang—the other one. "Damn, do you think they were watching?"

"No, I don't," I said. I had checked, especially while Anmar was finishing the phone purchase, no one watching the store, no cars slowly passing by and returning for another slow pass. No, I'm not perfect, but the Brande men aren't that smart either.

She answered it. "What? I'm still downtown." A pause. "Now?" Another pause. "Why?" A long pause and she put the phone away without saying good-bye, a line of worry on her face.

"What's up?" I asked.

"This is getting weird. Ellis wants everyone back at the house. Now. Donnie is going to come pick me up. You need to disappear. We shouldn't be seen together."

"Will you be safe?"

She looked at me as if no one had ever asked her that question before. "Yeah, I'll be fine. They know where I am; they know what I've been doing," then the ghost of a smile, "at least, mostly. Downtown, having drinks with a friend. Coming home when I'm called." She leaned forward and brushed her lips against mine, the barest hint of rebellion, but her lips were tense and hard.

"Call me," I said, pointing to her purse and her hidden phone. I turned and walked away. I didn't know how close Donnie—or his appointed goon—was and I didn't want to be seen. Especially if the goon was Junior Boy. I walked briskly away, the wrong direction for my hotel, but I planned to take a while getting back there. A block away, crossing the street, I looked back at her. The smile was gone, the worry lines that aged her in place.

The light changed. I walked across the street, past a building, and she was gone.

Chapter Eleven

If it weren't for planes and their schedules, I'd have left Atlanta right then. But I had a plane already scheduled and needed to act as if everything was all right and going as planned.

I occasionally checked my phone, but not obsessively, and rambled through the usual Atlanta tourist things. The aquarium—who doesn't love fish? A stroll in Olympic Park, but it was too hot for more than a slow stroll, then ducking into the air-conditioning at CNN.

I did look over my shoulder, trying not to be obsessive about it. But the Brandes stayed away in their suburban compound and I was left with the deflated August tourists.

Anmar didn't call.

Be patient, I told myself, the same advice I had given her.

The time passed. I was finally in the airport, finally heading home.

Checkout had come long before it was time to leave for the airport, but I had come here anyway. It was a concrete step on the journey home. Plus, I have learned the trick of dealing with the Atlanta airport. Hang out in the international terminal. Any of the trains will take you there after you've passed through security. It's much less crowded than the other terminals. I got through a couple of chapters of the latest Sara Paretsky book in peace and quiet, and had lunch without fighting for a table.

The time again passed and I headed to the gate for my plane.

I watched the people as I walked, no longer constantly looking over my shoulder. This was an airport. Even if Junior Boy saw me here, I was a traveler. Not to mention they don't mess with security in airports. Now I could watch the faces go by, people in a hurry or confused or both, people not aware they were being watched and how much I was amusing myself with my unsaid snarky comments. "Really, that outfit? No one even looks good in lime green leggings." "How long can you dither about what kind of water you want to buy? Oh, that long. Let me find another line." "Your suit isn't expensive enough for you to be that much of an asshole. Actually, no suit is."

She didn't register at first. Not after our one brief meeting. A very attractive woman coming my way. Jeans, a baggy T-shirt that didn't really hide her curvy body, but enough to proclaim she wasn't seeking male attention.

Holly Farmer, Karen's social worker girlfriend. She looked like she was getting off a plane, heading in the direction of the connecting trains. We were heading right at each other; she couldn't miss me.

"Hey, Holly," I said as I got near.

She looked up abruptly, surprised to see me. Then annoyed. Finally a smile, but it traveled a crooked line on her face, not reaching her eyes.

I didn't like this woman. I didn't know why. Maybe I thought she was taking advantage of Karen. Although I had no proof of that, nor did Karen seem to mind.

"Oh, hi," she said.

"Odd place to meet," I said.

She shrugged.

"How's Karen?" I asked.

"She's fine."

"You're not traveling together?"

"No, just a quick trip."

"Business or pleasure?" She seemed to not want to talk to me. Which made me ask more questions that I otherwise would have.

"Neither." Then again the crooked smile, not touching her eyes. "A bit of both. Visiting a sick aunt. Just a quick trip."

"I'm sorry to hear that. I hope she gets better."

"Karen? She's fine."

"Your aunt. Your sick aunt."

"Oh, yes. She'll be fine."

"Safe travels," I said, stepping aside so we each could pass.

"You, too," she answered, plunging into the crowd.

She doesn't like you, either, I thought as I got to the gate. I wondered why she lied about the aunt. Cheating on Karen? Or just wanted to shut me down and get on with it? Maybe she was jealous. Karen had carried a crush on me for a long time. Unrequited. Well, save for our very, very early acquaintance.

It didn't matter. Everyone who lives in New Orleans eventually ends up in the Atlanta airport. Maybe it was just Holly's turn. Who names their kid Holly Farmer?

My plane was on time.

I was happy to be home, pulling up in front of my house. The comfort of familiar. I officially gave myself the evening off. It was technically still early enough that, had I been diligent, I could have headed to my office, made case notes on the progress. I didn't know who Aimee Smyth or Sally Brand were—if they existed, but I had been hired to find a sister. The money was in my bank account—although if I expensed the Atlanta trip, that would take a chunk from it. I'd look for a sister, but a real one, and one I suspected I knew where to find.

But I didn't want to deal with that today. Didn't want to think about what to say to Joanne, didn't want to think about Anmar Brande, if I had helped her with encouraging her rebellion. Or hurt her by giving hope that was all too likely to be false. I would give myself a night of thinking without really thinking about it all.

But the night didn't last very long, and I was soon staring at the morning sun.

I was too much of a coward to head directly to Joanne, instead went down to my office.

Decent coffee, I told myself. I hadn't had enough of it in the last few days.

Of course I had to check all my email, even though I had checked it on the road via the wonders of modern technology. Then had to make a grocery list since I needed to make a food run sometime today.

It's cruel to delay a blow that must fall.

Andrea Brande wasn't going to reply to Anmar's text message.

I called Joanne. Maybe I could do this over the phone. It would be harder for her to ask pesky questions than in person. She was out. I left a message.

She called back a few minutes later. "I'm in your neighborhood. I'll stop by your office."

No! "I'm not in my office," I said.

"Then why am I talking to on your office line?"

"Call forwarding."

"I need to pee. I'll be there in about ten minutes." She hung up.

Damn. The last thing I wanted was for her to trap me here. She could ask all the questions she wanted. I couldn't stalk out of my own office.

I busied myself by tidying up. At least the place could be clean even if my thoughts were jumbled.

All too soon I heard her at my door. She didn't bother to knock, came in and headed straight to the bathroom.

After fortifying myself with another cup of coffee, I ensconced myself behind my desk, the only barricade in the room.

She came out, found a paper towel by my coffee stuff, and dried her hands, taking her time.

"So what's up?" I said, unable to let the silence build too long.

She threw the towel away, then sat down on the other side of the desk, pulling the chair so it was at the corner and less directly across from me.

"I wanted to apologize about Saturday night," she said.

Saturday seemed so long ago. My unplanned attendance at the Brande party.

"Torbin's show," she added. Then said, "How can you drink coffee on a day as hot as this?"

"I stay in air-conditioning," I answered. Then to her real point, "I was out of town. Otherwise I would have been there." We both knew I was lying.

"It's not fair," she said.

"It's not your fault," I answered.

"No, but I could have…done more to tamp it down."

I really hated it when Joanne decided to have an honest talk with me. Oh, yeah, good for the soul, but not so much for my current mental health. Yes, there were issues here that involved our friends and I was doing my utmost to avoid them. This would be a much better conversation to have in the evening when I'd mellowed myself with a nice snifter of Scotch, instead of a caffeinated morning.

"It doesn't matter," I said briskly.

"Yes, it does. The last thing I want to do is take sides."

"I hadn't noticed." Sarcasm font.

Joanne sighed. "I'll be the first to admit I haven't been perfect about it. It's been...too easy to just let things flow. Like everyone talking about Torbin's show and Nancy and Cordelia deciding to go to it. I could have shut it down."

"How? It's a public place. They can go where they please." I didn't look at her, staring into my coffee as if its black depths might have answers.

"That's it. They go where they please. You conveniently find work to be absent."

"We make our choices," I said tersely. I was so focused on how to tell Joanne who the body was, I'd forgotten about the mess in my personal life. I wasn't happy to be shoved back into it.

"They're the couple; they're two, almost like they have two votes to your one. I don't feel I've been a great friend."

"It's not like I want you to choose."

She ignored my sarcasm. "But that's just it. We are choosing. We're doing it by default. Nancy says she'd like to see Torbin perform and no one says no. No one points out that he's your cousin, you were planning to go and if you both go—"

"All eyes on the awkward exes," I finished for her. "Do you sit with me or with them? Do we put a bunch of tables together with me on one end and them on the other? And we each wonder about who sits where? Look, Joanne, I get it. But New Orleans is a small town. At some point we run into each other."

"Yes, you do, but it should be neutral ground. Saturday needed to be about Torbin's performance and us having a good time..."

"Not watching the two exes meet for the first time," I said for her.

"Well, it's not fair to put us all in that position, especially you. You should have been there. I could tell Torbin was upset you weren't."

"Well, then Torbin should have..." I didn't even know what Torbin should have done.

"Not that you weren't there—he understood why you avoided it. But that you felt you couldn't be there. You were polite enough to keep the elephant out of the room and let him do his show."

"Who knew I was so noble?"

"Or at least aware enough of everyone else around you."

"You don't like her, do you?" I asked.

Joanne looked out the window. I thought she wasn't going to answer. Then she sighed and said, "I'll deny I ever said this. But...I think she feels she has to win this unspoken battle. Make us Cordelia's friends."

"Sounds like love to me," I said. Big sarcasm font.

"Not my idea of it. But I've noticed how she crowds you out—inviting us over for dinner, making plans so our time is taken with them and not you. Saying how fun it would be to see Torbin and pushing to go."

"No one pushed back."

Joanne was again silent. "Danny did. Said you'd be there. And Nancy pretty much said what you did—it's a public space. That it didn't seem fair to miss the fun." Joanne paused. "She's…very nice. Not pushy in the way loud people are. Just nice and reasonable."

"Aunt Greta," I said, the prim and proper aunt who took me in after my father died. "She was always nice." And blind to everything except what she wanted to see.

"Yes, sort of like that. No easy place to say no. Or even 'wait a minute.'"

"It's okay, Joanne. You're not expected to be the savior of the world. I could organize dinner parties as well and invite everyone over."

"If you wanted to play that game. I suspect you'd be much better at it than she is. I appreciate that you're not."

She smiled at me. I even smiled back. I didn't tell her the truth—I would have been happy to play the game, but I was too tired and busy. I could barely think about what to cook for myself, let alone organizing and cooking for all my friends. "Well, maybe I should pick up pizza and invite you all over."

"Maybe you should. Or we should all go out some night. In any case, I will do better to balance things and not be swept along with the tide." She stood up.

"You might want to sit," I said.

She cocked an eyebrow at me.

"Work," I said. "I might have a name for the woman in the morgue."

Joanne sat back down. "Do I want to ask how you got a name when we've found nothing?"

"Probably not," I admitted.

"Illegal hacking?"

"No. But it's going to be messy."

She pulled a notepad from her brief case.

"Andrea Brande, from Atlanta."

"Where you were this weekend?"

"Yes. A daughter of the Brande family, who are probably well known to law enforcement in the area. They have very traditional ideas about sex roles."

Joanne, as I suspected, didn't just take the information down but instead starting questioning me. I finally admitted where I'd been. I left out a few things—like Anna-Marie's name and our flirting. I talked about the party and Donnie and Ellis and Junior's not-so-romantic advances. And my response to them.

At the end, she looked at me and said, "You beat the crap out of a mobster?"

"Mobster's grandson," I corrected.

Then I saw the repressed smile playing at her lips. "I can't say I approve, because I don't. You could have easily disappeared and never been found."

"I'm not that easy to get rid of," I replied.

"Okay, so you think it's the twin of the woman you met. Possibly the same woman who was in your office?"

"I think so. I'd have to look at them side by side to be sure," I said.

"But why?" Joanne said, putting down her notebook. "Why hire you? Put down money for a house with Karen? Then die?"

"Her family killed her to keep her from breaking free. She knew too much. Maybe she thought New Orleans was far enough away."

"Sounds naïve for someone who grew up in a mob family," Joanne said, shaking her head.

"Yes, it does. Maybe she only saw what she wanted to see."

"Awful thing to do to someone in your family," Joanne added.

"Nothing like blood hatred added to contempt for women. She may not be the first woman in the family killed for not being docile enough."

"We're not positive it was murder," Joanne said.

"What do you mean?"

"Overdose. Fentanyl."

"Wait, she was an addict?"

"We're not sure. Not much evidence of track marks. Just a few needle sticks. No signs of long-term or regular use."

"Someone gave her a hot shot," I stated.

"Possible. But it'll be hard to prove. Even with…the amount she had in her."

"Meaning someone wanted to make sure she overdosed."

"Probably," Joanne admitted. "That's our working theory, but as I said, it's hard to prove someone intentionally murdered her that way."

"It's not likely the Brandes will cooperate," I said.

"They would have reported her missing by now if they had any thought of that. Not expecting they will. But we can check ID other ways. Forensics these days. A woman in her forties, no children, good teeth, clearly taken care of."

"Wait, forties? Andrea Brande is in her late thirties."

"We don't have a birthday. Possible they're off by a few years. We'll check."

"What else do you know about her?"

Joanne paused. I was a civilian and she wasn't supposed to talk to me. Even if I had just handed her a big chunk of info—the name and a connection to a major crime family. "Her purse/wallet was taken but none of the jewelry, so it seems more like trying to hide her identity than a robbery. She was found in an empty lot, near the bridge."

"That's not a great place to dump a body," I said. Yes, there are a lot of industrial lots, but many of the homeless live under the bridge and it's a major traffic route.

"Interesting, isn't it?" Joanne said. "Someone who didn't know the city well enough to know it's not really a deserted area. Two homeless women said a late-model silver/gray SUV stopped there around two a.m. They said it stayed long enough for them to wonder, then it suddenly sped off. They let it get away, then went to see. Once they got close enough they saw the body. Neither had a phone, so they didn't tell anyone until they saw a shelter worker they knew. Shelter worker called us."

"So she was out on the street, what five, six hours?"

"First patrol got there around five, so not that long. If the women are right about the two a.m. drop."

I was silent. Knowing Anna-Marie, I now felt like I knew the woman. Enough to not want her lying on the side of an empty lot on a steamy night. Then I asked the question I knew Anna-Marie would ask. "Any signs of assault?" I hoped I wouldn't be the one who answered it.

"No sexual assault. Some bruising on her wrists. Could be someone grabbed her. But could also be from banging hard with the bracelets she wore. Some bruising on the torso. Some of it faded. Again, hard to know for sure."

"Nice ladies don't get bruised like that."

"They do if their husbands or boyfriends aren't nice."

"Or girlfriends. We're not immune," I added. Andrea Brande wouldn't be the first woman to assume another woman was safe and find out the hard way she wasn't.

"No, we're not," Joanne answered. Then briskly, "That's all we've had so far. A body that someone should miss—dentist visits, nice clothes, in good health save for elevated cholesterol. Expensive jewelry."

"Not a body that should get dumped and forgotten."

"Unless the people who should remember are the ones who did it."

With a look at her watch, Joanne stood up.

"Places to go, people to see?" I said.

She nodded. "At least back to the office. I need to follow up on your lead—contact some people in Atlanta." She turned to go. "Thanks for the air-conditioning." Took a step, then turned and said, "How about a pizza night this weekend? I'll see if Danny and Elly want to join us. We can go out. You don't even need to clean."

"Sounds good," I said.

Joanne nodded, then left.

I sat back down at my desk. Knowing the details of her death made it real. More real than I wanted to know. Even a few hours on a hot summer night meant the insects were at work. I shuddered. Then took another sip of coffee. It was cold.

My phone rang. An unknown number. Atlanta area code.

Anmar's burner phone? Or spam from me being in the Atlanta area?

I answered.

"Hey, it's me," she said as if I would recognize her voice. Which I did.

"Hi, how are you?" I asked. I had been worried about her after the abrupt summons home.

"I'm okay."

"Where are you?" I asked, hearing noise in the background.

"Shopping at the mall. Donnie dropped me off. Thinks I'm here to get my nails done and pick out a few bangles." She added, "They're keeping a tight leash. Just not tight enough to dig through my purse and see if I have a phone not bought from Ellis's store."

"Keep lots of tampons. That always scares the men away." Then I asked, "Why? Do you know?"

"They talk and forget we're human enough to listen. Someone tried to divert funds from a family account. To buy a house in New Orleans."

"Really?" I said, glad to be on the phone, so I only needed to bend my voice and not my face to deception. "What's wrong with buying a house here?"

"It would have to be approved. It's not the house buying, it's the diversion of funds. Some deal with the accounts. Someone got into places they shouldn't."

"Could it have been Andrea? Trying to get away?"

Anmar snorted. "No way, she's not that stupid. If she had enough money to buy a house, she'd be on the first plane for Kathmandu...we always wanted to go there. Liked the name. Or at least Paris or London, a big enough city to disappear in and a long air trip away."

"Maybe she wanted to make a place for you to get away as well."

"No, not a house. We'd travel. We talked about it—late at night when no one was about. How we might make an escape. It was leave and keep moving. Nothing as permanent as a house. Especially one as close as New Orleans."

I didn't press it. Anmar knew her sister, but even people we know can have surprises in them. "Is that why you got called back? The accounts and the house?"

"Barn door with the horse long gone. Because someone decided to try something, those of us who didn't, get punished."

"Do they know who it is?"

"No. If they do, they're not saying, but I suspect they don't. That's why they're treating us all with suspicion. With Andrea missing, they assume she's part of it, so they assume I probably helped her. Too bad I didn't. They con and use people, so they think everyone does. They seem to feel one of us did it and is remaining around to pretend we didn't."

"Is that what you think?"

"I don't know what to think. Why buy a house so close? It's not like we haven't done things in New Orleans. It's almost like they wanted to be caught."

"But why would they want that?"

"Con and use. Ellis has mega millions, and he uses it to rule the rest of us. Do his bidding and you get a few nickels. Cross him or even displease him and you get nothing. Someone got tired of it."

"But why in New Orleans? And something like real estate?"

"I don't know. But Ellis and Donnie are running around and yelling at everyone. He never imagined anyone would dare cross him like this. If someone has access to one account, they might have access to others. No money, no power. My best guess is this is meant to rattle his cage, make him overreact. And distraction. While everyone is focusing on New Orleans and the house, it means they're not focusing on other things."

"It still makes no sense," I said, hoping to prompt her to keep talking.

"I don't know. All I can do is watch from the sidelines. You might be careful, I know they're sending some of the boys down to New Orleans."

"Junior Boy?"

"Is that what you call him?"

"He never bothered to introduce himself. Not the most polite behavior when escorting someone home."

"If that's all he did, you're lucky."

"He tried to grab me."

"Damn. I hope he didn't hurt you."

"Nope. This old lady knows how to fight. I don't suppose he admitted that I kicked him hard in the groin and left him on the ground moaning."

She barked a laugh. "No, he did not. Came back, muttered about needing to get some more vodka, and drove off in one of the big, black trucks."

As I had suspected, Junior Boy did not admit he'd gotten beaten up by a girl. "Ah, well, I was long gone by then."

"Good for you." Then in a whisper, "Donnie's here. Have to go."

And she was gone.

My conscience wasn't easy about deceiving her. I'd never said I wasn't a private detective. But I never said I was either. I had presented as someone who stumbled into the party. I knew things she needed to know, but I couldn't tell her. I hoped that I'd be relieved of that burden, that the police would be the ones to break the news to her. And that she'd find some way to escape to a safe place.

I could also wish to ride a unicorn home from work. And world peace while I'm at it.

I pondered what she said about Junior Boy and possibly some of the other minions coming to town. Karen might need to worry, if it was her real estate deal they'd found out about.

But me? What were the chances? New Orleans isn't a large city, but it is a city all the same.

It was lunchtime. I'd worry about all this when I had a full stomach.

Since I hadn't done that grocery run yet, I'd brought nothing with me. My stubborn refusal to spend money at the coffee shop only to subsidize the rent they paid me meant I had to go out in the heat and get into my hot car. The other option was to walk five blocks, and it was too hot for that. Outside would not cool down; my car would.

Lunch. A shrimp po-boy. I'd eat a salad tomorrow. Today was a day to make up for too much bland, bad road food. I got back in my almost cool car and headed back to the office and its air-conditioning. Only mad dogs and New Orleanians would be out in weather this hot. And only because we had to.

I had to park farther down the street than I would have liked because a big, black SUV was doing suburban parking, leaving half a car length between it and the next driveway and another three-quarters of a car between it and the corner. Usually we can fit in three reasonable-sized cars there.

I was almost across the street when I spotted him.

What where the chances? Way too fucking good. Junior Boy was standing half in/half out of the coffee shop door.

He looked up.

Saw me.

He wasn't expecting to see me. His face showed surprise, then consternation.

"What are you doing here?" he blurted out.

Brazen through it. "I live here!" I said, doing my best outrage. "What are you doing here?" I shot back to him.

"None of your business."

He didn't know who I was, I realized—other than the woman at the party. He had the address of my office but didn't know I was M. Knight, Private Investigator. I don't hide I'm a woman, but I don't advertise it either. Junior Boy hadn't done his homework—I doubted this was the first time.

"I'm calling the cops," I said.

"Now, wait a minute." He took a step toward me. A look of remembered pain crossed his face and he stopped. "I don't want nothing to do with you."

No, I didn't correct his grammar. Too many missed homework assignments for me to bother. "Then what are you doing here?" I again demanded.

"Working. Gotta track someone down."

"You need to leave! Or I will call the cops."

"I don't give a damn about you. I'm not here for you," he argued.

"Well, I am here and I live here!"

"In this building?" he asked, the wheels of thought too clearly turning across his face.

"No, a few blocks down. I'm here for the coffee shop. I'm a regular." Never mind the po-boy tucked under my arm. He wouldn't know what it was.

"You know a guy named M. Knight? Works in this building?"

Stupid on steroids. A woman you recently tried to assault is not going to answer your questions. "No clue. I will call the police. I should have reported you in Atlanta. I can't believe you'd follow me here with some bullshit story about work!" I was shouting, hoping the hipsters in the coffee shop would get a clue that all was not right just outside their door.

"Look, bitch, don't you dare call the cops on me." He flicked his windbreaker back to show the gun tucked in his belt. Of course wearing a jacket, in this weather, was the road to heat stroke. Between the temperature and his agitation, he was turning a steaming shade of pasty pink.

The big question for me was if he was stupid enough to shoot me here on the street with multiple witnesses. That would so ruin my lunch plans. I decided to ask, "What are you going to do? Shoot me here on a busy street?" To prove my point, a bicycle tour came around the corner and slowly rolled past.

He looked like he was thinking. Very slowly.

I pulled out my phone. Then shouted, loud enough for the bike tour to hear, "And you can see a typical New Orleans robbery, right here on the street. Notice the big lug with the gun and the woman he's robbing."

"Shut up!" he said, clearly still not doing much in the thinking department.

The bike tour kept rolling, thinking this was all part of the show.

"You need to be quiet right now," he continued. "I got work to do. Go get your coffee and get away from me."

"No fucking way! You assaulted me!" I started dialing my phone. I could at least get the ambulance and the cops on the way before he started shooting.

He reached for his gun.

"Problem out here?" Melba, the transgender barista, was standing in the door. Holding a shotgun. She cocked it.

He recognized the sound. Turned to look at her.

She aimed it at him.

He looked at it, back at me for a second, then finally thinking kicked in and he ran as quickly as he could to the black SUV, ruining his mob boy cred by dropping the keys, having to fumble around in the chicken bones in the street before retrieving it and jumping in his car.

I could have gone up and gotten my gun in the time it took him to finally drive away.

I high-fived Melba. She smiled in return.

"Never know when you might need a little persuasion," she said.

"You do know how to use that?" I asked, being the responsible landlord I was.

"Two tours in Afghanistan," she said.

"Glad you're on my side," I said.

She nodded and headed back in. Maybe I'd have to start getting coffee here when she was working.

I headed back upstairs, locking my office door in case Junior Boy decided to return. I wanted an undisturbed lunch.

But before I took a bite, I called Karen. It went to voice mail. "This is Micky. Call me. It's important." I debated calling again and telling her to be on the lookout for a beetle-browed man wearing a windbreaker. But that snippet of information might not be enough to be helpful.

Then I did the right thing and called Joanne as well. Also voice mail. I left a description of Junior Boy and the vehicle he was driving and let her know the Brandes were in town.

Then I ate lunch. My po-boy was getting cold enough as it was.

What the hell was Junior Boy doing here? At my doorstep, no less. Karen and I were pawns in this game. Whoever was doing this either was incredibly sloppy or had deliberately led them to us. That they knew about the house and about me argued for the latter. If Andrea was the dead body in the morgue, who was the live person doing this?

"Too many damn Brandes," I muttered, taking another bite. I wanted to call Anmar and ask her more questions about her family, but didn't dare. The last thing she needed was for her secret phone to ring with Donnie sitting beside her.

That brought me back around to the central question—at least as far as I was concerned—why me and Karen? Which Brande would know to pick us? Which one of them could be connected to the queer circuit in New Orleans? Andrea maybe, but she was out of the picture.

Unless she wasn't. Joanne said the woman in the morgue was in her forties. Andrea Brande was the same age as Anmar, late thirties. Not a huge difference, but maybe it wasn't her.

Except for the resemblance.

Damn, damn, and double damn. Next time Anmar called—and I hoped she would—I would ask for a picture.

After finishing the last bite, I sighed and got up. Back out in the heat. I needed to find Karen and warn her. Her fancy espresso machine wouldn't be much protection.

I took my gun with me, stuffing it (safely) into a small shoulder bag. I was not wearing a jacket, not in this heat.

Hot car indeed. Almost cool by the time I got to Karen's.

A big gray Jeep was parked in the shady area, and today's parking memo was to take up as much space as possible. It left three-quarters of a car between it and the next car, and half a car from the driveway. All in the shade. I found a partly shaded spot down the street.

Stomping up the steps to let her know I was coming, I leaned on the doorbell.

And again.

Nothing.

I trotted about the side. Her car was here.

Back to the porch, again on the doorbell, a long, annoying peal.

Sweat was dripping down my nose and into my eyes. "Five more seconds and you can take care of yourself," I muttered.

Four and a half seconds later the door opened.

Karen's dress—or lack thereof—gave me a good idea of what had kept her from the door. It was two p.m. and she was in a bathrobe, her hair tousled.

"Who is it?" someone called from inside the house. Holly? It sounded like her voice.

"Micky! What are you doing here?"

"This is not a social call," I said. "You might be in danger."

"Danger? What are you talking about?"

I was standing out in the heat, sweat now running down every part of my body. "I won't be long, but can you let me in so we can talk?"

Karen sighed and stepped aside for me to enter. I came in just enough to let the door close. And get out of the heat.

Holly came down the stairs, even less dressed than Karen, wrapped only in a towel. In the five minutes I'd stood out on the porch they'd had time to get dressed.

"Let's go sit," Karen said, and without waiting for an answer, turned and headed to the back of the house, but instead of going to the sunroom—and its exposed windows—she stopped at the breakfast nook and sat at the table there.

I considered whether to sit or remain standing. I didn't want to be lounging around with two almost naked women.

"Holly, be a dear and get us some sparkling water."

Holly was a dear and fetched three bottles of trendy water. She sat at one end of the table, with Karen at the other, leaving me no choice other than to sit between them.

Oh, well, I've been with more naked women than this, I told myself as I sat. Admittedly the ice-cold water was welcome.

"I'm only here to warn you," I said.

"Of what?" Karen cut in.

"The woman. The house deal. It's all involved with a crime family in the Atlanta area."

"Really?" Holly. "That sounds like a not well made TV show."

I ignored her. "It does sound crazy, but a big guy showed up on my doorstep earlier today, looking for me."

"And how do you know he had anything to do with this family?" Holly asked.

I looked at her, the emotions in her eyes not matching those on her lips. Or maybe I just didn't like her and was reading it in. She was a young woman, younger than both of us. Do-gooder social worker trying to protect Karen.

"It'll take too long to explain," I said. "Research, talking to cop friends. Long story."

I'd run into Holly Farmer in the Atlanta airport—right when the Brandes were calling everyone home. Another quick glance at her face. No, it wasn't there; more olive in her skin tones, a delicate arch to her eyebrows, hair light chestnut rather than the dark almost black of the Brandes. And gray eyes, not their hazel or brown. I could see no resemblance to the Brandes in her.

I continued, "I don't know how it's all connected, but it has to do with the house, the woman who was at your office. Did you look at the picture I sent you?"

"I was supposed to recognize anyone from that?"

"It's security video."

"Not a good picture. No, I didn't recognize her, but it was too out of focus for me to recognize anyone. And she was at your office as well. Was she the one you saw?" Karen said.

"Possibly," I replied. "We're still not sure it's the same woman. Or that she's the one in the morgue."

Holly didn't react. Presumably Karen had already told her about her traumatic trip there. Most people perk up at things like dead bodies and morgues.

"But why? How can I be in danger? I didn't do anything."

"This is sounding more and more like a soap opera," Holly said. "Evil twins?"

"Maybe," I said, hiding my irritation. The sooner they let me finish, the sooner they could get back to doing what they were doing. "Someone tapped into an account for the crime family for the house, and it seems that person wasn't supposed to. So they are on the hunt. You might be collateral damage."

"Karen, this is crazy. She can't know this."

Karen worried a fingernail, then said, "Micky is usually pretty accurate. It might not hurt to—"

"To what?" Holly said. She didn't like that Karen was listening to me and not to her. Jealous much?

"I don't know, maybe just be more careful."

Holly reached across the table and took Karen's hand. "I'm sorry, you're right. This sounds crazy to me, but it's never a bad idea to be careful. I want to make sure you're taken care of."

Ahhhh, happy ending. Maybe if I weren't so cynical, I'd do better in the dating department. They were looking at each other in a way that was a cue for me to go.

I stood up. "Be aware. Big, black SUV. Or possibly a silver SUV. Tall, unibrow goon with a gun, but not very bright. Call me—or Jo—the cops—if anything happens."

Holly crooked a smile at me. "Thanks for the warning." I couldn't tell if it reached her eyes or not.

She and Karen remained sitting, holding hands.

I snagged my water bottle and let myself out.

The half shade covering my car had moved on, leaving it in full sun.

At least the water was cold.

And the car cooled down by the time I got home, my chosen destination. In case Junior Boy came by the office again, I didn't want to be there. And it was after three. It's a rule if it's over ninety-five degrees and in August you get to go home early.

I paused in the street, looking for the snake. Maybe it had slithered off to a bayou by now.

The poster still stared at me.

"Excuse me," someone behind me said.

I turned abruptly, not expecting anyone and being too prepared to jump away from a hiss.

"You're Michele Knight, aren't you?" she asked.

Short, middle-aged (okay, around my age), hair a light brown, almost washed out to blond. Casual professional clothes. The kind of person who is from the health department to tell you about a measles outbreak in your area.

"Yes, I am," I said slowly, having no idea what someone from the health department would want with me. My brain flittered to wondering if she was another Brande, whole different lineage. Maybe I should have lied and given another name. But she seemed to know me.

"You can't keep the house, you know," she said.

Now I recognized her, the brief glimpse I'd seen once, at a distance. Nancy Forgettable Last Name. What the fuck?

She forged ahead. "It's half Cordelia's. Dr. Cordelia James. Really more than half since she made the down payment."

"Wait, who are you?" I said tersely. I knew who she was but needed time to think how to respond. Other than shoving her into the street and cursing her out.

"My name is Nancy Olden. I am—"

I cut her off. "I know who you are. Cordelia sent you here to tell me she wants her half of the house back? Why isn't she here?"

"She…she's busy."

"You're doing this behind her back," I guessed.

"No. She's been meaning to do it, but with the new clinic building and everything, she hasn't been able to, but it needs to be done."

"So, she knows you're here, right?" I demanded. "Call her on the phone. I want to speak to her."

"She's busy," Nancy said. "She was afraid you might be upset with her and get into an argument that would do no good."

I took a step toward her, enough to make us uncomfortably close and to let me look down at her. I was pissed. My guess was Cordelia didn't know Nancy had undertaken this mission. It didn't seem like her to send her girlfriend (partner? wife?) to handle this in her stead. But people change with new people.

"And she thought I wouldn't get upset at a stranger showing up with no warning to tell me to get out of a house I've lived in over a decade? A stranger who put no money whatsoever into the house?" I took another step. She moved back. "A stranger who never waited all day for the plumber or crawled under the house to look for our cats, who hasn't paid a single penny on the mortgage? She thought that would be just fine?"

Nancy backed up, this time a full yard. "It has to be dealt with," she said, her face getting red. It could be the heat; her hair was damp and her underarms soaked. It might be anger. Or it could be her finally realizing she hadn't really thought this through. I gave her credit (small, very small) for not turning tail and running. She repeated, "It has to be dealt with. You can't keep living here like you own it. Cordelia—Dr. James needs to be treated fairly."

I almost asked if she called her Dr. James when they were having sex, their pet orgasm name. But I noticed Torbin and Andy out on their steps, watching the show.

"Fine," I said in as controlled voice as I could. "You tell 'Dr. James' to come talk to me about it. And tell her not to be such a goddamn coward to send you instead. She has my phone number; it hasn't changed."

"I had hoped you would be reasonable," she said, trying to save face. "I can see you're not."

"I am being reasonable. That's not the same thing as giving you what you want. I'm sorry you can't tell the difference. This is not your house. This is not your business. You need to leave."

"But—"

"Leave," I said, a low growl. "Now."

She opened her mouth to say something, but Torbin interceded. He was walking down the block toward us. "Nancy, this isn't a good time," he said.

She had enough sense to realize she was outnumbered. She turned away from me, nodded briefly at Torbin, then walked stiffly to her car, outrage with nowhere to go.

"What the fuck?" I muttered to Torbin.

She pulled away, driving a late-model sedan.

He sighed, then took my arm and led me to his house.

"What the fuck," I repeated as we got to his door.

"Andy," he called as we entered. "Stiff drinks. Very stiff." To me he said, "Well, that was classy."

"The highest," I muttered. I didn't know if he was referring to me or her, so I added, "She caught me unawares. I wasn't ready for that conversation."

Andy handed me a tall, frosty glass. Probably a vodka and tonic, but I didn't care. I took a long sip.

"She's been moaning about living in a condo, sharing walls. And how nice it would be if they lived right down the street from us."

"What the fuck," I said again. It would be my motto for the night.

"I love Cordelia, Nancy seems nice," Andy said, adding, "when she's not being too pushy, but I'd prefer you on our block than them."

I smiled at him. "Thank you." I took another sip. It was strong. A good idea. "Do you think Cordelia sent her to talk to me?"

They exchanged a look. Torbin said, "Never say never, but about as likely as a freak snowstorm here tomorrow. Nancy sees her role as being a doctor's wife, taking care of everything. If Cordelia doesn't get to it, Nancy takes it on."

"Like I never did."

"You had your own life, your own job," Torbin pointed out. "And you did wait for the plumber and search for cats who bolted out the door. You just weren't…"

"Her housewife," Andy said. "Well, it's true. She doesn't have a job, doesn't seem to want to get one, seems to prefer taking care of her woman."

"Didn't the women's movement get rid of that?" Torbin said.

I took another sip. "She is right. I don't own the house outright. Cordelia and I bought it together." I finished my drink in one big gulp.

Andy took my glass to refill it. I held my thumb and forefinger close together to indicate going lighter on the vodka. He nodded.

"She may be right," Torbin said slowly, "but it's not her house. I would be very…angry if they did anything to force you out. Cordelia deals with it or she doesn't."

"Thanks," I said, giving him a hug. He returned it, holding me tightly as if to show he wasn't going to let me go.

"Group hug," Andy said, putting the drink down to join in.

"Wait, I need my drink," Torbin said, pulling us halfway across the room to get it.

"I need mine," I replied, pulling us in the opposite direction.

"No, mine," Andy said, dragging us a different way, at which point we were all laughing too much to keep holding on.

I finished my drink. They were going out to a drag show out in the 'burbs.

I left, with them waving me good-bye with a "What the fuck!" cheer.

CHAPTER TWELVE

I let the sun get mostly down, and sobered up slightly, before walking to R&F. Tomorrow was salad day, so tonight could be fried catfish night and I could avoid the dreaded grocery run for another day. I needed to eat something filling, and this was the easiest option. Plus I could sort of call it work by checking on the security cameras.

"Hey," Rob greeted me as I entered. "Long time no see."

"Out of town. Anything happen while I was gone?"

"In the world? Or here at the bar?"

"The world I know about—as much as I want to know. Anything here?"

Two drop-dead-gorgeous men draped their arms over Rob's shoulders. One was a redhead, the other brown with distinguished gray. Both underdressed even for August, but with the bodies to get away with it.

The redhead said, "Is this the hot damn cute lesbian you were telling us about? The ever so butch security expert?"

I shot Rob a look.

"I cannot tell a lie," he said. "Indeed it is."

"Should we tell her?" Gray/brown said.

"Do you have names?" I asked. I didn't want to risk calling them by their hair colors out loud.

"Nickname is—duh—Red," said the redhead.

"Do you have a real name?"

"Zgorski. Kristopher Zgorski."

I coughed. "I'll call you Red. And you?"

"Nickname is Prof—Professor."

"Real name?"

"Milton Wendland. Do not call me Milt. All or nothing."

I sighed—softly. "We'll go with Prof as well. How'd you get that?"

"I teach gender studies at a university I will not name since they don't know I occasionally dance."

"You're a professor and you dance in a bar?"

"Oh, my dear. I could pay to go to a dreary gym. Or come here and get an even better workout and be paid for it. I didn't get a PhD because I'm dumb."

I looked at Red and said, "And you're a trainer for the Saints?"

"No, the Falcons." He kept his face perfectly legit for a long second, then broke out with a deep laugh. "No way, not the Dirty Birds." New Orleans and Atlanta are major football rivals with pet names for each other. "Like the Prof, I like the hours here and getting a workout. I'm a travel writer. Resting here from a week in Rome. Can't stay in all day starting at a computer screen."

"But we saw something strange," Prof said. "Over the weekend. We were both up on the bar—it gives you a nice view of the room—and these two women came in."

"First thought," Red said, "was they were a couple, although one was young and hot and the other a bit older."

"Sugar mamas happen, too," Prof said. "But they didn't act like a couple. Looked around a bit, then split up and took up posts in opposite ends of the room."

"Like they're casing the joint," Red added.

"Or waiting for someone," Prof said.

"We do two more dances; they're still there. I watch Mary go over and see if they want a drink—asked both—and neither gets anything. I can see that Mary is watching them from behind the bar, so she thinks there is something strange from their behavior."

"They hang out for another minute or so, then both leave at the same time, but separately."

"Drug deals?" I asked.

"Not that we could see."

"Did anyone else leave around when they did?"

"Huh, I didn't notice," Prof said. "But by then we were on a break and down from the bar."

"About what time?"

"After eleven, but before midnight," Red said.

"Let's go to the videotape," I suggested.

We all trooped into the bar office, Mary joining us as well.

I pulled up the video for around that time. It was only for the outside, but we should see them as they left.

Tedious minutes of people walking past the bar. I sped it up slightly but couldn't have it go too fast otherwise we might miss them.

"There!" Red said.

I paused the tape.

"Yep, that's her," Prof seconded.

I stared at the tape then started it again in slow motion. Aimee Smyth. Or Sally Brand. Or whatever her real name was. She walked partway down the block, then paused, now a blur in a dark patch. A man joined her. Maybe it was just his size, but he reminded me of Junior Boy. At this distance he could have been Junior Boy. Except this was from Sunday night, when JB was likely in Atlanta nursing a few bruises. They talked briefly—or waved their hands as if they were talking. She handed him something. And he gave her something in return. But it was impossible to see more than that.

A second figure emerged from the bar, a brief glimpse of the back of her head, but she knew there was a camera and quickly put on a ball cap and looked down, her features hidden in shadows. She kept her face away from the camera. Taller than the first woman, but I could see little of her.

She joined them only briefly enough to take something from the man, then kept on walking down the street and out of camera range.

A minute later, Aimee/Sally followed her.

The man walked toward the camera.

"Oh, that's trouble," Mary said as he got closer.

I paused the tape to get a better look at him.

Nope, not Junior Boy, not even close. Except for the size. "You know him?" I asked.

"He's not welcome here and he knows it," Mary said. "We think he's the one who sold the cut dope someone almost overdosed on."

"Why do you think that?" I asked.

Rob said, "Saw him doing a drug deal in the bar. Blatant, like this is just a bar, who would care if one more drug is added. I told him to get out and he gave me attitude. I went out to smoke a cigarette—yeah, I know, bad habit I'm trying to break, but being yelled at by a drug dealer was a trigger. He was still out there, taking money from someone and handing him something. He smirked at me, like what was I going to do. So I called the cops on him. That got him to scurry away. Too close to the police station."

The major station on Rampart was only a few blocks away.

"What happened?" I asked.

Mary sighed. "The usual. The police came, but he was gone."

"Told us to call again if we saw him."

"You're going to solve the case, aren't you, private dick Mick?" Red asked.

"A private dick; I want one of those," Prof added.

"Sure, on it right away," I said. "The case, that is."

They drifted away and I started obsessively going through all the video from the last week. Mary was kind enough to bring me a fried catfish plate without me even asking for it. Or she knows me too well. And beer to wash it down.

Nothing.

And nothing.

What did it mean? Aimee/Sally—of the Brande family?—was clearly up to no good. Dealing drugs? Quite possibly. But why the ruse with me and Karen? What did that gain her? Maybe as Anmar said, to throw the family into turmoil. Again, why? If she was running drugs, she was making good money. Unless she was making good money for Ellis and wanted more of a cut.

But I suspected she'd gone rogue. The Brandes liked the women in the kitchen—and bedroom—not on the streets dealing.

On the video a large silver SUV drove by.

A minute later another one. Then another. Everyone is now driving large silver SUVs. I had just started noticing.

I finally stopped counting large silver SUVs.

Druggie made another pass by, but he was just walking, didn't stop, didn't even smile at the camera. I hadn't gone to great lengths to hide the cameras—part of being a deterrent is being visible, but they weren't something the average tourist would notice either. I paused the tape to get a better look at him. Big, but a lot of weight in his stomach. He didn't look in shape. Greasy dirty blond hair, starting to recede. A large square face, jowls beginning to droop that showed how he would age. I guessed him to be mid-thirties, but a hard mid-thirties, drugs, booze, and a few stints in jail. I sent a picture of him to my phone.

Then back to nothing and more nothing, save for drunken tourists singing off-key. After the fourth bad rendition of "When the Saints Go Marching In," I got up and got another beer.

The Prof and Red were dancing on the bar. Both were far better than the average bar dancers, helped by them looking like they were having fun.

I got my beer, stretched, and then headed back to the office. I had only a little more to go. It was probably only fifty more silver SUVs and off-key singing, but I needed to be sure.

It was black SUV night. Five in a row.

Nothing.

Off-key singing. Someone with a boom box—did they still exist?—playing Big Freedia. Much better taste in music.

Holly Farmer.

Wait. I rolled the tape back. Holly, Karen's girlfriend, was walking down the street, heading this way. It was a brisk walk, as if she was headed somewhere. She looked up, directly at the camera.

She looked away and kept on walking, going past the bar and into the night.

I looked at the time stamp on the video. 10:36 pm.

Not crazy late. This is the French Quarter, and everyone goes to the French Quarter at some point. She walked down the street, that was all.

But not with Karen.

Even when Cordelia and I were together, we did things separately. Besides, Holly was a social worker. Maybe she was doing social worker things.

Maybe I was tired. I finished the last few hours, speeding the tape to get through the drunken tourists.

Nothing and nothing.

Saturday night. Torbin entering the bar in the early evening with a stuffed garment bag of his costumes. Andy, his partner, following with another suitcase in one hand and a wig stand with a long blond wig on it.

Drunk tourists.

Some sober tourists for a change.

Joanne and Alex, bantering and happy, dressed in shorts and T-shirts appropriate to the night. I was used to Joanne in clothes for her job, sensible suits, black pants. I can't remember the last time I've seen her knees.

Danny and Elly joining them at the door, also in shorts, also laughing and happy.

Joanne looks up at the camera, spots it, has to realize they're in it. Does nothing. Not worried about it.

They hang outside several minutes, laughing and talking. I can see the hands and mouths move, but it's picture only, so I don't know what they're saying. "Good thing Micky isn't here; we can have a relaxed time."

No, they are not saying that.

Joanne looks at her watch, then down the street.

More talk.

Danny looks at her watch.

Alex shrugs. Elly says something to Danny. Then Danny to Joanne, and she and Alex both nod.

They head into the bar.

Three gay male couples, holding hands or arms around each other. They enter the bar.

One nervous straight couple, the man with a death grip on the woman's hand as if to prove to the world he is straight. I want to tell him we don't care. They hurry down the street into the night and away from the demon queers.

More people coming into the bar, transgender, gender fluid, men in dresses, women in fedoras. Yes, even some straight folks. Everyone is welcome here.

Empty street.

Drunk tourists.

Lost tourists, consulting a map that they keep turning around. Probably also drunk. They wander off, still looking at the map.

A tall woman I recognized even in the dark distance. Her gait, how she holds herself. A shorter woman beside her, one I now recognized.

They come closer. They also stop outside where Joanne, Danny, Alex, and Elly waited. But don't notice the camera. The professionals—and the crooks—know to look for it.

Cordelia looks at her watch, points to it to the woman with her. The woman says something back. They are late, and Cordelia doesn't like to be late.

At least when we were together she didn't.

She pulls out her phone, texts someone.

They wait outside.

"They've gone inside; they got tired of waiting," I say to the days-old tape.

Cordelia looks at her phone screen, then points inside.

The woman shakes her head, not a no, but disappointment as if she thought they should have waited, and follows Cordelia into the bar.

The street is now empty.

I speed through the rest of the videotape, watching them blur by later as they leave. I don't slow it down. I don't care, really, I don't.

No more Aimee. No more man she dealt with.

Nothing.

I got up and got another beer.

I took it back to the office, but there was nothing else for me to do. I'd rolled the videotape and all it did was add more confusing details. No, I reminded myself, it gave me more information, and eventually, with enough information, it would make sense.

Aimee Smyth was not the dead woman in the morgue. That only made it more likely it was Andrea Brande. Too young to die, too young to leave her twin alone in a family that didn't want her to exist. I both hated and was relieved I couldn't tell Anmar the hard news. If I were a better person I'd find a way to do it, find a way to be that hero. But I'm just a flawed, fucked-up person, no magic bracelets available. Maybe with enough information, I could save myself—Karen along as collateral benefit. If it was just Karen...no, no hero here.

I took a sip of beer. Then another. I'd save who I could, and at the moment I wasn't sure that would include me.

I finished the beer.

Aimee Smyth wasn't the woman in the morgue. But how had her jewelry ended up on the dead woman? Did Karen and I see two different women? Or the same one? How was Aimee involved? She looked like the women in the Brande family, so I was assuming she was part of them. Was she ringleading this? Or the front for one of the men?

And why the fuck were Karen and I involved with a family feud in a crime family in Atlanta?

Time for another beer.

My phone rang.

Joanne.

I debated not answering, but I had called her. And she needed to know Junior Boy was in town.

The beer would wait.

"Hello?"

"Sorry to be calling so late," she said.

"I'm up, and it's well before midnight."

"And you're at home," she said, hearing the music from the bar.

"Work. Security for a bar."

"Which one?"

"R and F—Riley and Finnegan's," I say but she should know that; she was just here.

"You did the security there? The camera setup?"

"Yes."

"There are no cameras inside," Joanne, the police officer, says.

"The owner didn't want them. He wanted it to be a safe place for the people that come inside. We're covering the outside, back garbage and delivery area. Plus a panic button under the bar that goes directly to the police as well as a switch that can remotely lock all the doors."

"Okay, that's not too bad. But if something happens inside..."

"Like police detectives in ratty shorts and a T-shirt that says 'Suck the heads and pinch the tails'?"

"I do not have a T-shirt that says that."

"A video camera and a little editing and you could," I pointed out.

"So, you called me?"

"Remember that mob goon from Atlanta I told you about?"

"Yes?"

"He was at my office doorstep earlier."

"What?"

"Yep."

"What happened?"

"I told you he was stupid, right? Too stupid to do any research. Somehow he had my office address so was hanging out in the doorway to the coffee shop. But he didn't know I'm M. Knight, private detective. He thought it was a guy."

"But he's seen you before."

"Oh, he recognized me. Only as the woman at the party who kicked him very hard in the groin. I threatened to call the cops; he was instructed to find M. Knight, so he showed a gun and threatened back."

"Glad to know you're still alive."

"One of the coffee shop workers has a shotgun. She explained things to him."

"Hope it's licensed."

"She did two tours in Afghanistan."

"Close enough," Joanne agreed.

"I warned Karen," I said. "If he's visiting me, he might be visiting her."

Joanne sighed. She was still working, and the info I was giving her meant she would work longer. "I'll have a car drive by her house on a regular basis. And yours."

"I doubt he knows my home address."

"Maybe not, but not a risk I'm willing to take."

I didn't argue. I'd fought Junior Boy once; I didn't want to fight him again. Surprise wouldn't be on my side this time. "But there is more. I was reviewing the videotapes from the bar. I saw the same woman who was in my office meeting with a known drug dealer."

"Are you sure?"

"As sure as I can be, short of seeing her face-to-face. The reason Rob, the owner, wanted additional security was that someone in his bar almost overdosed from fentanyl and he wanted to keep that out of his place." I told Joanne what the dancers had told me, seeing her and another woman in the bar, catching her on the camera as she left and meeting with someone who had been banned from the bar for selling drugs, possibly the overdose one.

Joanne was silent for a moment. "Not sure how this fits, but eventually we'll figure it out." She asked for the videotape. I said I'd make a copy as soon as we hung up. I'd make sure to include some drunk tourists so she could enjoy what I enjoyed.

"More information is always better than less," she added.

I wasn't so sure; there were things I didn't want to know.

"Any progress on ID'ing the body?"

"Sent to the PD there for records; haven't gotten them back."

"Could they be on the take?"

"No. Or not likely. These things take time across jurisdictions. Any more great revelations?"

"Isn't that enough?"

"More than. Let me get on with it. I'll update you when I know more."

She was gone. I put the phone down and stared at the live feed. An empty street.

There were raucous cheers from the drag bingo going on in the bar. I found the section of tape, made a copy, and sent it to her.

I stared at my empty beer bottle. Stood up to get another one.

Then sat down again.

I didn't need another beer; it wouldn't solve anything. I needed to use the skills I had developed over the years as a private detective and my brain to solve this, to save somebody, maybe just me. Maybe Karen—and Holly—they seemed happy. Maybe Anmar. Andrea was probably already lost.

I stood again and left without looking at the video feed, took my empty bottle back to the bar, waved good-bye to Mary, and exited.

The night was sultry and close, the air either an embrace or a ghost wrapping itself around me. It had cooled to barely bearable, fine for sitting outside with a cold drink in hand. But I had none, only the blocks to walk home, and the air weighed me down.

The sidewalks were empty, traffic on Rampart was busy, people cocooned in the comfort of their cars. The new streetcar jangled by, a slow blur of red in the humid night, few people riding it.

How do I even save myself, I thought, one step after the other, only me walking this deserted street. Maybe that's the answer—one step at a time, with the desperate hope that I'd have time to take all the steps needed before... Before what? It might have been easier if I knew we were in danger. Yes, they were killers—Andrea Brande in the morgue proved that. But me? Karen? Were we pawns already used and we'd soon be left out of it? Pawns about to be played, killed, or brutalized? If I knew we were in danger, that would give me direction and action. I needed to know, and right now I didn't know and couldn't know.

"Damn you all," I muttered.

I heard footsteps behind me.

I quickly crossed to the median, between the two streams of traffic, then glanced back.

A waiter heading for home.

He passed and the night was silent and still, the air thick, as if waiting for a storm to clear it.

I turned the corner to my house.

The street remained empty. I marked my passing with sweat, leaving fat drops on the pavement. An ephemeral passing. The rain or the sun would take them away.

I walked slowly the last block, looking for snakes, both human and reptile. But the street was empty, not even a cockroach scudding by the garbage cans.

Then I was home, with no answers save to sleep on it and hope tomorrow had some. Or at least to find a few more steps to take in the right direction.

CHAPTER THIRTEEN

As I poured my morning coffee, the sun slipped away, clouds gathering, heralding an approaching storm. The weather report agreed, warning of a front moving through with possible severe thunderstorms, a line of rain almost over us.

I sighed, emptied my coffee out of the cup and into a travel mug. I wanted to be in my office before it was pouring down.

The first drizzle greeted me as I left the house, with fat raindrops just starting as I parked outside my office—no black SUVs hogging the space this time. I dashed in and managed to remain drier than I had been with sweat the day before.

Thunder boomed as I opened my office door.

Seconds later rain splashed against the window.

I drank my coffee as I did my usual morning routines, checking voice messages, checking email, checking the news and the weather. No messages, the usual heartbreaking news of the world, and the weather promised rain all day, enough to flood streets.

I drank more coffee, then again read over all the case notes, from the first ones when Aimee Smyth stepped into my office.

A split in the Brande family, one side trying to get money/power from those who currently had it. A woman dead in the morgue, likely Andrea Brande, who supposedly had decided to take a vacation from her family but hadn't returned, and no one had heard from her. Karen as a real estate agent and me as a private eye, pulled into it. We had a part in the scheme to get the money from Ellis and the other Brandes in power.

After the third read-through, I sat staring at the last page. What was I not seeing?

Or maybe there was nothing to see. Too many puzzle pieces still missing.

The homeless woman said it was two women who had dumped the body. Aimee and the other woman in the bar? Were they doing it for the men? Or even men dressed like women?

Damn it, all I had was speculation and that was dangerous, possible to weave the story I wanted, and not the one that was real.

If it was two women, it was more likely Aimee and Madame X. Since it was Andrea Brande rebelling and presumably dying for it, it was most likely something to do with the Brande family.

Aimee Smyth and Mad X killed Andrea Brande, and they involved both me and Karen.

Why?

Part of a plot to steal from the family. But what was the plot? Why hire a private eye to search for a most likely fictional sister? Why put money down on an expensive house and then disappear?

Aimee wanted to hide her trail. If she stole from them, she'd want to leave as little to track her by as possible. Maybe hiring me was a test to see if Sally Brand, or someone with a name close to that, could be found. So far I'd discovered nothing. If she was real, could she be that well hidden? Or maybe Aimee wanted the Brandes to think the dead woman was her—that would explain the jewelry and how it went from Aimee to being on the dead woman. Karen and I both knew that a woman who looked like the women we'd seen was now in the morgue. If the Main Brandes—Rebel Brandes vs. Main Brandes—were meant to know about the body in the morgue, that might explain why they somehow knew about us. Junior Boy talks to M. Knight. M. Knight tells of a woman in her office who is now dead. Or they find Karen, same thing.

The rebel is dead; the money she stole hidden and gone. The Brandes give up looking for her.

If it was that simple, all Karen and I needed to do was play our part, point them to the woman in the morgue. If they claimed the body, they might know it wasn't Aimee, but were they likely to do that? The Main Brandes might think they had their answer and be more than happy to have as little to do with a dead body as possible. If Anmar was right, they had little reverence for the women in the family. One who had scammed them could go to an unmarked grave.

All speculation. And even if it was right, I'd already mucked up their plot. I'd been to Atlanta and knew more about the Brandes than I was supposed to. I'd given Joanne the name of the woman in the morgue, and once she was officially identified, it would be game over for Rebel Brande and her merry band of women. Or men.

Maybe it would have been better if I hadn't tried to interfere.

Except that Andrea Brande would go to a pauper's grave, her killers would get away with it, and Anna-Marie would think her sister abandoned her. The innocent—as innocent as anyone in this mess—would be the ones who lost the most.

"I will outsmart you," I vowed out loud.

My phone rang. I didn't recognize the number or area code.

"M. Knight detective agency," I answered.

"I'd like to speak to M. Knight," the raspy voice of an old man.

"Speaking."

Silence. Then, "You're a woman?"

I'd heard the voice before. "Who is this?"

"Were you in Atlanta last week? Spying on us?"

Shit. Ellis Brande, hiding his location by using a number that wasn't from the Atlanta area.

"Who is this?" I repeated.

"It doesn't matter. I need information from you."

"It matters to me," I retorted. "I don't give information to people who won't even tell me their name."

"I'm going to make you an offer you can't refuse," he said, his voice confident, dismissing me.

A real mobster had taken mobster lessons from fictional mobsters.

"Tell me who this is or I'm hanging up. You're sounding more and more like a stupid prank call." I could be dismissive as well.

"Do not hang up; you will regret it. We know your name, we know where you work, we know what you look like, and we know where you live."

"Do you know the name of the Rottweiler sitting at my feet?"

"Don't bore me. I'm a busy man."

"And I'm a busy woman and you're boring me," I shot back.

Ellis Brande did not seem to know how to deal with a woman who wasn't subservient—or at least willing to play the part for him.

"I've been told you took on a case for a woman who is trying to cheat our family out of a significant amount of money. I need to know where she is."

"I have no clue what you're talking about, and even if I did, my clients are confidential."

"I have a check that was made out to you. It came from my account. You cashed it."

Well, more information, and not welcome information. Aimee had given them my info—and presumably Karen's—via checking account. Stupid? Or intentional?

"Fine, send me a copy of the check and then we can talk."

"That is not how I do thing—"

"It's how I do things," I cut him off. "Send the copy."

"Your life is in danger," he said.

"Is that a threat?"

"Yes, both from me and the woman who hired you. You get to choose who you take on. You should know I'm far more powerful and the one you don't want as an enemy."

"At least according to you." But I was tired of this, so I added, "So what is this offer I putatively can't refuse?"

"You tell me everything you know about this woman, including where she is, and we will leave you alone."

"Wow, what a generous offer," I said, bold sarcasm font.

"Do not mock me," he snapped.

"Okay, who should I mock? Your suck-up pal Uncle Donnie? The little junior goon you sent around here yesterday who got scared away by a transwoman? Oh, did he tell you I beat the shit out of him after he tried to grab me? Or was he too ashamed to admit an old lady kicked him in the balls and left him moaning on the ground? You think you know everything about me? I know everything about you. You're a second-rate crime family out of the backwoods of Georgia and so derivative you take your cues from made-up movies." I doubted he read the book.

"How dare you!"

"It's easy, Ellis Brande. You and your goons were too lazy and stupid to research me enough to know I am a woman. You've underestimated me every step of the way. If there are going to be regrets, they're going to be on your side."

"You fucking bitch!"

Yep, old Ellis lost his temper, which was what I'd been pushing for.

"You goddamned bitch! You will do as I say. You were hired by either Andrea Brande, Salve Smyth, Sabrina Jordon, or Hannah Foster. I know it was a woman. She's not as smart as she thinks she is. She's been seen. I need to know which one and I need to know it now, if you want to live to see the sun rise tomorrow."

"I'm not going to see the sun rise tomorrow," I said. "Not that much of a morning person. Your threat is as empty as Junior Goon Boy's head." I laughed.

"You do not mess with the Brande family! We are the most powerful crime family in the South! My people are everywhere! We could be outside your door even now!"

"Everywhere, right? But which are on your side and which are willing to exploit this to take your money and run? You can give the orders, but who knows if they'll be obeyed."

I could almost feel the anger coming out of the phone. I'd kicked him in the metaphorical groin—he was no longer the powerful man he desperately needed to be, and his family was willing to stab him in the back.

"No one dares disobey me!" he roared. "Especially the women! I control everything! All the money comes through me. If they want any of it, they have to come to me and beg."

"Guess someone got tired of begging. How'd they get control of your account long enough to write me a check?"

There might be a heart attack on his side any time now.

I added, "Maybe Uncle Donnie helped them. He's the type who would do anything a pretty young woman asked. Or maybe he's tired of always asking. Or begging. Is Junior Boy really that stupid, or is he screwing up on purpose? You have no clue, do you?"

"They would never betray me!" Protesting too much. Ellis knew someone betrayed him, and now everyone would be suspect. Maybe letch Donnie was loyal, but he was an evil bastard, and I was fine with two evil bastards going after each other. "It was a mistake, no one can really get to the accounts."

"Ah, of course. A mistake that someone got into one of your accounts and wrote me a big check and put money down on a much nicer house than you have. Mistakes like that happen all the time."

He was too enraged to notice my sarcasm.

"It was a mistake for someone to try to cross me. I will make an example of them! Anyone who helped will regret it. No one crosses Ellis Brande! Especially a woman. The accounts are safe now, no one can get to them. Soon they'll be where no one except me can find them."

"So if you croak, the family has nothing?"

"They deserve nothing without me! I built it all, little help from my father, but everything everybody has is because of me, and if I want to take it away, I can! No one will know where the accounts are! No one!"

"Clearly they need to be in a safer place than they are now," I cheerfully agreed.

"Enough of this! Tell me what I want to know."

"Sure," I said. "The woman who hired me lied through her teeth, gave a false name and fake phone numbers, and I haven't been able to contact her. As to her whereabouts, someone who looks a lot like her is now in the Orleans Parish morgue."

A gasp from his end. "Do not lie to me!"

"Call the coroner's office. Ask them to send a picture."

"If you are lying, you will pay!"

"Nope, Girl Scout's honor, all true. Call the morgue in Orleans Parish and ask about the unidentified woman there."

Ellis was nowhere near as dumb as Junior Boy, but that didn't mean he was a genius either. The last thing he wanted to do was call anyone in the legal system and ask about a dead body related to him. Crime family/dead body and the cops would be sniffing about with bloodhounds.

"Get me a picture of the woman and we will leave you alone," he finally said.

"Excuse me? Why don't you just leave me alone?"

"I need to know who the woman is, and not through official channels."

"Oh? I don't recall volunteering to be your errand girl."

"I've already paid you good money."

"No, I was hired to search for a fake person. I did that much longer than the money warranted. Nothing left in the bank for extra tasks. Even if I wanted to do them."

"Don't make this hard on yourself," he threatened. "I need to know by the end of the day."

"Or what? You're going to send Junior Boy wannabe mobster around again to get run off by a transgender woman and all of us to laugh at him? Yeah, scary threat."

There was silence from his end, except for raspy breathing. *Should have given up those cigars a long time ago.* Ellis had no backup when his threats didn't work. Not a good criminal strategy—or even a legal one—just one tool in the toolbox.

More breathing, then, "I will pay you the same amount you were originally paid. Send me that photo by the end of the day."

"Sorry, not interested. I don't work for known criminals. Bad for the license. You can try Scotty Bradley—oh, wait, he doesn't work for criminals either. And he's still in Italy. Send Junior Boy."

"Do it or you'll regret it!" Back to threats. Boring.

"I have an idea. I have a lot of cop friends. I can tell one of them the woman is likely to be one of the Brande family women, and all they need to do is send to Atlanta for dental records of all the women in that age range. I keep my license and you get your ID."

"Don't you dare!"

Oops, too late. Not that I'd tell him that. He'd find out soon enough. Maybe I could be in Italy by then. "Then sorry, cannot help you."

"You will regret this!" he thundered. Sound and fury, signifying nothing.

"Sorry, got to run, my next client, an assistant DA, is here. Good luck with your problems." I hung up. Ellis was only going to repeat his threats, and I was bored with them. Plus I had no doubt that he wasn't alone and was already giving orders to make me regret it. Maybe they would even be carried out. I needed to think and not just rely on their incompetence and stupidity. Guns make even stupid people dangerous.

Ellis had given me the real names of the women who were likely involved in this. They could still be working with some of the men, but clearly they had left the kitchen. But were they being used? Or were they getting free? He had let me know they'd used an actual Brande family account to lead the Main Brandes straight to me and Karen. It didn't explain why we were the chosen ones, but it did explain how the Brandes knew who we were. It also meant we were in danger. The Main Brandes would come after us to find out who had betrayed them. Ellis knew only threats, and that meant he was likely to believe in breaking kneecaps—or worse—to get what he wanted.

Karen should go into hiding. Maybe I should as well, but I hated the idea. It would mean I could do nothing here, and it would also mean I'd have to put the rest of my business on hold. A week or two of not working meant a week or two of earning nothing. That would make for a very unhappy bank account.

I sighed. I needed to call Joanne again. I needed to warn Karen. Again.

I needed to do the same searches I'd done for the fictional Sally Brande for the women Ellis mentioned. The latter task was more appealing, but my conscience demanded I do the other two first.

I dialed Joanne.

And typed in the first name. Salve Smyth.

Voice mail. "Call me ASAP. More stuff on the case."

I dialed Karen as the search results loaded.

Voice mail again. "You are in danger. The crime family is desperate to know who the woman in the morgue is. Desperate in a bad way. Might be a good idea for you to go far away for a long vacation."

In a week or less Joanne should have the dental records and make an ID. That would screw both the Main Brandes and the Rebel Brandes in ways that should make both me and Karen irrelevant. We just had to survive until then.

Salve Smyth had once been Salve Brande until she married Harden Smyth. Harden was doing hard time for drugs, three strikes—he had five—and he was out. He'd be released when he was seventy-two if he was a model prisoner.

They had one child, a daughter. If it was Salve who had reinvented herself as Aimee, she might have good reason for running away from the Brande family. Good rationale and some bad choices. Whatever her reasons, one woman was dead, and she had put Karen and me in danger. For all her faults and cowardly choices, Anmar Brande only hurt herself.

I found a wedding picture in the newspaper, but it was close to twenty-five years old. Salve had been seventeen when she had married.

Salve was an identical twin, with her sister Sabrina.

Shit, how many fucking identical twins did this family have?

The wedding picture was enough to let me know that Salve was a generic Brande—dark hair, square chin. But in thirty years, she could be Anmar, or the woman in the morgue, or the woman in my office. Or someone else entirely, her almost name thrown in to add more confusion just in case I stumbled on it. The Brande women only seemed to get their pictures taken at marriage.

Eight months later, she had a child, a boy. Three months later, he died, tragic accident in the bathtub. At least, that's what the newspaper reported. Another eight months and another kid. The girl. This one survived. Harden Smyth spent five years in jail just after she was born.

Sabrina, her twin, also married young. Also a blurry wedding picture. She married Harden's cousin, Haydel Jordon, another hard-looking man, a deep meanness around his eyes. She managed a bare smile for the camera, but it was hard to find joy anywhere in the picture. Maybe it was just the fuzzy newsprint. Maybe. If she was lucky.

He did two years in prison shortly after they were married. They also had a daughter. She was named Hardeen. Lovely.

Haydel was more jail prone than his cousin. Or stupider. He was back in just six months after he got out. Car theft. More stints in and out. Then a short paragraph—knifed in the shower in prison, left there to bleed out. No one held to account.

The women faded away. No more notices. No jail time, no more marriages. Or maybe only the first one merited mention in the newspaper. I could find very little information about any of them. No occupation, no college graduation. Nothing to hint at what kind of people they were, even as vague as majoring in biology or English. Women who lived in shadows.

Hannah Foster was a first cousin to Salve and Sabrina. Daughter of Phoebe Brande and her husband, Marlin Vincent. Another blurry newsprint picture of her wedding. Married Hubert Manred. A pharmacist. She was seventeen.

Too many Brandes to keep track of. I sketched out a family tree.

Ellis was the oldest of five brothers—and three sisters. One of his brothers died in a car wreck; another in jail, supposed overdose. Back in the day when overdoses weren't so common. His youngest brother was father to Salve and Sabrina. That would put them both at around the right age for the woman in the morgue, late thirties to early forties. Before he died in the wreck, his brother managed to pop out a few kids as well, and his oldest daughter was the mother to Hannah Foster. Again, putting her in a possible age range for the dead woman, late thirties.

Hannah married again—no mention of what happened to Hubert— still, as all good Brande women, young, at nineteen. Unlike the other Brandes, she and her husband looked happy in their wedding picture. Dominic Foster. He was tall and handsome, more Mediterranean than the pasty white of the Irish Brandes. He listed his profession as accountant. Two years after they married, they had a daughter, Ellicia Halley.

Too many E and H names. My eyes were itching and blurry.

I sat back and stared out the window. The August sun glared. I got up and pulled the blind to shade it out, then sat back down.

All four of the women Ellis Brande named—Andrea Brande, Salve Smyth, Sabrina Jordan, and Hannah Foster—were possible, at least in age range and vague looks, as the woman in the morgue. But I only had his rant to include the last three. Anmar had confirmed her twin was missing and had not contacted her.

I glanced at my watch. It was well past lunchtime. The searches had been time consuming.

I needed a break, and lunch was calling my name.

My stomach was in mid-growl when my phone rang.

It was Joanne calling my name. I needed to talk to her.

I gave her a quick rundown of my conversation with Ellis Brande.

"And you're still sitting in your office like they're not trying to kill you?" was her response. She added, "Go somewhere safe, where they can't find you."

"Hey, I hear the cops are driving by every once in a while. I should be fine."

I heard the frustrated sigh. I was meant to. "Do not blow this off.

Yes, they're well over the stupid line, but stupid men have killed a lot of people."

"I know, but I also don't want to be run out of town. My boss doesn't give me a great vacation plan. I don't work, I don't eat."

"At least vary your routine. You might want to stay away from places they know about—like your office—for a few days."

"I'll carry my gun."

"Humor me. I have enough gray hair as it is."

"Then go completely gray and it will all match, no straggling brown left to fade away."

"Don't do it," she said. "Don't blow it off and act like the hero. It won't do you any good and it won't help the situation. You can come stay with me and Alex. But no more 'I'm tough' bullshit."

"Maybe I am tough," I said.

"You are. You're not bulletproof. Come over, spend a few days with us. You can keep working. You can help me with the case."

It was tempting. Joanne was right. I needed to be hard to find for a while. And it would be fun to hang out with her and Alex, as well as throw around ideas about this case. She usually kept strict police protocols about sharing with civilians. She was offering a lot, which was a sign of how worried she was. There was just one problem.

"If I'm in danger and I stay with you and Alex, I put you in danger as well."

"I'm a cop, I can handle it."

"Alex isn't." To keep her from arguing further, I added, "Look, Joanne, you're right. I'll find a place where no one will look for me. But I can't put my friends in danger."

"Do it now. Promise? Let me know where you are. I want daily check-ins."

"Agreed." Then I rushed to the question I really wanted answered. "Any word on getting an ID on the body?"

"Still waiting. They're hunting down the dentist. Hope she had at least a few fillings."

"Maybe I can find a way to ask."

"Don't. The more you stay out of this, the better. Call me later and let me know where you are."

She hung up. I knew Joanne was going to do the same thing I'd done, search the names Ellis had blurted out, just with better police resources.

Don't underestimate them, I reminded myself. Maybe Ellis was angry and had given something away. And maybe he was angry and still cunning enough to drop names to lead me into a labyrinth.

I grabbed my laptop and the sturdy messenger bag with my gun as well as other PI tools like cameras and disguises and headed down the stairs. I did not need to be easily findable.

I stopped in at the coffee shop, ignored my growling stomach to maintain my vow not to subsidize them. Melba was there. I caught her eye and said, "If you see that guy around here again, call the cops ASAP. Gangster from Atlanta, up to no good."

"Can I shoot him in the butt first?"

"I'd say yes, but I'm not the final authority on that."

"Got ya. I'll keep it legal." She winked at me.

I paused in the door to scan the street before heading to my car. The most danger was another bicycle tour spouting historical nonsense. "And on the corner is the original location of the House of the Rising Sun, where Louis Armstrong got his start in jazz."

"Only credulous Yankees would believe that shit," I said loud enough for the last two cyclists to turn their head in my direction.

No sign of Junior Boy. Maybe Ellis decided to send the D team instead of the F team, and their plane was delayed in Atlanta.

I headed to the one convenient place where no one would ever look for me, a new national chain coffee shop location that had just opened on Elysian Fields. We have plenty of good local coffee shops and I would always choose them. But hidden I needed to be, so hidden I was. Plus I could find something I could call lunch and use their Wi-Fi to continue my searching.

After getting a large iced coffee, Bucket of Latte—it was too damn hot for anything hot—and a tired-looking turkey sandwich (Turkey SourBucks), I set up at the most out-of-the-way table, my laptop screen facing the wall so no one could see it.

I went back to the Brandes. As best I could given their scant notice, I searched all the Brande women, daughters, wives, cousins.

Two more iced coffees later, to earn my table, I had gone through most of them. Anmar was right, some did disappear. Or died young. Domestic violence? And a family that closed ranks around the men?

I didn't have the time or energy to look up death rates and ages for women during those years. This was from the '60s on, not before clean water systems and vaccinations.

What would it be like to grow up in a family like that? Warped, a looking glass world with right and wrong upside down? Stealing and cheating are good, and being honest and kind are bad. Be loyal no matter how little it's returned. There is one big lottery we're all forced to play: who our parents are. Win at it, with decent people who know how to love and nurture and provide what's needed. Do okay, with parents who aren't perfect but do their best. Lose, and end up with the broken people who break you as well.

From the Brande family tree, they had scattered a number of broken people around.

But the main thing I was looking for was candidates for the dead woman. How many in the age range? How many could I find enough photos for—even the blurry old newsprint wedding ones, that would confirm they carried the Brande looks?

I had my answer. The women Ellis Brande had mentioned. He had slipped up and given me their names, not misled me.

At least I knew and didn't have to keep looking over that shoulder.

A slow pile of information, some guessing, some firm ground. With enough stepping stones, I could find my way through this swamp.

I also needed to find a place to stay, at least for tonight. With a sigh at my bank account, I chose one of the big convention hotels. They would be anonymous and would have security. Even if I was cursed enough to pick the one Junior Boy was staying at, they'd be able to handle him. No, they weren't as tough as a transwoman who had served in Afghanistan, but they'd do for a crook that dumb.

Ellis's threats—and Joanne's warning—had spooked me. I drove by my house, going around the block to case any unfamiliar cars, before running in to grab enough stuff for a couple of days. One advantage of a blistering summer is that no layers or even long pants were needed.

As I handed my car keys to the valet, I reminded myself that as expensive as this was, it was cheaper than my funeral. Even if I was cremated. At least this was the butt end of summer, as inexpensive as it gets down here.

After getting to my room, I called Karen again. Still voice mail. Karen was a rich heiress, but you'd think a social worker would have other things to do besides sex. Or maybe she was at her real estate office. Even so, she should be answering her phone.

Then I called Joanne.

She answered, in her car, from the background noise. Usually she'd let me go to voice mail if she was driving.

"Update," I said. "I'm in one of the hotels on Canal Street. The heat has melted my brain; I can't even remember which one. I can look it up—"

"That's fine; you should be good there."

"I've tried to call Karen several times and not gotten an answer. I'm worried Junior Boy might have paid a visit."

"You stay put. We'll look into it. I can find her. I'll call—some people to get to her."

Call Cordelia, who was her cousin, with enough messy family ties that Karen would respond to her. "Okay, let me know. I'd hate to think I'm in a high-class hotel and she's dealing with Junior Boy all by her lonesome."

"Right."

"Plus, if he's coming after her, it means they're not half-assing this. There is a rebellion in the Brande family and no way to know who's loyal to whom. If Junior Boy is diligent, he's sided with Big Daddy Brande."

"Could be," Joanne said. "I'll let you know when I've talked to Karen. Stay put." She hung up.

I ordered room service. What's another twenty-dollar hamburger on top of valet parking and a high-end hotel night?

I paced the room, but it wasn't big enough to give me any release for my tension. The hotel did have a fitness room, but my hasty packing didn't include workout clothes.

Joanne was right, I needed to stay here. Even if this was Junior Boy's place, we wouldn't see each other if I stayed in my room.

I turned on the TV. The weather report was that it was hot, that it would stay hot for at least the next week. With afternoon showers likely. Hot and wet.

I turned the TV off.

My hamburger arrived. I tipped an extra five. My offering to the gods that I would never have to bring hamburgers to whiny guests. It was food, better than the turkey sandwich of the afternoon.

After eating, I opened my computer.

What case was I truly working on? I'd been hired to look for a lost sister. Just a random ruse to get me involved? Or was there a larger purpose behind it? Salve Smyth could easily be called Sally, and she had been a Brande. If she was Sally Brande, or had been, why send me to look for her? She hadn't been Brande for decades, instead likely going by her married name of Smyth. Unless she was Salve Brande-Smyth. I redid the search on her, under all combinations of those names: Salve, Sally, Brande, Smyth, Brande-Smyth.

Oh, interesting, Sally Brande-Smyth opened a small dress shop in Biloxi a decade ago, about ninety miles east of New Orleans on the Mississippi Gulf Coast. The name was High Fashions.

Businesses have public records, licenses, etc.

"And you thought I wouldn't find you," I muttered. Of course, she'd done her best to make it hard. Given me the wrong name and wrong location.

High Fashions seemed to do mostly high-end gowns. Sequins 'R Us. Yes, we do a lot of Mardi Gras balls and other glitzy stuff, but that hardly sounded like a viable business model. Indeed, they were often late with property taxes and were taken to small claims court on a few occasions for not paying bills.

Ah, criminal complaints. Neighbors called in several times about noise and trucks coming in late at night. Love smaller town newspapers, they give the juicy details. A neighbor was quoted as saying, "All kinds of trucks at all hours of the night. This is a nice neighborhood, and I don't want people I don't know skulking around after midnight."

Two years ago the police raided it on suspicion of it being a front for drugs. They found one bag of marijuana that the owner—presumably Sally—claimed had been left by a disgruntled employee. A little more searching and I found the case was settled with them paying a fine, but no jail and no guilty plea. Nothing criminal on her record.

Six months ago the store closed.

Now the neighbors were complaining about them not keeping the property up. "Weeds growing everywhere. Seen a big snake there last week. Never were good neighbors. Forgot that folks lived on the street behind the store. Noise and parties all night."

Probably not drugs. My bet was money laundering. High-ticket items that can come and go. Buy a cheap knockoff and claim it's a ten-thousand-dollar designer dress. Local cops weren't likely to know a Versace from a Kmart.

Where had Sally Brande-Smyth gone from there? The property records from the store listed its address as the one on record. In the morning I could get the computer grannies on her financial records— not technically legal, but people always spend money and you can always track them through their money.

On a hunch, I checked to see if her abusive husband was still in jail. Released six months ago on good behavior and overcrowding. Was she hiding from him? Or going to him?

Three months ago he died of an overdose, found by an abandoned warehouse on the outskirts of Atlanta.

That didn't sound like a joyous reunion. Was he no longer needed in the Brande family? Or did Sally prefer the single life?

Or maybe he just overdosed. In prison for a long time, gets out and lets loose. But doesn't know the drug scene anymore and gets bad stuff. Or takes his usual dose, now too much.

But too much of a coincidence to not be related. Sally is doing a nice little money-washing business on the beach. Hubby unexpectedly gets out of jail. She closes the shop. He dies three months later.

Someone arrives in New Orleans claiming to be her sister and wants to look for her.

All hell is raised in the Brande family, with one side trying to steal from the other.

I picked up the phone to dial Joanne.

Then dialed another number. It rang but went to voice mail. Interesting she hadn't discarded the phone yet.

"Sally Brande aka Salve Brande-Smyth most recently was running a high-end dress shop in Biloxi. Probably a money-laundering operation. It closed just when her husband got out of jail. Short-lived reunion, as he died of an overdose three months later. Thought you'd like an update on the case you hired me for."

She would not call me back, of course. But she had played me for a fool, and I was pissed. If she ever checked the messages—it had to be a disposable phone—she would know I had tracked her down.

My phone rang.

Joanne. She didn't bother saying hi, just, "Karen and Holly have been over in Pensacola, enjoying the beach. I told them to stay there.

Karen says she has to be back in a few days for a big real estate deal, but she'll stay with...friends."

With Cordelia, the sensible family member she usually turned to when she needed something. But I didn't ask and Joanne didn't tell.

"Okay, good to know. Did she mention if she'd seen anyone like Junior Boy?"

"She said no, nothing out of the usual." Changing the subject, she said, "You're still at the hotel, right?"

"Yes, even got room service to not stick my nose outside the door."

"Good move. Stay there." Office noises in the background. "Got to go."

I let her hang up with a quick good-bye. I could fill her in about Sally Brande tomorrow. I wondered if Sally/Salve was back in Atlanta with the Brande family, or lying in the morgue. Two overdoses in a family that ran drugs but didn't seem to use them raised questions.

I yawned, glanced at my watch. Not late by my usual standards, but I should just go to bed and think about it all tomorrow.

My phone rang.

I didn't recognize the number until I did.

She had called me back.

"Hello," I answered.

"We need to talk," she said.

"We are talking."

"In person. Can you meet me at your office?"

"At this time of night? No. Where are you? We can meet around there."

"I'm not in a place to meet. Your house?"

"In public," I stated. Curious as I was, I wasn't stupid curious.

"I'm trying to not be seen. It's not safe."

"One of the hotel bars on Canal Street? They are full of tourists and conventioneers," I said.

"No, that's too risky."

"Why?"

"I'll tell you when we meet, can't talk much over the phone," she said.

"Okay, where should we meet?"

"I don't know," she said sounding exasperated. "I don't know the city. Someplace out of the way."

I did a quick inventory of the bars I knew. Damn, I knew a lot of them. "How about a local place in the Garden District?"

"Where's that?"

"Away from the French Quarter and Canal Street, but not too far to get to. Connie's Alligator and Bait Bar, on Felicity near St. Charles." I gave her the address. "It is a local place, no tourists around. It'll be safe."

She reluctantly agreed.

I shoved my shoes back on. Thought of calling Joanne, but Connie was a country girl who used to be a marine biologist in the swamps of Florida. She kept at least two loaded guns behind the bar. And knew how to use them.

I got my car out of the valet parking. Another generous tip to the expense, but if you can't afford the tip, you can't afford the place.

I wanted to get there before…Aimee? Salve? Sally? Maybe I could get her real name.

Connie's was well off St. Charles, on the less trendy side, although more gentrified day by day. Alligator and Bait Bar was both a joke and a signal this wasn't a place for craft cocktails. Yes, there was a stuffed ten-foot-long alligator hanging from the ceiling.

"Well, well, stranger, long time no see," Connie greeted me as I entered.

"Ms. Jarvis, you're too far uptown," I bantered. "Gotta cross Canal Street."

"What can I get you?"

"You're behind the bar? Where's Greg the Red?"

"Cat rescue." Greg was a muscled, tattooed, big motorcycle kind of guy. She elaborated. "About six months ago, he found three kittens hiding from the rain. Took them in. Now he and his bruiser friends climb trees to rescue cats on their days off."

"Wow, who knew Mr. Greg, Mr. Red the Man, would be a cat dude."

"Strange world," she agreed.

"Whatever local brew you have on tap."

She nodded and poured me a beer, a nice wheat one. I gave her ten for a tab and a tip and found a table in the back. It was a slow night and pretty empty, after-work people gone home and not the trendy place where the glamour kids showed up around ten.

About fifteen minutes later, Aimee arrived. The same woman who was in my office, but different. A mask had been removed. Or added. This woman was wary, looking around, scanning the room the way one does when looking for danger, not friends. I waved her over.

"Would you like anything?" I asked, a skein of politeness.

She glanced at my beer. "They have any decent liquor in this place?" With another glance up at the alligator.

"Depends on what you mean by decent," I said. "The usual brands. Probably no single malt Scotch or small batch vodka."

"Dewar's on the rocks," she said.

I went to the bar, bantered with Connie for long enough to remind Aimee I wasn't her waitress, then returned with her drink and another beer for me.

"How did you find out—what you found out?" she asked.

"Who are you?" I countered. "You didn't give me your real name when you hired me and did your best to send me on a wild goose chase."

"It doesn't matter." She shrugged and took a sip.

"Let me narrow it down. Are you Andrea Brande, Salve Smyth, Sabrina Jordon, or Hannah Foster?"

Her eyes widened in surprise. "How do you know those names?" she asked in a harsh whisper as if worried about being overheard in this empty bar.

"I'm good at what I do. You used me, tried to set me up for your crime family to find, lied to me, wasted my time. None of that makes me happy."

She looked down, swirled her drink. Another mask slipped in place. Or another one came off. "Look, I'm sorry. This is complicated."

"How?"

"It's hard to explain."

"Ellis and the purse strings?"

Again the look of surprise, well hidden, a slight widening of her eyes, straightening of the lips. "How do you know this?"

"Like I said, I'm good at my job. Who's the woman in the morgue?"

"What…what woman in the morgue?"

She was good. Believable if I didn't know better. "The woman who had on the same jewelry, except the really nice piece, and clothes you wore to my office. The same ones you wore to put money down on the house. Or are you going to tell me some strangers mugged you, stole all your clothes and most of your jewels—except the really good ones—and they were wearing masks so you can't even tell if they're men or women."

"It is complicated."

"Start explaining it to me, or I go to the police. I have several cop friends on speed dial."

She looked down again, then at me. She made a decision; I just didn't know which one. "You know about my family?"

"Some."

"You said Ellis Brande, so you know. They are not...well, women are supposed to be barefoot and pregnant. Or sex toys. Get a little older...and we're less useful."

"Got it. But that doesn't explain you showing up in my office."

"No, it doesn't. It's not...easy to get away. Ellis doesn't let anyone out of his grasp, not without his permission."

"But you—or Salve—managed to run a store in Biloxi for years."

"Yes, I did. But only because it was useful to them. You were right; it was a money-laundering business. I had to report weekly, turn over all but enough to keep me fed and clothed."

"You're Salve—Sally Brande—Smyth?"

"Yes, yes, I am. I never thought...you'd find me. I hired you to make sure I could no longer be traced by that name."

"But you can be, although I have to admit it wasn't easy. You'd get by with all but the most thorough search."

"It got worse."

"Your husband got out of jail."

She looked at me, not bothering to hide her surprise this time. But she continued, "Yes. I had hoped that would never happen. As long as he was in jail, I was in a safe limbo—properly married as Brande women are supposed to be, but no husband to throw me around when he felt like it. Or beat up our daughter."

"Why did you marry him?"

"I don't know. Oh, I do, he seemed strong and confident, could protect me from the Brande men. But there was no one to protect me from him. Jail was the best thing that happened to me. When he got out, he wanted things to be the way they were. Me always available to him, cooking his meals, wanting sex when he wanted it, taking his blows and insults without complaint. But I couldn't be nineteen again."

"How convenient he overdosed so soon after he got out."

"I didn't do that. Women don't touch the drugs. Not ladylike. He might have started using in prison. Or…he wanted his place back and other Brande men had taken it."

"You're suggesting that one of your family members killed him?"

"It wouldn't be the first time. Inconvenient people have a habit of disappearing. Rumor is there's Brande property in the hills of Georgia, kept only as a place to dump bodies where no one would look."

"Really? Do you know where it is?"

"No clue. Not even sure if it's real or not. But we came from the hills and hollers, and sometimes justice is given the old-fashioned way."

It didn't matter. There would be property records, and the police could search for them.

"So, your husband conveniently gone again, this time for good. You had nothing to do with it. Why run now?"

"I'm no longer married. Ellis was suggesting I 'take care' of Uncle Donnie." She made a face.

"Isn't he already married?"

"Of course. But marriage doesn't bind men the way it binds women. Brande women must be faithful—even to jailed husbands. But Brande men—and their buddies—can wander as much as they like. Donnie was bored with his wife and assumed since I was now free, available, I should be available to him."

She made a face and took a sip of her Scotch.

"So rather than wait a few months for Donnie to get bored with you, you decided to start a civil war in your family?" I was deliberately pushing her. I wanted her off-balance—and to let her know I wasn't playing by her rules.

"He's an ugly man. Oh, he plays nice, but sucking up to Ellis has a price, and he makes sure those below him pay it. And once he was done, it would be some other old fart Ellis owed favors to—a seventy-year-old who isn't rich enough to get a twentysomething woman, so has to settle for those of us in our forties. Women are bargaining chips in this family. Some of us got tired of it."

"So what's your end game? Ellis knows about the account you

used to pay me and put a payment on the house. I presume that's part of the play. How does that break you free?"

"Are you sure?" Then, "It's complicated," she said. Another sip of her drink.

"You involved me in your 'complicated' scheme. I need to know the truth."

"The truth?" She looked up at me, set her drink down. "The truth is this is a brutal family, we're held in gilded cages—yes, nice clothes, a big house. But only if we submit. And do it with a smile. I can't do that anymore. I can't stand to watch younger generations of women seduced into it, seeing the pretty things, the money things, and not the ugly, violent underside until they're trapped, no easy way out."

"You want to escape, but only if you can get enough money to continue the comfort," I challenged. "Nothing like 'get on a bus for as long as you can ride, then clean rooms or serve burgers' for the Brande women."

"So easy for you to judge. They would hunt us down. You can't escape from the Brandes on a minimum wage job a hundred miles away. Ellis is getting…increasingly desperate to hold on to power. Upping the consequences for displeasing him. It was now—or I'd conveniently overdose. If I was lucky."

"What if you went to the police? Witness protection?"

"Please, I've been part of this family since I was a baby. Drugs put in my stroller to smuggle them. Not interested in going to jail for a decade or so."

"What are you intending to do?"

"I can't tell you. Really, I can't."

I guessed, "Ellis is moving the accounts, all the paperwork to access them. He says no one will ever find them again. But he's too old and infirm to manage it all on his own."

She stared at me. But then she said, "It'll be soon and then this will all be over. But I can't tell you more. I'm taking too much of a risk just talking to you." Again, the look around the room, hard wariness in her eyes.

"One of you is dead, lying in the morgue as they search for her ID. What happened?"

"A lesson in disobeying the Brandes."

"Witnesses said they saw two women dump her body."

Her face closed down, to hide the emotions. Or contain them. "No, it wasn't us! We're not killers. We're trying to escape the killers."

"But she was killed here in New Orleans. Not Atlanta."

"We think they traced her here. Ellis monitors our phones. A grandson is down here, setting up a drug operation. Maybe he found her. She might have slipped up and answered her phone, forgetting he would trace it. I don't know. I just know…I wish it hadn't happened. I wish…we'd been able to save her. But now you see they will kill us. Even if we stop now and go back, we'll pay. We have to escape."

"What role am I playing?"

"It's done. To see if you could find me." She said it too quickly.

"Except you used an account that Ellis was monitoring and it led them to me. And Karen Holloway. They want to know where you are. A polite no doesn't deter them. I've had to leave my house and hide out. Doesn't seem done to me."

"That wasn't intended," she said. "We had timed it so he wouldn't reconcile the accounts until, well, until it wouldn't matter."

"But he did. Why?"

"I don't know. Maybe someone got scared and tipped him off."

"Which means he knows what's going on."

"No, we've been careful. Kept the entire plan to only a few. Others had a task or two to complete but didn't know how it fit in."

"You're stabbing him in the back and someone is doing the same to you?"

"We've been taught to survive. Look, it's almost over. Keep hiding out for the next few days. You'll be safe. Once I'm free, I'll send another check to pay you. I just need you to keep this between us for the next few days—a week at most. It's to free the Brande women—at least some of us. We can't do this any other way."

She reached out and put her hand over mine, her expression beseeching. Begging.

I wondered if it was the begging she had learned to survive in the Brande family.

"You have to make sure no harm comes to either Karen or me."

"I'll do my best. I can't control them, their violence. Do your part to stay as safe as you can. Speak to no one. Please help us get away." She let go of my hand.

"Let me call Karen and warn her." I started to pull out my phone.

"No." She again reached for my hand, this time to keep it away from using my phone. "The less she knows, the safer she is." She quickly added, "We can give them misleading information, let them think the house deal is a blind alley." She kept her hand blocking me from my phone. "We should have done this already. It'll be taken care of in the morning. The last thing we want is more people to be hurt."

"Okay," I agreed, moving my hand away from my phone and her hand.

"Please don't tell anyone," she said. "That's the best way you can help us."

"How will I know when it's safe?"

"I'll call you," she said. "You deserve to know. As soon as it's safe I'll call you."

She stood up to go.

I did as well.

"I need to get a ride," she said as she headed for the door.

"I'll wait until you're picked up," I offered.

She smiled and nodded. The habits of someone doing this for her were hard to break.

I gave Connie another ten to cover both our drinks on the way out.

Salve was on the curb, looking at her phone. "Car should be here in a minute." She looked down the street, then said, "That was a nice place. I'm glad you suggested it. Kind of place it's pleasant to stop by. No pretensions."

"Like I said, for us locals. Comfortable. Plenty of places to get fancy cocktails."

We were just making conversation, strangers forced to spend a brief time of transition together.

A large SUV pulled around the corner and slowed as it got closer.

My hand traveled into my messenger bag.

But Salve smiled and said, "This should be it." She opened the rear door as it stopped. "Please tell no one until I've called you," she said, then closed the door.

The windows were tinted; I couldn't see the driver, but she seemed okay. I waved them off, then headed to my car, at a pace appropriate to the heat still lingering in the day.

Once they turned the corner and could no longer see me, I ran, jumped into my car, and pulled a quick U-turn, thankful for a small car with a tight turning circle, then sped after them.

I only managed to get my seat belt on at the next corner, just in time to see them turn uptown on St. Charles.

Had she told me the truth?

Yes.

Had she lied?

Yes.

I knew from what Anmar told me about the rancid misogyny of the Brandes that her tale of the violent men and the way they treated the women—and the acquiescence of the women to spare themselves—was true. Certainly enough to cause a desperate plan to escape. But Salve was a survivor, and she had so learned the tricks of surviving in that family, she couldn't unlearn them in a lifetime.

Were Karen and I really safe now? Maybe. But I couldn't assume Salve could make it so. Maybe she thought she could—and could be wrong. Or maybe she was saying it to avoid the truth. She had used Karen and me, and all the king's horses and all the king's men couldn't protect us now.

The SUV continued up St. Charles for about ten blocks, then turned right, into a residential block.

I slowed, then turned to follow. It was dark and I didn't want to lose them.

The SUV was stopped at the end of the block.

I pulled over and turned off my lights as if coming home. I quickly scrabbled in my bag for my good camera.

I took as many pictures as I could of her as she got out of the SUV and went into the house on the corner. I got a couple of shots of the license plate as well. Probably just one of the rideshare drivers, but better too much info than not enough.

I gave her a good five minutes, saw a light go on in an upstairs room, then I drove down the block, making a note of the address. Something else for the computer grannies to run down for me. Again, probably innocent, but better to know.

Then I drove back to my hotel. Of course, Canal Street was a jam of traffic and the usual drunk tourists trying to make it across all those lanes of insanity. Plus cabs stopped to pick up the drunk tourists. All this added an extra fifteen minutes of sitting in traffic before I got to the hotel.

Another tip to the valet, and I was back at my home away from home.

I stopped in the hotel bar—scanning it just in case Junior Boy was there—to get a drink, asking for it in a go-cup to take to my room. A vodka and tonic, shelf brand. Good Scotch would cost about half a bottle of even better Scotch here. I had some limits on my spendthrift ways.

Back in my room I took a sip of my drink.

I debated calling Karen. But she was safe in Pensacola, ensconced with her social worker girlfriend. If they weren't asleep, they were otherwise busy. I also thought about calling Joanne, but she was surely asleep. And I'd have to admit I'd gone against her orders to stay in the hotel.

I was caught in half promises and partial lies. Salve was right in trying to get away from the Brande family. She was also right that most of them were criminals at this point, accessories at the very least. Between a big rock and a very hard place. I had no qualms about them screwing over the boy Brandes, taking the money and running. If they broke a few laws that mostly affected lawbreakers, I could shrug and walk away. I doubted Joanne would be so sanguine. She did have to pay attention to the pesky details of the justice system.

But Ellis had seemed taken aback about the body in the morgue. If his side of the Brande family had done it, he would have already known. Might even have hinted it could happen to me, since he was so fond of threats. Or he was not surprised at her death, but surprised I knew about it. Or other Brande men were involved, going behind his back.

Was there a double-cross to the double-cross?

The Brandes wouldn't keep their dirty money in the local bank where all the tellers would recognize you. It almost had to be in the kind of overseas accounts that were anonymous. Anyone with the account number and access codes would be able to get to them.

Salve hadn't given me the details, but her hidden expression made me suspect I'd gotten close to it. Ellis kept a close watch over the accounts. Maybe not close enough to prevent someone from getting access to one of them, enough to write a few checks. Enough to scare him into making the hasty decision to move them. But like most Brande men, he didn't think much about the women, so forgot how much they would notice and see.

For as big an upheaval as moving the power of the family—the money, even if it was only a pile of paper—there would be signs, tension, terse whispers, odd phone calls, the signals women would have to recognize to survive in a family like this one.

I had grown up in a broken family. My mother, far too young at sixteen to have a child, forced away when I was five because of her "unnatural acts"—ones I had inherited from her. The man I called my father, although he wasn't, killed in a car wreck when I was ten. Taken in by a pious aunt and lump of an uncle who never noticed how their children treated the bastard interloper. Especially my older cousin.

I left when I was eighteen. With help, a band of women who gave me a place to stay, got me into college, the armor of an education to help keep me safe.

I knew what it was like to have to survive in places you weren't supposed to survive.

I knew how desperate you could be to get out.

I also knew desperation could make you do things that weren't kind, and if you were desperate enough, you could justify anything.

My conundrum was how much of what Salve told me was true? Did she really have nothing to do with the murder? Had the plan been for Karen and me to be brief pawns and safely bypassed? Or were we disposable?

I wanted to sit in a room with Anmar and Joanne and be honest. But Anmar didn't know I was a private eye, and if I revealed it now, she might—with good reason—decide not to trust me anymore. If I told Joanne what I knew about Salve, she would be bound to bring her in for questioning and possibly send her to jail. Or back to the Brandes.

I was at a dark crossroads with no signs and no clear direction.

Except to sleep.

I hastily finished my drink, stumbled through the usual, and was in bed just before midnight, the party still going on the street below.

CHAPTER FOURTEEN

Between the strange bed, the strange thoughts in my head, and the street noise, I hadn't slept well.

And no solutions had come with my dreams. Instead I focused on the more immediate decisions of the day—where to go and what to do. I had only booked one night in the hotel, so needed to check out in a few hours.

My office wasn't safe. Possibly my home would be okay, but there were no women with shotguns downstairs there. If they knew where I lived, I'd be alone.

I made a few decisions. I would hold off calling Karen and Joanne, give Salve a grace period of doubt.

I did call the computer grannies, a group of older women who rented the second floor of my building—at a rate set back when the area was down at heel and not trendy—and did computer work. They had discovered that sitting at a desk with large, bright screens to read was a perfect job for those with arthritic knees, attention to detail, and a knack for sleuthing online. In return for the reasonable rent, they cut me a deal on their work. Plus they were a motley crew of women, save for all being fierce feminists.

I gave them the info on Salve and her business, asked them to track her finances.

"Hack, in other words?" she asked. She was one of the newer grannies. My brain raced for her name. Lena Smith. She swore Smith was her real name.

"Just see what you can find," I hedged. No, I would not be asking—outright—for illegal stuff.

She gave a low, conspiratorial laugh. "I'm sure I can find something. Call by the end of the day, I might have a few details by then. Probably tomorrow, though."

I threw in the SUV license and the address, saying they were probably legit, or at least no worse than an unlicensed home vacation rental. But that wasn't my area of enforcement—unless they were next door to me and throwing late-night noisy parties. I thanked her and hung up.

I looked at the pictures I had taken last night. Not great light, and some were blurry, but I got one good shot of her as she came under the porch light. Better than the earlier security camera shot. I sent it to Karen, no explanation, just asking if it was the woman she had seen.

I would give Salve the time she asked for. But I would still keep digging. I couldn't risk my life or Karen's on the word of a woman who had already lied to me.

Damn, I had forgotten to ask her what she was doing talking to a known drug dealer. Although that meant she didn't know my connection to the bar and my access to the videotapes.

That gave me a direction to go in. I could hang out there, ostensibly to check the recent surveillance. It was an office, had a secure internet connection, and would be safe enough, close to the Rampart Street police station, and Mary was also ex-military and not to be messed with.

I checked out of the hotel and drove the short distance there, finding unmetered parking two blocks away.

I scanned the streets, knowing where Salve's wariness came from, the constant threat hovering just out of sight. Like a snake, miss the hiss and you're hurt.

Only heat-bedraggled tourists. When we say humidity, we mean slap you in the face with a hot, wet blanket humidity.

The bar had just opened, the floors still damp from being mopped. Only Mary and Ali were there. I got a club soda and went to the office.

The same verge-of-heat-exhaustion tourists were on the video screen as I'd seen on the street. At least they were too hot to sing "When the Saints Go Marching In."

I switched from the live feed to the recordings of the last few days, speeding it up to get through and also because it was fun to watch people furiously duck walk.

At least for the first half hour.

The second half hour they just looked stupid. Probably as stupid as I looked sitting here staring at them. There were a few drug deals, but all down the block, looked mostly low key, a bag of weed. A woman getting into a car. The same woman getting out ten minutes later, tucking a folded bill into her bra.

All in all, a slow time on Rampart.

My stomach growled. Hotel room coffee and a granola bar I'd brought with me wasn't much breakfast. Fortunately it was also lunchtime in the rest of the world, and the bar had started the grill up. I was good—sort of—got the blackened chicken salad. Yeah, with dressing on the side even. Mostly salad day was tomorrow, but every once in a while it ended up being today.

Then back to the video feed. I didn't think I'd see anything, but at least this was a place to be. I had to wait until three to check into another hotel. There was little I could do until I heard from the computer grannies. I still didn't want to call Joanne, as I didn't want to out and out lie to her by talking to her and not mentioning I'd met with Salve. Or did she go by Sally?

If I ever talked to her again, I'd ask her that as well.

And maybe you won't solve this, won't figure it out, will just get by with hiding out until the Brandes have other, more important enemies to fight.

I came to the end of the recorded material and switched back to the live feed. More tourists dripping sweat.

Two homeless women trudging toward the camera, a small shopping cart between them. They moved slowly, trying to stay in the shade. They paused as they came to the door, holding to the shade under the awning. One of them disappeared and came inside.

I opened the door of the office.

"I have a dollar," she said. "Can I get some water for that?"

Mary pulled two ice-cold bottles of water from behind the bar and brought them to the woman. "Keep your dollar. Too hot to go thirsty."

"Thank you, you are such a dear." She hurried out the door.

Mary saw me looking. "About once a week or so. City is cleaning out under the bridge where they usually stay, forcing them onto the streets. They're on a waiting list for housing, but it can take forever."

"Yeah, it wasn't easy before Katrina, but it's so much harder now, a lot less housing stock and so many places are being gentrified."

"I try to give the women a bottle of water and a meal. Even if it's just a bag of chips to take with them."

"You are a dear," I said. I went back to the office, retrieved my plate, and took it back to the kitchen area. No one was going to clean up after me.

As I passed back by the bar Mary said, "These two claim they saw someone killed last week. Seemed upset enough that it might be real."

I nodded. "I guess that happens too much in this city as well. The safe places don't let the homeless hang out."

"No, they don't," Mary agreed, then went to help a customer.

I headed back to the office, then stopped. Two homeless women. Usually staying under the bridge.

I turned to the door and headed out. They were gone. They couldn't have gone far. I rushed back into the office and reran the last few minutes of the video. Easier in the air-conditioning to see where they went than running up and down streets.

They continued down Rampart, sucking down the water. A very tall man was walking toward them. Oh, fuck. Junior Boy.

And behind him the man Mary had noted as a drug dealer. The women noticed them, two large men on an empty street. They huddled against the side of the buildings as if they could be small enough to escape notice there. Rabbits seeing wolves.

The drug dealer stopped and the woman closest to him put up her hands as if in protection.

He smiled at her. A leering, ugly grin.

She shook her head. He kept smiling and took something out of his satchel. A baggie with white stuff in it.

Both women shook their heads.

He held out the bag.

One woman again shook her head, then held out the dollar they had offered for the water. Showing it was all they had.

He waved it away. Handed them the bag. Kept smiling. Like he was a benevolent god.

Junior Boy was watching. It was hard to know if he was an amused bystander or a participant. If Druggie didn't know Junior Boy, it didn't seem likely that he would be handing out drugs in front of him.

Druggie left the two women looking at the bag.

Junior Boy followed along, enough behind Druggie to not be clearly together, pausing at our door long enough to stare at the rainbow, trans, and leather flags outside. He tried to spit, but was too dehydrated by the heat to do more than drip down his chin. Yes, we know you're heterosexual, now go wipe your face.

The two women hadn't moved, as if wondering why the wolf had left them a present.

Then they said a few words and headed across Rampart to Armstrong Park.

I jumped up and ran into the bar. "Mary, Ali, do you still have naloxone here?"

They looked at me.

"Yes, of course," Mary said.

"Here," Ali said, grabbing a box from under the bar.

"Grab two doses and follow me," I said.

Ali and Mary looked at each other. "You go," Mary said. "I'll stay here. Should I call the police?"

"Call an ambulance," I said, already at the door.

Ali followed.

We ran across the street, ducking through the traffic. I headed to where I'd seen them enter the park.

We rushed through the arch, into the sculpture area. Too open, they would be somewhere hidden. Congo Square was to our left, a few musicians there. I turned right, to the pond and islands.

"This way," I instructed Ali.

I headed for the biggest tree, with bushes around it.

Saw a foot sticking out, then the gleam of the shopping cart.

I heard an urgent whisper. "Sharon, Sharon, you need to wake up. It's too much. Stand for me."

One of the women was lying on the ground, the other kneeling beside her. The woman on the ground, presumably Sharon, wasn't moving, her eyes closed, her breathing raspy and shallow.

The kneeling woman looked up at us, the same scared expression on her face. "We're okay," she said quickly, as if fending off a blow.

"No, you're not," I said. "It's bad stuff. We have naloxone. She needs it."

"You're not police?" she asked.

"No, we're not," Ali said. "I train people at the needle exchange on how to do this," she added, getting on one knee next to the comatose woman.

I'd read a pamphlet and it was supposed to be easy, but I was glad to have someone else who really knew what they were doing.

I took the other woman by the arm and helped her stand out of the way. I had questions, but now was not the time. I needed to gain her trust first.

"She's Sharon?" I asked.

The woman nodded.

"And you are?"

"Margaret," she said, her eyes never leaving the woman on the ground. "We didn't mean to, she's struggled so long, was doing so well. But...we got kicked out of the place we had under the bridge, a group of us together all looking out for one another. Two nights ago. Now we take turns sleeping. Haven't eaten in almost a day. Hot and tired and hurting, walking for so long. And...she just wanted to get away from it all for a few hours." She started crying.

"Hey, Margaret, I'm Micky and that's Ali. I drink more than I should, especially when problems pile up and I just want to get away from them."

She looked at me briefly, then back at her friend. "She was doing so well. Three months now. We might get a place to stay, a real apartment, in a few weeks."

The two women were younger than they had first appeared, probably mid-twenties, old enough to have made mistakes with consequences but young enough to get past the consequences.

"Who was the man who gave you the bag?" I asked.

She again looked at me. "You sure you're not a cop?"

"I promise I'm not a cop. I'm a private detective." I took out my license to show it to her. She looked it over carefully, squinting as if she needed glasses. She handed it back to me.

The woman on the ground sputtered and thrashed onto her side.

"Sharon!" her friend called.

"What the hell?" Sharon muttered. "Where am I? Why is it still so fucking hot?"

"You're in the park. It was bad stuff. You looked like you weren't coming back."

"What the hell?"

"You were given a bad dose," Ali said.

"That bastard," she muttered. "Should have known better than to take anything from him."

A siren wailed, coming closer.

"I'm okay," Sharon said, trying to sit up.

"No, you're not," Margaret said. "Let's take a rest. We have the cards now."

"The cards?"

"Medicaid. We got signed up over at that new place on Elysian Fields. So we can get care."

Ah, yes, Louisiana had expanded Medicaid a few years ago.

The siren stopped, just outside the park.

I loped out from the trees far enough for them to see me and waved the EMTs over.

They were quick and professional, the woman EMT telling Sharon, "You're way dehydrated. Let's take you in to check you out."

"I need to go with her," Margaret said.

The two EMTs looked at each other.

"I'll give you a ride," I offered. Everyone nodded at my solution. I had my motives, of course, other than being a Good Samaritan. I had questions Margaret and Sharon might be able to answer.

She, Ali, and I followed the stretcher out of the park, watching them load it in. Then Ali headed back to the bar and I led Margaret to where my car was.

"You think she'll be okay?" she asked as we got in.

I turned on the AC full blast and opened the windows to let the hot air escape. It was blistering and, well, sleeping on the streets isn't the most attractive of odors.

"She'll be okay," I said and pulled out. Then added honestly, "At least for now. Once the overdose is reversed, it's okay. It's just the next steps are hard."

"Yeah, I know. She's been really good, too."

"You don't use?"

"Did once. How I lost my job and my home. Got a record now. It's hard to get a job with a rap sheet."

"Yeah, it is," I agreed. "What are you good at? What kind of work have you done?"

"I wasn't good at much, stupid kid, fooling around when I should've been studying."

"High school? College?"

"One year in UNO. Dropped out before I could flunk out. Yeah, I know, I need to go back."

"You need to take care of yourself. Maybe that's the way, maybe not." It felt like she was saying what she thought I'd want to hear. The hustle of survival, give the right answer and you get a meal or shelter for the night. Thinking that I had already judged her. Maybe I had. I said I drank too much as a way of bonding, admitting we all make mistakes. But I had a career, a house, all the trappings of middle-class comfort. I hadn't lost any of that to a bottle. And maybe I wasn't any better, just luckier. I didn't have the genes that sent me down into the addiction hell hole. It's so easy to refuse a vice you're not tempted by, then judge others because they are. In truth, there but for fortune.

If I was going to use her, I should be honest about it. "I want you and Sharon to be okay, but I'm also working on an investigation that might involve the murder you witnessed."

"No, no, we didn't see a murder. A car stopped. They put something big out. That's all we saw."

"You saw enough that the two of you were given a bag of bad stuff. You weren't meant to wake up."

"But...we didn't see anyone."

"Do you know the man who gave you the drugs?"

"Yeah, he's a badass. Trouble from the sun to the moon."

"Trouble in what way?"

"Vicious. Hurts people because he likes to. Some dealers are okay, businesspeople like. They sell you a product, at enough to make a profit. They don't try to fuck with you. Not him. Saw him steal a hit from a guy desperate for it—going into withdrawal, then dangled a bag in front of him and made him pay everything he had, a special gold coin, his mother's wedding ring, stuff he'd kept no matter how hard it was. Heard about him beating the crap out of an old man to show others they'd better pay him. Man hadn't done anything to him, hadn't bought nothing. Just in the wrong place."

"You buy from him?"

"Not no more. Did a few times a long time ago. But he'd give you crap and charge too much. Most have learned to avoid him if they can."

"But he's still dealing?"

"New and stupid folks arrive all the time."

"Any idea why he might have given you the bad dope?"

"He works for anyone who'll pay him. He likes to hurt women." She shuddered as she said it.

"Has he hurt you? Or Sharon?"

"No. Not till now. He took a young girl, small build, maybe sixteen, just out on the street. Dragged her behind an abandoned house. We could hear her screams."

"No one called the police?"

"No phones to call. By the time they came, he was gone. We couldn't help—at least that's what people whispered—and it'd piss him off. She was too new to have friends, anyone who'd risk for her. Not pretty, but surviving out there isn't pretty."

"Why'd you take the bag from him?"

"Stupid. Thought he was going to hit us at first, but then he says he's got new stuff, wants to get the word out. Giving out a few free samples. Send people to him. Too good to be true," she said with a disgusted shake of her head. "We wanted to believe it, so we did. I thought Sharon would be okay, just once to get away from the heat and how her feet hurt and hunger. Just once, then we'd be good again."

She started to cry.

I pulled into the parking garage at the hospital, the new one that had replaced Charity.

"You still have your chance. You can still be good again. Take a day or so to recover. They should let you stay with her, claim you're her sister."

"Cousin, but we grew up together."

That explained the bond. It didn't feel sexual, but there was more of a connection than just the streets and a hard life. "That should do. Stay with her and you both get a few days off."

"Just being here in your cool car is nice," she said.

I didn't think it was very cool, barely tepid, but at least not the blazing heat of an August afternoon. "Can you tell me what you saw? Every detail you can remember?" I nosed into a parking spot, then turned the AC up another notch.

"Just what I said. Middle of the night. We heard the car go by. Usually no traffic back there even in the day, nothing at night. Watched it drive down the road. Then it stopped a ways away. Both doors opened, but the engine stayed on. They opened the back and took something big out, dumped it on the side of the road, then left."

"You told the police you thought they were women?"

"One was tall but had long hair, the other was shorter. Guess we assumed long hair was a woman, and no man would be that much shorter than a woman, so it had to be another woman."

"Could it have been a man with long hair?"

"Maybe...but they didn't walk like men, you know what I mean? Or maybe we just assumed from the hair and saw everything that way. That one was tall, so probably not a woman."

"Taller than I am?"

She shook her head. "I don't know. Just know one was taller than the other and that made him look tall."

"You called the vehicle a car?"

"It was one of those boxy things."

"SUV?"

"Yeah, that. The ones people buy to drive off-road, only they never do."

"The more off-road it looks, the slower they go over bumps in the street," I groused.

She laughed. With a smile she wasn't bad looking, had good teeth, a wide, generous mouth.

"More square or more rounded?" I asked.

"Square, corners, no curvy lines."

"Really big and bulky? As big as they get? Or less so?"

"Big, but I've seen bigger. Like them Army ones."

"A Jeep?"

"Like that, I think. It was dark, we weren't paying that much attention, not like we knew what they'd throw out."

"Just tell me what you can remember, what comes easy. If you can't recall, that's okay, say so. Sometimes asking questions helps you with details. Can you give me another five minutes?"

"Sure, honey, you get all the time you want, if I can sit and be cool."

She was giving me what I wanted, but her foot was tapping. She wanted to check on her cousin.

"On the street, that other man, big and tall, have you ever seen him before?"

"Not often."

"But you're seen him? Here in New Orleans?"

"Yeah, here. Nowhere else to see him. Not like we vacation often."

"With the drug dealer? Or by himself?"

"Yeah, together. Think they work sometimes. Druggie does stuff for him."

"Why do you think that?"

"Street sense. See them together and someone gets a beating."

"Murder?"

"Maybe. Maybe Druggie was the tall one. With a wig, since we know what he looks like."

"Would he dump a body there?"

"Well, I guess not. Unless he wanted it to be found. He'd know a bunch of us were camping around there. We'd see it right soon."

Her fingers were now tapping.

"Is there a way I can get in contact with you if I think of something else?"

"Yeah, usually once a week, I go for group. People like me, working through it. Place on Claiborne and Elysian Fields. You can find me there. Or leave a message with my counselor. Name is Cindy Espinosa." She dug a battered business card out of her bag and handed it to me. "She's been real helpful, a kind soul."

I took a photo with my phone and handed it to her. She seemed relieved to have it back in her possession, as if a touchstone to her recovery.

"Let's go find Sharon," I said.

We got out of my car, into the blanket of heat, the garage and concrete holding it in.

Once inside, we found our way to the emergency room.

"We're looking for Sharon..." I turned to Margaret for her last name.

"Pas. Sharon Pas. I'm her cousin, first cousin, but more like sister, Margaret Baughman. We lived together mostly growing up."

The woman just nodded, looked at her screen, then gave us directions to where she was.

A woman in scrubs looked up as we entered.

"Family," I asserted, claiming our right to be there.

"She okay?" Margaret asked.

The woman, Dr. G. Rodger, I read on her tag, said, "She'll be okay, but we'd like to keep her overnight, make sure she's stabilized. Dehydrated, close to heat exhaustion, a bad blister that's infected on one foot."

"Be okay if I stay with her?" Margaret asked. "She can get agitated in strange places."

The doctor nodded, deciding a calming presence was more important than any rules.

"We're going to move her to a room in a little bit," Dr. Rodger said.

I left the cousins holding hands, Sharon's face relaxing once Margaret arrived. I went in search of food. Both for myself and for them.

By the time I'd gotten a pile of things—a couple of sandwiches, chips, and a few healthy options like apples, bananas, and a carrot/humus combo—Sharon had been given a room.

I dumped the pile on the bedside table.

Margaret's eyes lit up. "You didn't need to do that." But she was already unwrapping a sandwich.

I felt guilty. It was so easy for me to walk into a grocery store, order a pizza to be delivered. "I was hungry," I said, taking a sandwich for myself.

I stayed long enough to eat and not be rude. I wanted to ask Sharon what she'd seen, compare it to Margaret, but now was not the time. She was tired and drained. Maybe I'd get a chance later. Maybe I wouldn't.

Maybe none of it mattered.

I gave Margaret a twenty dollar bill as I left. Sharon would get fed, as a patient, but Margaret wouldn't. A few more sandwiches.

Except someone wanted these two women dead, and the only likely reason was what they had seen.

None of it made sense. If Druggie had dumped the body there, he would have wanted it to be found quickly. Which was what happened. Unless he/they hadn't planned on anyone seeing the actual dumping and were worried Margaret and Sharon might have noticed something that could lead back to them.

And how were Druggie and Junior Boy involved? Had Ellis ordered the hit on the rebellious Brande women? Left Junior Boy to arrange it? And Junior Boy turned to Druggie, his pal? Maybe Ellis was surprised because the body wasn't supposed to turn up. Junior Boy had fucked up again, by leaving a dead woman to end up in the morgue, attracting police attention.

I sat in the parking lot, letting my car cool down. And trying to come up with a place to go.

Junior Boy was still in town, and staying close enough to Rob's bar, he could walk there. He didn't strike me as the long walks to nowhere kind of guy.

I-10 was a rush hour mess, so I took Airline Highway out to, you guessed it, the airport. There were a number of hotels out there, with rates far below those around the French Quarter—as well as free parking lots. No one would look for me there.

Once checked in, I first took a shower—it had been a long, hot day—procrastination to avoid doing what I needed to do.

Call Joanne.

That Junior Boy was in town and involved with Druggie, who had a reputation as an enforcer, argued that Salve was telling the truth, she was trying to escape, with enough money to get well and far away, and the Brande men were trying to stop her.

Joanne needed to know someone had tried to kill the two witnesses to the dumping of the woman. Maybe they knew something they hadn't revealed to me. It was possible the police told them to keep some details back.

She answered on the first ring.

I recounted what had happened, the bad drugs, the overdose.

She listened without interruption.

"I'll check with security at the hospital and let them know to be on the watch, although it would be beyond crazy to try anything there."

Nothing was beyond crazy in this mess, but she had a point. Too many people around and no quick escape to the street.

She also said she'd ask Druggie to be picked up and held for as long as they could. And if they could, pick up Junior Boy, aka Elbert Brande, for questioning. I offered to press charges for his threats at my office.

"Let's hope we can take you up on that," she said.

I gave her the details of what Margaret had told me and asked if there was something more, something the police didn't want released. A reason to kill them.

Joanne said she'd look over the interview again, but she didn't remember anything worth killing for. There was no ID, not even a good description of either the people or the vehicle.

She asked where I was, and I told her.

"Good," was her response.

I didn't tell her about talking to Salve. I was more on the side of the Brande women than the letter of the law.

We hung up.

I stared at the bland hotel room. Between this and my Atlanta trip, I'd spent way too much time in hotels.

What was I missing?

If Karen and I hadn't been pulled into this, I could walk away. But I was stuck in a hotel out by the airport, and somebody needed to pay. Even if not literally pay. If Salve kept her promise to send me money, maybe I could manage to come out ahead at the end of this whole mess.

The hasty sandwich had been a while ago. I passed time by driving around, checking out the eating options out here—not a part of New Orleans I have explored for culinary purposes. A lot of fast food. I ended up with takeout from a Vietnamese place—and stopping at a daiquiri shop. Yes, you can buy them and drive away, although technically you're not supposed to actually be sipping while steering.

Back in my room, I ate, I drank, I tried not to obsess over the case, let things ferment in my brain with hopes the subconscious would perform a miracle. TV was boring. I tried to read, but nothing kept me engrossed enough. *Next time I swing by home, I need to get workout gear*, I told myself. A good session in the fitness room might help with the nervous energy.

Shortly after ten, just as I was contemplating giving up and going to bed, my phone rang.

An Atlanta number.

"Hey, stranger on a train," Anmar greeted me. "Is it too late?"

"No, not at all. How are you?"

"I should be polite and ask how you are as well, but as usual I'm calling because I can't really call anyone else and I have to talk to someone."

"I'm fine, so consider the question asked. What do you need to talk about?"

"How crazy everything is. Remember the hotel we met at for a drink? I'm staying there now. Escorted here by Donnie. For reasons I don't understand, they wanted no one—especially any of the women—at the compound. But he called just now, demanding to know where I'd been, like he hadn't just dumped me here in the late afternoon."

"What did you tell him?"

"The truth—fortunately—that I was here the entire time, got room service for dinner. Told him he could check the GPS on my phone—the Ellis phone, not this one—to check."

"How often does this kind of thing happen?"

"That's just it. Never. I've never been sequestered like this. I'm wondering if they're murdering someone there—or 'making them talk'—and they wanted to make sure there were no witnesses. Except that kind of stuff doesn't happen where we live."

"Where does it happen?"

"Honestly, I don't know. Mostly because I don't want to know. Yes, I'm a hypocrite, I live in a crime family and do my best to keep my eyes to the ground and my ears plugged. That way I can pretend it's just harmless, victimless crimes, like gambling."

"Drugs, sex trafficking," I pointed out.

She sighed. Then took a wavering breath and said softly, "Yeah, I know. If I really thought about it, really knew what it takes to buy the big houses and fancy cars and expensive booze, I'd hate myself. So, I have conveniently walled off my conscience."

"What do you want to do about that?" I prompted.

"Think about it tomorrow. Right now I'm trying to know if I can lay low here in the family-approved hotel or if I should hightail it to the airport and get on the first plane out."

"Do you think you're in danger?"

"Something is happening, and it's big. Ellis is screaming at Donnie and Donnie is screaming at everyone he can scream at. Andrea has disappeared and I don't know where she is. Before she left I could talk to her about this. And now...I can't. Something must have happened to her. She was my twin...my almost me. At times we'd switch places and pretend to be each other. We lived on the same path. If something happened to her...it'll happen to me." She started to cry.

"Anmar, you're still here. If anything did happen to Andrea, it took place before all this. Horrific to say, but women get hurt and killed too often. That could have happened to her, it could have nothing to do with your family."

She sniffled and said, "That's not much comfort."

I said gently, "Would you prefer that I tell you everything will be okay? That she'll return any day now?"

"No," she sobbed. Then said, "Maybe. Maybe I need that fantasy for tonight. To think I'll go to sleep and wake up and she'll be back, brimming with stories of her adventures."

I wanted to tell her that Andrea might well be in the morgue. It would only help because it would give her the answer, finally let her start on her path of grief instead of the purgatory of hope. I didn't. Maybe it was the right thing to do, or maybe I was a coward. Like her, I wasn't going to look too closely at my choices.

"I saw a woman here in New Orleans who looks a bit like you, although she appeared older," I said. "At a distance. I snapped her picture. Can I send it to you and see what you think?"

"Yes! You think it might be her?"

"She doesn't look quite like your twin, but I was struck by the resemblance."

"Send it."

I fumbled with the phone, trying to not hang up. I'm not a member of the multitasking generation. Finally I figured it out and sent the photo.

Then waited.

It was a full minute before she replied. "No, that's not Andrea. It looks a lot like Sabrina or Salve, but why would either of them be in New Orleans?"

"No clue," I said. "Would there be any reason for them to be here? Anything to do with what's going on?"

"No…but I don't know. I'd not pick Salve or Hannah as the ones to anger Ellis."

"Why not?"

"It's hard to explain…but you can see it in their eyes, their face. They hide it from the men, but you can tell who wants to go along and who has to go along."

"Like you?"

"Yeah, I guess. I toe the line, but I don't like it. As a teenager I used to get the shit slapped out of me. I learned…to be respectful enough to not get hit. The last time…I did it and Andrea got punished. They confused us."

"She resent you for that?"

"I said she should have told them. But she said it wasn't too bad—just her head being held underwater in the pool—and she was happy to have fooled them. She called it an experiment. If they were that close and couldn't tell us apart, it meant we could trade places. I think that was when I became careful. One thing to bring it on myself, another to bring it on her when she didn't deserve it."

"Did you ever fool them? Deliberately confuse them?"

"Yes, we actually got good at it. We'd plan things. We'd go out around the same time, then one of us would come in at the appointed time, then change clothes, sneak out the window, and come in again to make it look like we both had returned. It's how we got away with seeing girls. Act like we were going out together and then came back together while one of us stayed out all night. The amazing thing is we never got caught."

"That's pretty impressive."

"Or they were pretty stupid. Two left. Two came back. No one looked beyond that."

"Did Donnie tell you how long you're to stay in the hotel?" I asked.

"He said a day or two. But that was when he dropped me off. When he called just now, he told me not to leave and threatened they would check my phone."

"Good thing we got you another phone. If you want to go out, you can just leave the family phone in your room."

"That's an idea. Be nice if there was someplace I wanted to go."

"Maybe tomorrow."

"Look, I'm sorry I called you," she said. "This isn't your problem."

"No, it's not. But it's okay. I can listen. You're missing Andrea right now. I'm not a replacement or even a substitute, just a live human. I would like it if you would call and let me know what's going on. If you have to camp out, you can hide with me in New Orleans." In my lovely airport hotel.

"Thanks. Probably not far enough. I think they're doing stuff there."

"Stuff?"

"The usual criminal stuff."

"Why do you think that?"

"A few beers and they get loud. Heard them talking about expanding to Houston. And one—oh, you know him, your escort—said he'd hate to give up the girls in the French Quarter."

That would explain why Junior Boy was here and why he was consorting with Druggie. It didn't explain why I'd seen Salve with him.

"So if any of the women—or anyone—was trying to get away— they're not likely to come to New Orleans?" I hoped she wouldn't wonder at my questions.

"Not as a final destination, that's for sure. Too bad, it's one of my favorite cities. Andrea and I used to go there as often as we could. Neither of us can sing, but she liked to constantly prove it with karaoke. Well, now I'm back to me and it's late."

"Later where you are." I pointed out our different time zones.

"Yes, but I'm not a working girl. I can sleep in tomorrow. There's not much else for me to do."

"True," I said. "But call me when you can. Let me know what's going on."

"I will. You sleep well."

"Hey, weird question. Do you know anyone named Holly Farmer?"

"Holly Farmer? Someone really named their kid that?"

"I guess so."

"I don't. Good thing. I'd probably snigger every time I heard her name. Why?"

"Long shot. Saw her here in Atlanta."

"It's a big city? She in the business?"

"No, a social worker."

"Don't know too many of them. That's just so weird."

"What do you mean?"

"It was an ongoing joke between me and Andrea. We met a man named Al Pine and after that we'd come up with names like that. Sandy Beach. Pearl Ring. Dyna Mite. Rumor Mills. But, no, I don't know a Holly Farmer. We got extra points if it was a real name. Maybe someday I can tell that one to Andrea."

We said good-bye.

I finished my daiquiri.

CHAPTER FIFTEEN

The problem with airport hotels is that some people need to wake up and leave long before the sun has left Australia. And they seem too sleep deprived to remember how to shut a door quietly.

I looked at the clock and put a pillow over my head. Sheer willpower got me through another hour of sleep.

Then a long shower—I wasn't paying the water bill—and dressed enough to go downstairs for breakfast.

Ellis had moved his accounts. That was my bet on why Anmar was sent away. He wanted as few people around to see as possible. My next bet was that all did not go as planned. Or at least as Ellis had planned. That was the reason for Donnie's panicked call to Anmar to make sure she was still in her room.

Oh, to be a rat running around the Brande house this morning.

This might be good news for both me and Karen. If the Brande rebels had succeeded, they would be focused on finding the accounts and not bothering us.

I had a second cup of coffee.

My phone rang.

Anmar's Atlanta number. I answered and got up to go back to my room.

"Hey, sorry for the early-morning call after the late-night call," she said.

"Are you okay?" I asked.

"Yes, but I wanted to warn you. The Brandes are heading to New Orleans."

"How do you know this?" I asked, getting on the elevator, ignoring the family of ten asking me to hold the door while they crammed in and held up the elevator for another ten minutes as they jostled with their luggage. I had watched them take that amount of time crossing the lobby.

"I ran into Halley, my cousin, also stuck here, in the lobby. She was in a chatty mood. Told me Ellis lost control of the accounts and there was a rumor they were heading to New Orleans. She said five SUVs sped out in the early morning hours, heading that way."

"Did she say why they think it's New Orleans? And who it might be?"

"I asked. She wasn't that chatty. Or her sources weren't as good as she hinted."

"Would she be in a position to know?"

"She might. We bonded as queer kids, but she's younger, twenties. She's more, well, interested in the family business than Andrea and I ever were. She's done some stuff, mostly courier to the beaches. But I think Ellis has finally clued in that she's smart and Junior Boy—your name for him is perfect—isn't. I think she has ambitions to be the first major female mob boss."

"Is that likely in your family?" I keyed the door into my room and its privacy.

"Delusional, I'd say. But she's not asking me. Yeah, she's smarter than they are, but I can't see any Brande man taking orders from a woman. Fifty years too early. If ever."

"What did she say exactly?"

"That Ellis and Elbert had fucked up—she likes to use 'fucked' a lot, to prove she's one of the boys, especially when there are people around to be shocked like a hotel lobby—and someone snatched all the account info. But the snatchers weren't so smart either. They dropped an address."

"That sounds like everyone is trying to outstupid everyone else." I sat at the desk, bracing my phone between my shoulder and ear so I could get a paper and pen to take notes.

"Yeah, I can see why it made Halley gleeful, it proves how smart she is. She even said that—that she'd never be this stupid. But the point of my call is they are heading to New Orleans and I wanted to warn you. If you see a convoy of big black and gray SUVs, head the other way."

"New Orleans isn't the sprawl of Atlanta, but it's still probably big enough we're unlikely to cross paths."

"I know," she said quickly. "I'm just...I know it's paranoid. But I've lost Andrea and...I don't want anyone else hurt. I think there's going to be a bloodbath in the family, seething resentments of years' standing with a finger on the trigger. I feel helpless and stupid here. This is what I can do, at least give you a warning you probably don't need."

"Better to have it and not need it than need it and not have it. I have friends who are in the police department. I can call them to be on the lookout."

"I don't know," she said. "That feels like ratting."

"Better to let them shoot it out?"

A wavering breath. She was emotionally on edge. "You're right. Jail is better than dead. It might be the best place for most of them."

"It might free you," I pointed out.

"Unless I join them. Accessory, all that. No, I didn't do anything. But I can't claim innocence either."

"Did she tell you the address?" I asked. Joanne would find that helpful information.

"Yes, but we were in the lobby and she rattled it off. Something with a C?"

"Claiborne? Carrollton?" I named two major streets.

"I don't think so."

"Calhoun? St. Claude?"

"No...not familiar."

I couldn't think of any more C streets. I'd have to look at a map. "Anything else? Time frame?"

"Afternoon, around three, Halley said."

"So the rebel Brandes got the accounts and accidentally left an address and time for their gang to meet up?" I said.

Anmar was silent for a second. "You think they planned it?"

"It's really stupid or really smart," I said.

"But why?"

"Because they're on a plane to Paris and the rest of the Brandes are driving to New Orleans."

"They may be stupid but not that stupid. Airport is the first place they look. They sent six guys there to cover the ticket counters.

According to Halley, Ellis moved the accounts around midnight. So late enough at night few flights were leaving."

"Halley knows a lot about this."

"Junior Boy talks to her, and he thinks he's next in line. I know he runs things by her, mostly to steal her ideas and pretend he thought of it. Besides, she's been relegated to female purgatory, stuck here in the hotel with me."

"Unless it's just her phone in the hotel," I pointed out.

"She's clearly not in New Orleans. Or on the road to anywhere else, if I saw her just a few minutes ago in the lobby," Anmar pointed out.

"It just sounds—"

"Crazy? Welcome to my family."

"Anything else you can tell me?" I asked.

"Why?"

Oh, now she finally started to wonder at my questions. "To pass on to my police friends. The more they know, the more they can do to stop it."

"Something C, around three. Convoy of Brande men heading there. Junior Boy is already there. Oh, but Ellis didn't tell him yet, because he's worried Junior Boy will blab. They'll call him when they get to town."

"She told you that?"

"Said her contact wanted to make sure no one else called him either."

"Ellis thinks he might be behind it?"

"Maybe," Anmar said. "He's paranoid as shit now. No one is talking to anyone, except we're all talking but aren't supposed to be. But I doubt he's organized or smart enough." Then she said, "Oh, shit, my other phone is ringing. Uncle Donnie."

"Call me if you learn more."

She hung up.

I looked at my scribbled notes, then tried to order them. Rebel Brandes had ambushed Ellis at around midnight and gotten the account briefcase. Ellis seemed to have relied on stealth, not strength, probably only one or two people with him. He and Uncle Donnie wouldn't make a formidable team. Rebel Brandes had maneuvered him into moving the accounts, so they were ready. Once the "nonessential personnel" were sent away, they knew it would be soon. All they needed to do was wait. The usual, surprise and ski masks. They jump Ellis right outside his house. Smash and grab. Get the briefcase with the account info. It could be fairly compact, a pile of paper, all in one attaché.

They were either stupid—always possible with the Brandes—and accidentally dropped a piece of paper with the rendezvous location and time. Or it was a setup, meant to decoy the Main Brandes to look where the Rebel Brandes were not.

Salve? Was this her?

Or was Junior Boy trying to take over?

Could there be multiple factions of Rebel Brandes?

My head hurt.

It bothered me that New Orleans was part of the plan. If the address was an empty lot, what were the chances Ellis would come after me and/or Karen?

Damn, damn, damn. Like Anmar, I felt trapped here.

Okay, call Joanne.

A phone seemed such a small, powerless tool.

Voice mail.

While I left a message for her, a text came in.

Anmar. *Donnie checking on me. I asked what was going on and he told me to stay here and hung up.*

I started to text her back, but my phone rang.

Joanne.

I gave her the latest update.

"Oh, hell," was her response. "Do you know how many C roads there are in this city?"

"Can't say I've counted them."

"Way too many. About half the uptown/downtown streets are Cs." She named the ones I already had, then added, "St. Charles, Canal, Camp, Clara, Carondelet, Constance, Coliseum, Chestnut, Convention Center, Chartres."

"Tell me you're looking at a map and don't have all the streets memorized in alphabetical order."

"I am looking at a map. These are the major ones in Orleans Parish. Add in smaller ones, the suburbs, the Westbank—a lot. Too many for us to have any chance of patrolling. Except blind luck."

"A convoy of black and gray gas guzzlers."

"Every day. People like their big vehicles." She added, "You did the right thing to call, and I'd prefer the info to nothing. Just being real."

"Reality checks are always fun," I said.

"You need to stay out of this," Joanne admonished me.

"I'm encased at a hotel by the airport. I'll see if I can get it narrowed down any more."

"That would be helpful. Just stay where you are while you do it." She hung up.

I texted Anmar. *Thanks for the update. St. Charles or Camp?*

I looked at my watch. Just coming up to ten a.m.

The Brande convoy was probably here by now. It's about seven hours, less if you speed and skimp on the bathroom breaks. They probably left about two a.m. or so, giving Ellis enough time to gather the troops. Probably napping now.

Or cleaning their guns.

The location is a decoy. An empty lot. What would they do next? I didn't see them giving up and going home. Search for me? Karen?

What if it was real? A shootout between the Rebel Brandes and the Main Brandes? That would be messy in a populated area. I carry a gun but try my best not to use it. People aren't stable targets, they run, they weave, they duck. A bullet keeps going whether it hits its intended target or not. Too many people shot by bullets not aimed at them.

I dialed Salve. No answer. No option to leave a message.

"Damn," I muttered.

If the site was real, they wouldn't escape. I was, I admitted, rooting for the Brande women. For them to con the mob, get the loot, and get away.

I didn't want them shot up.

Nor did I want them to disappear without a trace, leaving only me and Karen with any connection to them.

Anmar texted me back. *Sorry, they don't sound like it.*

I called the hospital to check on Sharon and Margaret and was connected to their room. Margaret answered. They were okay, but the doctor was there and she couldn't talk.

I plugged in my phone. It was getting a workout today.

Joanne told me to stay here, but the last thing I wanted to do was be stuck out in a hotel listening to the planes roaring overhead.

I texted Anmar again. *Clara, Carondelet?*

Then I stared at my phone, willing it to give me information. Narrow the street down. Another clue from Sharon or Margaret.

I paced the room. There are many things I do well. Waiting is not one of them.

A text. Anmar. *No. Ordered to go to brunch with Aunt Vera—also here at hotel. Can't show this phone.*

Damn.

I texted back, *Canal, Camp, Constance, Coliseum, Chestnut, Convention Center, Chartres? Text back when you can.*

Again, waiting. How long can brunch take?

Longer than I wanted to wait.

My phone rang. It almost jerked out of my hand since it was still attached to its cord.

Salve.

"You called me?" she said.

"You stole the account info from Ellis?" I asked.

"What? Where did you hear that?"

"It's not important," I replied. I was not going to tell her in any case. "A piece of paper with an address and a time was dropped during the heist."

"Wait. What? Are you sure?"

"I wasn't there, but a large group of the Brande men are here—or will be soon. They think it's real, not a decoy meant to misdirect them."

"How could anyone be that stupid?" she said under her breath as if not talking to me at all.

"Did you intend for them to find out? Or is it a mistake?" I asked.

"We thought we had gotten away. We just wanted enough money to escape, that's all. We are going to meet and divide things among us. Then go our own ways."

"Probably not a good idea to meet at the planned location," I said. "That does pose a problem for me. If Ellis gets there and finds nothing, he's likely to come after me and Karen Holloway as a desperate attempt to get information."

"But you don't have any."

"He doesn't know that. We might be dead before he realizes that."

"I'm so sorry. We never thought it would come to this."

"How do you know the tall, beer-bellied, dirty blond drug dealer on Rampart?"

That caught her off guard. Phones aren't good for questions like this, no body language, no expression. "I…don't know him."

"Saw you on a security videotape. He handed you something and you gave him something in return."

A pause, then, "Oh, him. What a scumbag. I didn't want to do it but felt I couldn't refuse. Elbert, Ellis's grandson, thought a woman wouldn't arouse suspicion. They think the cops view women the way they do. Not up to much besides baking and babies. He asked me to give him a payment. Elbert is expanding our territory here."

"What did he give you in return?"

"I don't know. A thick envelope. I didn't open it. I didn't want to know. Just handed it to Elbert. And then washed my hands thoroughly." She added, "Until I'm out of the family, I have to play along. Refusing tasks could be suspicious. It's not just me, but several younger women as well. I can't risk them."

"Understood. But back to our original problem. Unwelcome attendance at your meeting and them coming after me and Karen when no one is there."

"We…didn't plan for something this stupid."

"Most people don't."

"I have no way of contacting some of the people."

"You can't warn them?" I wondered if Andrea was one of them.

"No. To avoid risk, we've kept communication at a minimum."

"No burner cell phones? Anonymous emails?"

"We didn't think it was needed," she said slowly, digesting the enormity of the problem. Then quickly as if thinking out loud, "We had to be very discreet; our priority was to not let them know we were doing anything out of the ordinary. Only passing messages when we saw each other in our usual routine. Ellis gives us all our phones, so we couldn't use them."

"There are other phone stores in the Atlanta area," I pointed out.

"Yes, but he also reviews our credit cards. He'd notice another phone."

I thought of pointing out what Anmar and I had done, take a cash advance, but it wasn't helpful now and far too late. We needed to think about what to do, not criticize what hadn't been done.

"Are the others coming here by plane? Driving?"

"Driving, I think. We left it open, but again credit cards and plane tickets aren't wise."

No place to potentially catch anyone. New Orleans is surrounded by water, but even so, there are a lot of roads in and out.

"So, at least some of the people will show up and be met by a vengeful Ellis?"

"It's possible," she said, hesitation in her voice as if she didn't want to admit the cost of their blunder.

"Possible? What's to prevent it?"

"I don't know. I need to think."

"Where is the meeting? I can contact my police friends and have them be there."

"No! Please don't do that. That would only make it worse."

"How? The police can stop the killing."

"Or be killed. Ellis is old. He has nothing to lose. He's willing to go out in a blaze of glory. If the police are there, it will only make sure guns are fired. It'll be bad if anyone is hurt, but if a cop is shot or killed, this will never be over. We'll all be hunted."

I backed off. From the vehemence in her voice, Salve wouldn't give me the address, and we were no closer than looking at all the C roads in the area—and that wasn't very close at all.

"I know," she said, a change in her voice. "I can go there, claim to have found out about the plot. Give Ellis back some of the accounts and say that's all we can find. I'll pretend to be a good little Brande woman, doing service for her men."

"Will he buy it?"

"If he gets enough of the money back."

"What will happen to you?"

"I'll probably survive," she answered tersely. "Spend some time with Donnie to prove I'm really loyal to the family."

"That's horrible."

"Yes, but I will survive. And maybe get away in a year or two. At least some of us will be free."

"I'm sorry. Think about it. I can get the police there."

"It will protect you and Karen. Ellis will have no reason to come after you."

I might have to be satisfied with that.

"Where are the accounts now? Do you have them?"

"No, I don't. I've been here in New Orleans, pretending to work with Elbert. They'll be here soon."

"Before the meeting?"

"Yes, but close to it. Again, we have little contact. They can't know we're together. They think the women…are only loyal to their men."

"How many are you?"

"Too many. Around ten total."

"All meeting today?"

"Most, but not all."

I wanted to ask if Andrea Brande was one of them, but that would out Anmar as my source. "Ten people could get killed today!" I stated.

"I need to plan this," she said. "I can't talk anymore."

The line went dead.

Because I could think of nothing better to do, I called Karen. Salve said we would be okay. If she did what she was proposing to. On the phone she sounded like she meant it. But a few months of Uncle Donnie's attention might change anyone's mind. I wanted to make sure Karen was still in Pensacola.

Voice mail. "Micky. Call me when you get this."

I stared at the walls of the beige room.

"Goddamn it, Anmar, how many mimosas can you drink? It's lunch time. Brunch should be over. At least run to the bathroom and give me a quick text."

The walls ignored me.

I couldn't just sit here and wait. The future is not ours to see—but I could see some of the paths the next few hours would take. *Salve carries out her plan—and acquiesces to letting Donnie rape her for a few months—and Ellis goes along with it.*

Or Ellis doesn't go along with it, demands all the accounts back, and does things to Salve that make her talk.

I could still call the police on them.

I just didn't know where to send them.

Salve backs out. Something else happens and she isn't there. The accounts aren't there.

Ellis comes after me and Karen.

The future is not ours to see.

"This is a shit show," I muttered. I glanced at my watch. Just past noon. Past one in Atlanta. Brunch should be well over.

The chime of a text.

Anmar. *Maybe Constance or Coliseum? Co something sounds like it.*

Thanks, I texted back. *That's helpful.* Not much. They are both long streets, going from the lower Garden District all the way up to Audubon Park. I wanted to scream at Salve about being so stupid as to write down the meeting place, shove it in a pocket, take it to the ambush, and then leave it there. And at Anmar for not catching the most crucial piece of information.

I was angry and agitated. I couldn't fix any of this now, and my anger wasn't going to help.

Anmar texted back. *Sorry to take so long. Aunt Vera watched me like a hawk. With Andrea gone, they assume I'm in it with her. She insists we go shopping. Told her I needed to run to the room for the bathroom.*

I phoned. "Can you call Halley and get the address again?" I asked.

She was breathless when she answered. "I'll try. Being watched. It might be hard. Aunt Vera is a bulldog. She's not going to let me out of her sight. I had to claim I needed to take a big shit for her to let me come back here."

"Constance or Coliseum? Can you take a guess which one?"

"No, I can't. I'm...sorry."

"Numbers? A one or a nine?"

"Halley was rattling it off so fast. I couldn't seem too interested. I think she was testing me. If anyone is working for Ellis, it's her."

"Got it."

"Damn, Vera is knocking." A toilet flushed. She called loudly, "Just a second," mercifully moving the phone away from her mouth. "Have to go." I heard half a toilet flush again before the line went dead.

I called Joanne. "Constance or Coliseum," was my greeting.

She sighed. "That does help."

"Still a lot of blocks."

"Yeah, but not spread all over the city. Anything to narrow it down." Then she added, "You're still at the hotel, right?"

"Yes, damn it," I groused.

"Good, stay there." She was gone.

Because I'm contrary, I left the hotel—not that I had any place to go. I checked out—I might be back here, but it might be better to keep my options open, maybe go to another hotel. I put my bags in my car, a small one of essentials like underwear and my toothbrush. A larger one of my gear, cameras, disguises. My gun.

As I left, I decided I could pretend this was about lunch. I wasn't really hungry, but I couldn't stare at the beige room anymore. I left my car parked but kept my hand in my pocket on my phone, as if it were a lifeline.

The area wasn't designed for walking, with no real sidewalks. I settled on a gas station convenience store not too far away. Snacks and drinks. Nothing healthy, but chocolate was more important than well-being at times like this.

Not wanting to sit in my car, I returned to the hotel. There was a breakfast area on the mezzanine that was empty now. I could hang out there, using my recent guest status. I'd claim my flight had been delayed.

Back in the hotel the same family (or do they all look alike?) was clogging the lobby, kids jumping around, taking up space and parents oblivious to other people who might want to get past their progeny. I tried to walk past one kid twice, but he kept moving in my way.

I'm a big dyke and if I touch your kid, he will be infected and start wanting fashion dolls and sequins. No, I didn't say it. Grandma came to the rescue just in time to pull him out of my way. I let them file (slowly, so so slowly) onto the first elevator that came.

The second one was blessedly empty.

Just as I was winding my way through the tables, my phone rang. I jerked it out of my pocket, juggling the bag.

"Hello."

"You called me." Karen.

"Are you still in Pensacola?"

"No, I just got back. Traffic was horrible in Alabama. I'm late and rushed."

"Didn't Joanne tell you to stay longer?"

"Yes, but I have a major showing this afternoon and need to be here. She didn't offer to replace my income," Karen huffed. From the sounds I heard, she was unloading her car. "I'm in a rush. What's so important?"

How do I say this in twenty-five words or less? "Be very careful. There is shit going down, and it may blow back on you."

"Well, that's helpful," she said, slamming a car door.

"The dead woman. Her crime family kin are in town and looking for answers."

"I don't have any. I can't even say for sure she was the same woman in my office."

"These aren't the kind of people who listen to reason."

"Micky, have you lost it? This is sounding like a badly written TV show. I think this whole thing is some stupid coincidence and you're both blowing it out of proportion."

"There is a dead woman in the morgue."

"Who just happens to sort of resemble a woman who hired you and was interested in a house from me. We don't know if they're the same woman or not. We don't know for sure it's related. And now you're telling me she was part of a crime family and because someone who might not even be her spent a few hours looking at houses with me, they're coming after me?"

"I'm not saying they're coming after you. It's about money. One faction of the family has stolen from the others. Supposedly the rebel side is meeting somewhere here in the city. The other side found out about it. They fight each other, we're out of it. But if it's a trick, the other side might come after us as the only link to the thieving side of the family."

"Yeah, right." I heard keys jangling and a door opening. "Holly thinks this is loony and I have to say I agree with her. She thinks it's about you keeping in contact with me—"

"No—" I cut in.

"Because I'm Cordelia's cousin and you either want to keep track of her or get into my pants to piss her off," Karen overrode me. A suitcase was dropped on a wooden floor.

"What? That's even crazier than what I just said."

"No, it's not. You've warned me, thank you."

"Where is Holly? Can I talk to her?"

"She's not here. She had to leave, some social work emergency. I had to rent a car and fucking drive back by myself and now need to unload everything and get to my showing in about an hour."

"Goddamn it, I don't give a fuck about you or a fuck about

Cordelia. This is serious and your life might be in danger. I'm only trying to keep you from getting killed."

"Yeah, right. I have to go."

Getting pissy with Karen—as tempting as it was—wasn't useful. "Humor me. Reschedule your showing and stay home. Just for today. You can read about it in the paper tomorrow."

"No way. I've already rearranged things to be here for this. The buyer is only in town today and is very interested. If it'll make you happy, I'm too tired to do much else. Holly and I didn't catch up on our sleep these past few days. I'll come back here right after."

"Just stay away from Constance and Coliseum Streets."

Water was running in the background. "What? Really? My showing is on Coliseum, just off the Square."

"At three o'clock?" I asked.

"No, two thirty. I have to go. Holly is calling."

She hung up.

I stared at my phone.

Coliseum is a long street, with a nice section of it in the Garden District, the area Karen did real estate in.

The time wasn't right. It was three, not two thirty.

The Rebel Brandes wouldn't meet to divvy up the loot at a house showing.

Not if this truly was their meeting place.

What if Salve lied? After decades of living with the male Brandes, she would be practiced at it. Good enough to fool most people, especially over the phone.

Karen arrives at two thirty, opens the house for the showing. Client is late. She'll wait. Ellis and his troops show up at three. Karen, who they know was involved, is there. They assume she's part of it. She's alone with them in an empty house.

Her last thought will be that I was right.

Satisfying, but not helpful.

What if I was? Could I leave it? Call Joanne and tell her to detain Karen?

I glanced at my watch. Just after one thirty.

What if I was wrong? I'd look like an idiot.

Well, I'd done that before.

What if? What if? What if?

I called Joanne. Voice mail.

I stuffed the barely nibbled chocolate back in the bag.

I stared at the walls, beige down here as well, the empty tables, voices from the lobby below.

What if I'm right and Karen is walking into a trap?

What if I'm wrong and, like the proverbial butterfly flapping its wings, my interfering will prevent the Brande women from escaping?

What fucking if?

Joanne returned my call.

"Karen is back in town and has a house showing on Coliseum," I said.

"And you think it's related?" Sensible, of course.

"It could be. Big coincidence if it's not."

"What time is her showing?"

"Two thirty. Which means she'll likely still be there at three."

"Maybe. And it could have nothing to do with it. You haven't gotten any more info on the address, have you? To even be sure it's those two streets?"

I had to admit I hadn't. Now I was pissed at Aunt Vera and I didn't even know her.

"Okay, I'll call…around. Get to Karen, tell her I'm meeting her at three if she's still there."

"Okay," I agreed, understanding her code. Karen wouldn't answer if it was Joanne, so Joanne would call Cordelia, who would call Karen.

"It's far-fetched, but better careful than not," was Joanne's verdict.

"Thanks." But she was gone before I'd finished.

I headed downstairs. I couldn't sit still any longer.

I got in my car, cranked up the AC, but didn't go anywhere. On my phone I looked up Karen's real estate page, found the listing for Coliseum Square. Nice house, one of the old Greek Revivals, with the front columns and second-story balcony. A large lot. Described as elegant and quiet.

One sultry summer night Cordelia and I had walked there, hand in hand. Admiring the houses, admitting even in those less gentrified days we couldn't afford them. Coliseum Square is not really a square, about four blocks of a long narrow park, just wide enough to show a vista of green to the houses bordering it. We had gone out to eat—I couldn't even remember where—and didn't want to rush home, so had taken advantage of the night, moon full, to be together in one of those lulls of life, no "be" or "do" hurtling at you. Just our hands, slightly sticky from sweat, but enjoying the contact too much to care.

Why was I thinking of that now?

Because the house Karen was showing was the one we stopped in front of, admitted we might buy it if we could afford it. I said something like, "I'd get it for you if I could."

She had lifted my hand and kissed it, and replied, "We have each other. We'll always have each other. That's more than enough." She gently kissed me on the lips. She wasn't one for public displays; maybe it was the wine, maybe the night, maybe the moment. Held the kiss until the moon reappeared from a scudding cloud.

"We'll have always until we don't." I looked out the car window at the glaring light, sun beating down hard, the day brittle with heat. Damn it. *You are not getting my house. Your nurse girlfriend can get a good job, probably making more than I do, and between that and your doctor's salary, you can afford something like this. You have a cousin in real estate who owes you.*

I started my car and pulled out.

I could just drive until it was all over, a cocoon of cool air. Until three, then four passed. I'd sent out the warning. It wasn't my fault if no one listened.

Not my fault if Karen was murdered by the Brandes because she was doing her job.

I was heading back into the city.

It was a little before two.

Holly Farmer.

Cousin Halley. Another Brande queer girl.

What was her family name? I searched my memory, sliding onto the exit from I-10 that would take me to the Garden District.

Not Brande. One of the Brande women had married. A man named Foster.

Halley Foster.

Holly Farmer.

"Fuck," I muttered out loud. A little family in-joke with the name, perhaps?

Or was it just the coincidence of the two letters?

That would explain the one thing that made no sense—involving me and Karen. Karen clearly had mentioned my name, told Holly about me. They needed a private eye—or decided one was useful—and bingo, I was part of this. A big puzzle piece slipped into place.

Or was this too far-fetched, going into convoluted plot instead of what real crime was like, messy and stupid?

I exited the freeway, speeding past cars that were clearly lost tourists.

As soon as I could, I pulled over to the side of the road, then frantically looked through the security photos I'd sent myself from the cameras at Rob's bar.

I found the one of Holly, then sent it to Anmar. "Is this your cousin Halley? Important. Get back to me ASAP."

I pulled out again. It was just after two. I needed to catch Karen before she left. Her house was only a few minutes' walk from the showing—although she'd drive to avoid a few blocks of sweat. She could leave at 2:25 and be there on time.

I sped down MLK Drive, crossing St. Charles on a yellow light that was well on its way to red, then turned uptown to get to Karen's place.

The street was quiet, too hot for even wind to stir the leaves. I parked in the first available place, full sun, of course.

Then scanned the street. A big navy SUV was a few houses down, in the shade. Behind it a silver Jeep.

Holly got out of it, going to the back and putting a battered-looking briefcase in the locked compartment there. Social worker case notes with confidential information in them?

Sharon and Margaret had seen a gray Jeep-like vehicle dump the body.

I watched her go in, carrying a small suitcase and handbag with her, presumably from the beach trip she had been called away from. Called to where? Atlanta?

But leaving the briefcase in her car.

My phone pinged. A text.

Anmar. *Close. Or a twin and she doesn't have one. How did you get a picture of her? Aunt Vera is trying on clothes so I have a few minutes.*

Long story, I typed back. *Will update you soon.*

I got out, slinging my messenger bag over my shoulder.

I called Joanne as I walked across Karen's Garden District–sized lawn. Voice mail.

"Micky. You're going to be needed at Karen's house ASAP," was my message.

Either to haul me away for being an idiot. Or to arrest the criminal Brandes.

The door was slightly ajar. Holly hadn't fully shut it. Careless? Or did she need to leave quickly? Karen wouldn't notice since she would go out the back to her car.

I heard voices in the back. They sounded like they were coming from her big sitting room.

Karen. "You're back! I wondered what took you so long. Your aunt arrived just after I got here."

Holly. "Sorry, things took longer than planned, and traffic was bad. I know you have to run. But I'll be here when you get back."

I barged in. "No, she won't."

Three people stared at me. They were in the large sitting room off the kitchen. Karen, sitting on a couch flanked by two matching armchairs. Holly was standing across the coffee table from her.

Karen was first to speak. "Micky! What the hell are you doing in my house?"

Holly was next. "What the fuck?"

"Salve," I said to the third woman, sitting in an arm chair. "How interesting to find you here."

Her face was stone, as if she was willing it to be blank, given away only by a deepening line in her brow. She'd had so many years of hiding her emotions, it might be automatic. But I couldn't read her, and that worried me. She should be surprised or worried. Or even happy, if they were truly trying to get away.

It didn't look like she had any intention of meeting Ellis, though.

Then from the near corner of the room, behind me and the door I'd come through, another voice. "Micky?"

Cordelia.

Oh, fuck, oh, fuck, oh, fuck. What are you doing here? This is the last place in New Orleans you should be. You're in danger. Or about to see me make an utter fool of myself. I had called Joanne. Joanne had called Cordelia. Maybe she couldn't get Karen on the phone and had come over. Who the fuck knew? She was here.

I knew we'd run into each other eventually. This was as bad a place as any.

"Told you she couldn't keep away from you," Holly said, her mouth settling into a sneer.

"Holly Farmer—what a cute inside joke—social worker? Or Halley Foster, ambitious drug dealer?"

Cordelia said, "What are you talking about?" She left her chair to stand, flanking me. We were a ragged circle around the room, Holly, Salve, and Karen closer to each other, unconsciously using the coffee table as a barrier.

"She's lying," Holly said.

"Is this the unbalanced private eye you mentioned?" Salve asked calmly, as if she'd never seen me before.

"Why did you call her Salve?" Cordelia asked me.

"Her name is Sabrina. She's Holly's Aunt Sabrina," Karen said. "What is going on here?" Then she threw up her hands. "It doesn't matter. I have to get to the showing." To me, she added, "You need to leave."

"Don't bother. The showing is a fake," I told her. "Sabrina Brande. So it's your twin, the real Salve, who's in the morgue. Not the first time you've used her name." She had used Salve's name for the money laundering—and probably other times as well. If there was trouble, it would be Salve, not Sabrina, to take the fall. A cruel and ugly twist on Anmar and Andrea's game of switching places.

"I don't know what you're talking about," Salve/Sabrina said. Too quickly. She gave the Brande men what they wanted to hear, not real emotions. If she really didn't know what I was talking about, she'd be shocked at her twin sister being dead and in the local morgue. If she didn't know, she'd want to know. But her expression didn't change. She asked no questions.

Cordelia did look shaken, looking around the room as if to read their faces, then at me as if she also sensed something not right here.

"Look, this is crazy talk," Holly/Halley said. "I told you she had a screw loose. Looks like a few more as well. What kind of fantasy hero are you trying to be?" She didn't direct the question at me but at the audience she was playing to.

"I've called Joanne; she's on her way. She can sort it out," I said.

I was hasty in blurting that out. Until that moment I'd had lingering doubt, thinking I could be making all this up, conjecture on assumption on speculations and a few coincidences. If they were blasé, or even welcomed Joanne, I'd be wrong.

The expressions—fleeting and controlled on Salve/Sabrina, less so on Halley—told me otherwise. Sly. Sinister. Desperate. They would not wait for Joanne.

Holly put her hand into her bag. Going for a cell phone? Nervous habit? A syringe of fentanyl? A gun? Had we become expendable?

A split second. She knew what she was going to do.

I didn't.

Her hand was already in her bag. I could jam my hand into my bag and hope to come out with my gun before she did. If we started shooting, the bullets could go anywhere. Hit anyone.

Decide! There was no more time. Her hand was moving.

I threw myself across the room at her.

She turned at the sound, her hand almost free.

My fist reared back and I punched her in the solar plexus as hard as I could.

Then a quick blow with my other hand to her nose. I needed to hurt her, make the pain keep her hand away from whatever it was reaching for.

If it was a cell phone, I'd face an assault charge.

She went down hard, hitting the floor with a reverberating thud as she let out a strangled groan, blood pouring from her nose.

"Holly!" Karen screamed, jumping over the coffee table to her. "What the fuck!" she screamed with the barest of looks at me, her gaze on the blood dripping down Holly's chin.

She was too transfixed to notice the gun Holly had pulled from her bag.

Sabrina got up. I took my gun out and pointed it at her.

"Don't move," I growled.

She stopped but didn't sit back down, her face trying to hide anger, then desperation and resignation.

I kicked Holly's gun to Cordelia. She didn't like guns, but when we lived together I had insisted if we had one in the house, she needed to know how to use it. Reluctantly, she had agreed and we'd gone to the firing range several times. She was never happy about it. It was one of the fault lines between us—she was a doctor and saw the destruction guns did. On rare occasions I've had to pull the trigger in my line of work. A few times it saved a life.

She picked it up. Looked at it like it was a snake, then held it properly, flicking the safety off. I almost wanted to say "good girl," but knew she would not appreciate it.

"These two women are killers," I said. "Sabrina murdered her twin sister, Salve, to make it look like she was the one who had died. She killed Salve's husband as well and tried to kill the two women who witnessed them dumping Salve's body in an area of town that only looked deserted. They were sending Karen into a death trap to cover their escape. Do not let them move, hands, fingers, legs. Nothing." Some of this was conjecture, but I needed Cordelia to know these women were dangerous and deadly.

Cordelia looked grim, but nodded.

Halley groaned, then pushed Karen away. She tried to sit up, but flopped back.

"I won't let her hurt you again," Karen said, still kneeling at Holly's side. She was in love with her. Couldn't see that Holly didn't exist.

I took two steps until I was standing over her. I pointed the gun down at her, keeping Sabrina in the corner of my eye. "Do not move. Understand? I can shoot your knee out or you can cooperate."

"Cooperate," she mumbled, her hand over her nose in an attempt to stop the blood.

"Good. At this point it's your best option. The police are almost here."

I moved away, backing toward the door.

"You're leaving?" Cordelia said to me.

I nodded. "I have to. It's not finished. Loose ends. Don't let them move."

"Put the gun down and help her!" Karen demanded.

"She'll live," I said. "Get Joanne and the police here first." I looked at Cordelia, willing her to understand.

She gave a bare nod. She hadn't become a doctor to hold a gun on a bleeding woman. I had to trust she'd at least wait for Joanne. And knew enough to know a nosebleed usually looks worse than it is.

I grabbed Holly's purse and backed out of the room, keeping my gun pointed at them.

I didn't look at Cordelia again.

A siren sounded in the distance.

When they were out of my sight line, I spun around, running out of the house, thrusting my gun into my bag. As I ran down the steps and across the lawn, my fingers searched for Halley's Jeep keys.

Yes, a big honking key ring.

Andrea Brande was not the woman in the morgue, and there were still a few Brande women I could save.

I beeped her Jeep open, heading for the back. I had to fumble to get the key to the locked compartment, but it opened easily.

The battered briefcase.

I grabbed it and then ran back to my car. I paused just long enough to dial 9-1-1 and report a robbery in progress at Karen's address. I needed to make sure the police got there as soon as possible. Likely they were the siren, but I couldn't take the chance they weren't.

I started my car and drove away.

The siren sounded closer.

CHAPTER SIXTEEN

I was back at the airport, pulling into short-term parking. More expensive than long-term, but I didn't have time.

Only then did I open the briefcase. A small pile of paper, a few manila envelopes with account passbooks in them. A quick riffle through them told me it was the Brande family secret accounts.

I called Anmar.

"Micky! Are you okay?"

"Are you?" I asked.

"Yes, although it's gotten even crazier here. Aunt Vera abruptly dumped me back at the hotel. Told me…it was all over. And she had to get back to Uncle Billy to get away. She said I'd need to fend for myself."

"Do you have a passport?"

"What?" Not the question she expected. "Yes."

"With you?"

"Yes. Always. Just in case."

"Pack what you have. Check out. Meet me at the airport? International terminal."

"Yes…but…I have to buy a ticket to get in."

"Buy one. Anywhere. Late enough to give me time to get there."

"But what's going on?"

"No time, I'll explain there." I hung up on her.

Flights from New Orleans to Atlanta happen about every hour. I booked myself on the next nonstop, coming back on the last flight of the evening, carrying only the briefcase and a few things from my messenger bag—like chocolate—that I might want. I left my gun locked in the trunk of my car.

I was jammed in a middle seat as that was all that was left, but it was a short flight. Either no one was talkative or my scowl warned them off.

As the plane landed, I texted Anmar to let her know I was here. There were a number of other messages on my phone, but I ignored them.

She was in the food court in the international terminal. Few people at this time in the evening.

She looked at me.

Then saw the briefcase.

It was nice to see real emotion on a Brande woman's face. Surprise, shock. Wonder.

"How did you…?"

I took out my PI license and handed it to her. "I've lied to you. I'm sorry. But at the time I didn't think I could be honest."

She took it from me, strong emotions still moving across her face—fear, disbelief. Curiosity.

She handed it back to me.

"Your aunt Sabrina came to New Orleans. She called herself Aimee Smyth. She claimed she wanted me to find her long-lost sister Sally Brand, no 'e.' She also went to a real estate broker and put money down on a house. All from a Brande account she got into."

Anmar stared at me, then a slow comprehension entered her eyes. "Sabrina and Halley, of course. Go on. Elbert comes down there to get a foothold, so if it's New Orleans, Ellis might think he's behind it."

"Probably. A lot of this is just guessing. Their plan was to focus Ellis here and make him think the accounts had been breached."

"Uncle Dominic, Hannah's husband. He's an accountant. Ellis would let him do the work, but he was always watched. He could never write anything down."

"But he might have memorized at least one account number."

"They had a miserable marriage. Perfect couple on the outside, hate on the inside. He was the kind of man who would let her take all the risk."

"That provoked Ellis to move the accounts. But he was stupid and clumsy about it."

"Sending us all away, so even Junior Boy would know something was going on."

"Halley left Pensacola where she was with her girlfriend, went back to Atlanta, and organized an ambush on Ellis and grabbed the briefcase."

"But how did you get it?"

"They couldn't resist trying to prove they were smarter than we are. She named her sister Sally Brand. I did a lot of searching, discovered the Brande family from Atlanta, and the fictitious Aimee Smyth claimed to be from there. Then I found the name Salve. Probably turned into Sally as a nickname."

"Yes, we usually called her Aunt Sally. She's not involved, is she? She's…the kind one. So different from her twin. Sabrina is, well, always looking for her advantage. Sally was different, learned to be kind somewhere in that family. Too trusting, if anything. She was always happy to see us kids."

Anmar noticed my face.

I hadn't wanted to tell her, and now I had to. "I'm sorry, I think she's dead. She overdosed, so she just went to sleep and didn't wake up."

Her face crumpled, then she said, "But she didn't do drugs. Didn't even drink."

"I think she was killed. Someone, mostly likely Sabrina and Halley, gave it to her."

Anmar wiped the tears from her face, "But why?" she said angrily.

"I'm guessing, but the men can't tell the twins apart. What better way for Sabrina to escape than to have people think she's dead?"

"Damn," Anmar muttered. "Halley asked me how Andrea and I got away with going to the lesbian bars and having girlfriends. I told her how we fooled them since we looked so much alike. But Ellis would know Salve couldn't be involved."

"Maybe. She might have gone along. Or been taken by someone who didn't want to leave her with the Brande men. I think they messed up, not knowing New Orleans well enough. They left her body in a deserted location. A day or two in the heat…would make identification even harder. But there was a camp of homeless people there. I think they wanted the body found, but not as soon as it was. Sabrina claims to be Salve, and everyone thinks Sabrina is dead. But two homeless women prevented that."

"They found her?"

"Yes." I didn't tell Anmar that Salve might have still been alive. That was too cruel to add to the other cruelties she was hearing.

"Sally was kind. That was how we could tell her and Sabrina apart. They looked exactly alike but didn't act alike. It settled into their faces. Laugh lines for Salve. Anger and frustration for Sabrina."

"Seeing Sabrina again, alive, I realized it had to be her twin. As great as the family resemblance was, it wasn't Andrea."

"You thought it might be her?"

"Yes. I was pulled in to see if I could ID her as the client in my office. But I'd seen her for less than an hour, didn't know her well. Enough to notice the strong family resemblance when I saw you, but not enough to be sure."

"You think Andrea is still alive?"

"I don't know."

"But no sign of her in this mess?"

"No, none."

She looked down at her phone, then at me. "I got a text from a number I don't know. It just asked, 'are you okay?' I answered yes. That was hours ago. I've heard nothing since."

"You think it was Andrea?" I asked.

"I hope it was her. It's all I have left."

She had more questions. I did my best to answer them. The fake dropped meeting address to lure Ellis and his ilk to a confrontation that could get the attention of the police. How I figured out that Holly Farmer and Halley Foster were the same person, and with that everything fell into place. Halley coming back to New Orleans to get Sabrina, the plan for them to disappear with the briefcase into the sunset—or more appropriately, the dark side of the moon.

"But what would Halley get out of it?" she mused.

"Money and power," I suggested. "What she wanted all along. She was smart enough to know she'd always have to be second to a man if she sided with Ellis. This way she could be in charge and pay them back."

"Feminist murder. How empowering." She managed a ghost of a smile. I saw a hint of the woman she should have been. Strong, funny, able to take on the world. Maybe she could find her way there from here.

"What will you do now?" she asked me.

"Go home and face the music"—aka a lot of questions from Joanne and Danny.

"You broke the law for me."

"Let's say I stretched it. A bit. Returned property to the only family member not in jail, on the run…or no longer with us."

"I don't know how to thank you."

"Cash is always appreciated."

She laughed. She was a handsome woman when the worry went away.

"Serious. Pretend you hired me to find your sister and this is what I stumbled on. I'd appreciate having my expenses paid. I doubt Sabrina will give me more than the advance. I'm not asking for more than that. Things like today's airfare, the hotels."

"Done. As soon as I sort things out. That's probably a pittance to what's in here." She tapped the briefcase.

"It's not my family. They didn't damage me. The pittance will be plenty."

She glanced at her watch.

I looked at mine as well. "Planes to catch?"

"Soon."

"Where?"

"London. First stop, at least. Probably better to stay out of the country for a while."

"Probably." We stood up, then headed down the stairs from the food court.

"And where will you go?" she asked.

"Back to New Orleans."

"You could come to London, you know."

I smiled, sad, wistful. I wanted to fly away, a world of adventures. But there were too many things holding me to earth, to the sultry streets of New Orleans.

She smiled, too. Also wistful. "Thought I'd ask. Nicer to go with someone than alone."

"You'll find Andrea. I'll keep looking as well."

"Thank you."

We stopped, the moment before we had to go in different directions.

"My whole life I was raised to think I needed a hero," she said. "A man to come sweep me off my feet and take care of me. I finally learned to get over that, no heroes, only people. And now one appears."

"I'm no hero."

"To me you are. One I'll probably never see again." She leaned forward and kissed me. We held it long enough to be real. This time her lips were soft. Trusting.

Then she turned and walked away.

I watched her until she disappeared in a crowd of people getting off a plane.

Then I headed back to the domestic terminal.

CHAPTER SEVENTEEN

It was late, past eleven, when I got back to New Orleans. The one blessing was that I had no luggage, so could head directly for my car.

Even with the night, the day had barely cooled, the heat seeping into the concrete and asphalt as if waiting only for the sun to blaze again. End of summer with all the weeks before to leave a little more hot air behind each day until you felt caught in a sticky, sweating squeeze.

I was dripping halfway to my car.

Someone was leaning against it.

Joanne.

She looked exhausted.

She watched me as I approached.

"How long have you been waiting?" I asked.

"I used police resources," she answered, without really answering. "Found out which flight you were on, so got here in time to find your car. Checked which flight you left on and knew you only had time for short-term parking. You're giving me a ride back to the city."

"Okay," I said, as I opened the door. We both would be happier out of the heat.

"Where did you go?" she said as she settled into the passenger seat.

"An unrelated case," I hedged. "Had to courier a package to a client." I fumbled for my seat belt so she couldn't see my face.

"A briefcase full of Brande account info?"

"Joanne, that would be illegal, wouldn't it?" I started the car, put the AC on high.

"Probably," she answered. "But it wouldn't be illegal enough for me to worry about it if it went to help some battered Brande women escape."

"That's what you think I did?"

"A missing briefcase and you take a hurried trip to Atlanta? Leaving, mind you, a distraught Karen sobbing over her putative girlfriend and an even more distraught Cordelia holding a gun on them."

"I knew you'd be there soon." I pulled out of the parking space and headed for the exit.

"And the minute we arrived, that briefcase couldn't go missing."

"I did what I thought was right," I said. Lame. I didn't think I could explain why I'd given Anmar the money. Except Salve Brande had been murdered, cruelly and senselessly. For that cost, some of the Brande women—maybe just one—should get away.

"I know. One of the most annoying things about you. And one I admire the most. Stubborn integrity. Yeah, I'm a police officer, but I'm not here as one. I'm here as a friend. I wanted to make sure you're okay."

"Really? So if I confess it all, you won't arrest me?" There was no traffic this late at night, no line to pay at the exit.

"Your word against mine, doesn't get to probable cause," she replied.

"A trusted cop against a disreputable private eye?"

"We're women; we're lesbian. Not firm ground to stand on for either of us."

I sighed. She was right. I paid the parking tab. I quoted, "Feminism is the radical notion that women are human, too. Maybe someday."

"Maybe. But let's not worry about that tonight. I'm exhausted."

"I'm sorry; you didn't need to meet me out here." Only a few cars on Airline Drive; I pulled into traffic without pausing.

"Yes, I did. Like you, I have a few stubborn areas. I was not going to let you just slip away and leave me wondering what really happened."

"You first. Were you able to arrest Sabrina and Halley?"

"Yes, right now just fraud, but we're working to build more charges."

"Murder."

"If we can. Elbert Brande—"

"Junior Boy," I said.

"Perfect. Anyway, he's already doing his best to blame everyone else."

"You have him in custody?" I turned onto the access road to get to the interstate, the fast way back into the city.

"Oh, right, you've been flying all over the place."

"Just Atlanta."

"Halley and Sabrina set him up as well, telling him to be at the same house Karen was showing, right at three p.m. Guess they thought if both he and Karen were there, it would clinch it being the double-crossing part of the family."

"So what happened?"

"Ellis lost his temper and fired first before asking questions. Claims he was only firing a warning shot, but he winged Junior Boy in the arm. He wasn't hurt badly, but bleeding enough—and scared Ellis might fire a few more warning shots and kill him—that he looked happy to see us."

"You were there?" I merged onto the interstate.

"At the tail end, after I'd dealt with Sabrina and Halley—and calmed down both Karen and Cordelia."

"Well, I'm glad they're okay," I said as I passed a slow-moving truck.

"I'm sure they are, too. Or will be. Karen is still insisting Halley is innocent."

"Ain't love grand?" Traffic was light, as light as it gets on I-10. I continued my law-breaking ways and cruised over the speed limit. Joanne didn't seem to care. It was a long day and we were going home.

"Only when it really is love," she replied. "So, yes, a couple of SWAT teams converged just as the first shots were fired. They found Junior Boy whining and bleeding, pissed enough that he fingered Ellis right then and there as the shooter. They arrested them all. Junior Boy is selling everyone out, hoping he'll get leniency."

"So much for family loyalty."

"Their only loyalty was to the money and power. Take that away and it's everyone for themselves."

"What's the best exit to get to your place?" I asked. I didn't go to Joanne's via I-10 East.

"Carrolton. Get on Tulane and take that to Mid-City. And you're spending the night with us. I've already told Alex to make sure there is no cat vomit in the spare room."

"Thank you, but—"

"No buts. I need to sleep tonight, and I can't sleep if I have to worry about some extra Brande cousin stupid enough to come after you."

I didn't argue. I wouldn't admit it, but I didn't want to be alone either. And likely Alex would make blueberry pancakes in the morning. Even if Joanne had to work, it was the weekend. I simply said, "Thanks, Joanne. For no cat vomit. And not arresting me. And…being at the airport to make sure I was okay." I exited the highway.

"Wasn't even thinking of arresting you. The real reason I don't give a damn about the briefcase—and will swear you never had it—is that it righteously fucks the Brande men. They would have reclaimed any of the accounts we couldn't track back to criminal activity. It disappears, they get nothing. I like that as an ending."

I did, too.

CHAPTER EIGHTEEN

It was slight, the changing of the seasons here, the sun slanting at a different angle, a breeze that didn't feel weighted with humidity, small harbingers of time passing. Searing August slipping into September, sliding past the heat of what most places call Labor Day weekend and we call Southern Decadence, aka drag queens melting in the heat. Still hurricane season, but we were past the cruel dates, Betsy, Camille. Katrina. Anniversaries safely past until the next year. It was no longer jarring leaving my car to walk up the steps to my house.

I tore down the poster with the snake picture on it, still menacing as wrinkled as it was by the rain. Yesterday Torbin told me the truth—a resident disgruntled with the constant invasion of tourists in an illegal short rental had put them up as a tactic to scare them away. I would buy the most realistic fake snake I could and leave it on his doorstep. Revenge is a Southern tradition.

I threw the poster in my trash can and entered my house.

Tomorrow I was meeting Joanne, Alex, and Torbin for dinner and drinks. We hadn't decided where but would meet at my house. So this evening I needed to clean and tidy it up. No one admitted it, but a trade-off had been reached. Danny and Elly were probably meeting Cordelia and Nancy. A couple of weeks ago, I'd gone out with Danny and Elly, presumably Joanne and Alex taking their turn with what I was now—and only to myself—calling the "Uptown Couple."

The newspapers called them the "Bad Brandes" and the story was only now dying down. Until the reality TV show *The Real Mobsters' Housewives of Atlanta* aired, at least. I hoped I was making that up. I'd had to spend more time than I wanted in answering questions about what I'd done. But Joanne and Danny were kind enough to mostly keep my name out of the papers.

The New Orleans police had arrested everyone they could, with charges from Ellis's attempted murder to firearms violations. Atlanta law enforcement swooped down on their compound. Over the years they had gotten secure and sloppy, keeping the drug and sex trafficking account books conveniently available to them and therefore the police when they searched. They were now digging up the rural plot of land and had already found three bodies. Most of the Brandes—especially the men—wouldn't get out of jail for a long time.

Halley and Sabrina had turned against each other, both claiming they weren't the ones who gave the lethal dose to Salve. Forensics found traces in Halley's Jeep that proved they had used it to dump her body. They wouldn't get out of jail for a long time either.

The Brande women? Some of them stood by their men. Maybe they really loved them. Maybe it was the only life they knew and they were too afraid of starting again.

Some of the women didn't.

I picked up the mail and put it on top of the stack, smiling at a postcard from yesterday. I had learned to recognize the handwriting. She used only her new names, never the one I knew her by, never named the location. She was now Helmi Schausberger, and Andrea was Dawn Rhineheart. American, but from German ancestors. If I saw those names, I would know it was her.

Anna-Marie had made good on her promise to pay me. Several weeks ago an international money order arrived at my office. Maybe it was a pittance to her, but it was enough to cover my bills and cushion me through the fall.

She called on occasion but never told me where she was—the habits of mistrust die hard. Occasionally a text with a picture. An old city, one I didn't recognize, but sun, a large square, buildings with carved stone and high arches. A table in the shade of the dazzling light and a sparkling drink in her hand. Her smiling. A wide smile, happy. At times I still wished to join her, soar over the clouds and land in a place I'd never been before, where I could start with nothing to hold me to everything I had become. She had nothing to go back to, no choice but to go forward. Life held me here: Torbin, my job, my friends, the streets

I had trod on for my entire adult life, the sultry summers that gave way to the bright blue of fall days.

It could be somewhere in colonial South America or on the Adriatic Sea, a smaller city in Europe. A place where she could smile widely.

The text she received in the airport had been from Andrea. They had reunited a few weeks ago. She had risked calling me late one night—at least in my time zone—to tell me. Andrea had initially been part of the plot, but she quickly realized that Sabrina and Halley only cared about themselves and were using everyone else as padding to protect themselves. If she didn't agree with everything they wanted to do, she was in danger. She hid in a small cabin in Tennessee, one she picked at random from a tourist guide, and cut off all communications, afraid they could trace her.

They both had the same smile, hair that became easily windswept. But I thought I could tell them apart. Andrea's eyes were open and direct, Anna-Marie's held back, couldn't find trust as easily.

That call, when she knew her twin was alive, well, and on her way to join her, her voice was joyful. I tried to picture her, as happy as she sounded, her words flying over themselves in her exuberance to tell the news. "She's safe! I'm going to see her tomorrow! We're back together. Safe from them!" But I hadn't yet seen the pictures, the happy ones taken with Andrea, and could only remember the sad, longing smile she'd shown me. I settled for hearing the elation in her voice, letting her happiness make me happy.

Now that they were together, the texts and pictures were less frequent. That was okay. Expected. She needed to find her new life.

They had been in contact with two of the younger Brande women, told them to go to college, they would pay for it.

A few women saved.

I had mentioned Sharon and Margaret to them. Another money order, enough to pay rent and cover basics for about a year. They had agreed that I would dole it out in monthly allotments. It turned out that Sharon's family had owned a donut shop and she had worked there growing up. And the coffee shop that rented from me was now doing a thriving donut business. Sharon hadn't been good at school, but she was a genius with dough. She—and Melba—had made me break my vow to not buy things there. Bacon praline donuts, OMG. I kept it to once or twice a week by saying I had to go to the gym every time I had the donuts. So far I'd (mostly) kept to it.

The computer grannies had taken in Margaret. She was doing admin work, answering the phones, filing, and they were teaching her computers, workplace etiquette, and helping her start taking classes again.

Maybe a few more women saved.

There had been another letter in yesterday's mail. Handwriting I knew well.

I didn't want to open it.

Joanne and Danny had kept me updated—at least as far as they were willing to go without violating confidences. They had to be talking to Karen and Cordelia, and they wouldn't tell me everything.

Karen had insisted Halley was innocent and demanded I be arrested for punching her. Halley, true to form, was willing to play along and act the blameless victim. To the point that Danny grumbled I should have hit her harder. That lasted until Karen discovered Halley had used her credit cards for a few major purchases and taken over ten thousand from her bank account.

"Money usually does it," Joanne had said.

"Or it being proof that Halley really was using her," I'd replied.

With that damning knowledge, Karen had listened to the other side of the story, that Halley was sending her as a decoy into a dangerous situation, while she and Sabrina made their escape. Halley had said she'd stay at Karen's house with her "newly arrived Aunt Sabrina" and start supper while Karen went to the showing. Cordelia was going to tag along with Karen because she'd always wanted to see the inside of the house—and she didn't feel comfortable alone with Halley and an aunt she'd never met. Of course, the minute they left, Halley and Sabrina would have taken off. If no one showed, Karen would still be gone for close to an hour, plenty of time for them to be well out of the city. But they were planning for Karen to be caught in the crossfire. When/if anyone thought or even knew enough to look for them, they would have disappeared into the places money can buy.

The letter was from Cordelia. I left it unopened and took a shower and changed into a comfortable pair of jeans and a soft, deep purple V-neck T-shirt.

I looked again at the letter. Was it about the house? Demanding her share as her girlfriend had?

You could find out if you read it. I dropped it, then quickly picked it up again and tore the flap. It was on her personal stationery, small initials at the top, a thick vellum.

Dear Micky,

I looked up from the page. Those two words. Even if it was just a standard greeting, I never thought I'd hear those two words from her again. I looked down at the letter, the words blurring before I could focus again.

I don't know what to say. But I have to say something, don't I?

We need to talk, but I understand you might be angry. Nancy should never have approached you. The house is between the two of us, our names on the title. We do need to work that out somehow.

I should have written this sooner, but for so long I didn't know what to think. It became easier to put it off for another day, let things settle and sort themselves out. Who to believe. One story from Karen, Holly (or Halley) backing her up. It's only in the last few days, finally finding the time, finally talking at length to Joanne and Danny, that I know what you did. Maybe we would have been okay, although that didn't seem to be in their plans. And maybe you saved our lives.

I still can't wrap my head around it; how Karen got involved—and involved you—with such a heinous family. How easily it could have been different. I could be leaving flowers at her grave. Or in one myself.

There are no words to express how grateful I am, a grace I'm not sure Karen or I deserve. I won't even try.

Danny had to point it out, but if I had been killed, that would have solved the house issue. It would be yours and no one else could claim it. I can't look at the ways this cost you, putting yourself in danger when you were safe, taking the

*risk you were wrong, the hours of work to understand what
they were doing. I would be beyond churlish to make you
sell or move or anything impossible or even difficult. Sabrina
killed her own sister. That is the evil they were capable of.
You stopped them.*

*You were and always will be a big part of my life. I hope
we can be friends,*

CJ

The initials she always signed notes to me with. Not Dr. James, as
Nancy would have her be. Or even Cordelia.

I folded it and put it under papers on my desk, so I wouldn't see
the familiar handwriting as I passed.

I went out the back door to the small yard and sat, looking at the
horizon, the sun behind clouds.

After Katrina, the destruction, the heartbreak, I watched the
choices I made and others made and realized for some of us there was
no road back, not enough time in a life to regain what had been lost. The
house gone to the floodwaters, every memory, every stick of furniture
gone, thirty, forty years, some from birth to the levees failing. All gone.
And not enough years left to recover, to move on to a new life. Either
coming back here or Houston, Atlanta, the end of the refugee road trip.

Some of us would recover and did. The years allowed us that
mercy, the time to begin anew.

I now saw the world that way—who can come back? And who
only have a short road left?

Sharon and Margaret might be okay, if they could resist the
undertow of addiction, the damned genetic chemical demands that
took so many into a shadow world of need and desperation. They were
young enough to regain the road they had lost in their missteps.

Anna-Marie and Andrea would be okay. Late thirties. Enough
money to never feel want or the worry, the trickling fear of not being
able to pay the bills. Or the need to be someone you aren't and don't
want to be to survive.

Karen would be okay, although bruised. Halley was probably a
sociopath, confident, glib, smart (although with the fatal blind spot of
not considering she might be wrong), and attractive. Willing to say all
the words, like "love" and "forever," that would bind Karen to trust her,

believe her. Enough to be used by her. Just from Joanne's and Danny's reports, Karen had fallen hard and was still dazed that her world had so fallen apart. Poor little rich girl. She had so much wanted someone to want her for more than just her money. She thought she had found it.

Cordelia? I'd left her holding a gun on her cousin's girlfriend and aunt. Left her to pick up the shattered pieces. But I hadn't broken those pieces. She was unhurt, alive. That might be all I knew. I'd call it okay and leave it there.

The clouds scudded by, letting a golden shaft of light through. It fell first on my arm, then on my face. One perfect golden ray. I let it warm me until it slipped away again.

The seasons change.

And me? Where did I put myself?

I would be okay.

About the Author

J.M. Redmann has published ten novels featuring New Orleans PI Micky Knight. Her first book was published in 1990, one of the early hard-boiled lesbian detectives. Her books have won three Lambda Literary awards, with seven nominations. Her third book, *The Intersection of Law & Desire*, was an Editor's Choice for the year of the *San Francisco Chronicle*, which called Micky Knight, "One of the most hard-boiled and complex female detectives in print today," and was a recommended book by Maureen Corrigan of NPR's *Fresh Air.* Writing as R. Jean Reid, she has published two books in the Nell McGraw series. She lives in New Orleans.

Books Available From Bold Strokes Books

A Moment in Time by Lisa Moreau. A longstanding family feud separates two women who unexpectedly fall in love at an antique clock shop in a small Louisiana town. (978-1-63555-419-9)

Aspen in Moonlight by Kelly Wacker. When art historian Melissa Warren meets Sula Johansen, director of a local bear conservancy, she discovers that love can come in unexpected and unusual forms. (978-1-63555-470-0)

Back to September by Melissa Brayden. Small bookshop owner Hannah Shepard and famous romance novelist Parker Bristow maneuver the landscape of their two very different worlds to find out if love can win out in the end. (978-1-63555-576-9)

Changing Course by Brey Willows. When the woman of her dreams falls from the sky, intergalactic space captain Jessa Arbelle had better be ready to catch her. (978-1-63555-335-2)

Cost of Honor by Radclyffe. First Daughter Blair Powell and Homeland Security Director Cameron Roberts face adversity when their enemies stop at nothing to prevent President Andrew Powell's reelection. Book 11 in the Honor series. (978-1-63555-582-0)

Fearless by Tina Michele. Determined to overcome her debilitating fear through exposure therapy, Laura Carter all but fails before she's even begun until dolphin trainer Jillian Marshall dedicates herself to helping Laura defeat the nightmares of her past. (978-1-63555-495-3)

Not Dead Enough by J.M. Redmann. In the tenth book of the Micky Knight mystery series, a woman who may or may not be dead drags Micky into a messy con game. (978-1-63555-543-1)

Not Since You by Fiona Riley. When Charlotte boards her honeymoon cruise single and comes face-to-face with Lexi, the high school love she left behind, she questions every decision she has ever made. (978-1-63555-474-8)

Not Your Average Love Spell by Barbara Ann Wright. In this romantic fantasy, four women struggle with who to love and who to hate while fighting to rid a kingdom of an evil invading force. (978-1-63555-327-7)

Tennessee Whiskey by Donna K. Ford. After losing her job, Dane Foster starts spiraling out of control. She wants to put her life on pause and ask for a redo, a chance for something that matters. Emma Reynolds is that chance. (978-1-63555-556-1)

30 Dates in 30 Days by Elle Spencer. In this sophisticated contemporary romance, Veronica Welch is a busy lawyer who tries to find love the fast way—thirty dates in thirty days. (978-1-63555-498-4)

Finding Sky by Cass Sellars. Skylar Addison's search for a career intersects with her new boss's search for butterflies, but Skylar can't forgive Jess's intrusion into her life. Romance is the last thing they expect. (978-1-63555-521-9)

Hammers, Strings, and Beautiful Things by Morgan Lee Miller. While on tour with the biggest pop star in the world, rising musician Blair Bennett falls in love for the first time while coping with loss and depression. (978-1-63555-538-7)

Heart of a Killer by Yolanda Wallace. Contract killer Santana Masters's only interest is her next assignment—until a chance meeting with a beautiful stranger tempts her to change her ways. (978-1-63555-547-9)

Leading the Witness by Carsen Taite. When defense attorney Catherine Landauer reluctantly becomes the key witness in prosecutor Starr Rio's latest criminal trial, their hearts, careers, and lives may be at risk. (978-1-63555-512-7)

No Experience Required by Kimberly Cooper Griffin. Izzy Treadway has resigned herself to a life without romance because of her bipolar illness but wonders what she's gotten herself into when she agrees to write a book about love. (978-1-63555-561-5)

One Walk in Winter by Georgia Beers. Olivia Santini and Hayley Boyd Markham might be rivals at work, but they discover that lonely hearts often find company in the most unexpected of places. (978-1-63555-541-7)